D0103702

M.J. Hyland

How the Light Gets In

CANONGATE
Edinburgh · New York · Melbourne

First published in Great Britain in 2004 by
Canongate Books Ltd, 14 High Street,
Edinburgh EHI 1TE

This edition published 2005

Originally published by Penguin Books Australia Ltd, 2003

10 9 8 7 6 5 4 3 2 1

British Library Cataloguing-in-Publication Data
A catalogue record for this book is available on
request from the British Library

ISBN 1 84195 611 2

Typeset in 12/15pt Centaur by Midland Typesetters, Maryborough, Victoria
Printed and bound by Nørhaven Paperback A/S

Text design by Debra Billson, Penguin Design Studio

www.canongate.net

For

Richard Clements

1951 – 1999

Acknowledgements

The author gratefully acknowledges the kind support, advice and encouragement of Stewart Muir, David McCormick, Clare Forster, Danny Lynch, David Lumsden, Marion May Campbell, Evelyn Conlon, Sam Chesser, Fran Martin, Carolyn Tétaz, Alice and Arthur Shirreff, Jamie Byng, Karen McCrossan and Polly Hutchinson.

Without them, this novel would not have been written.

Part One

Part One

I

In less than two hours this aeroplane will land at Chicago's O'Hare airport. It's lunchtime. My window shutter is open, the sky is vast and blue and the earth is brown and flat. The air hostess has delivered my drink and my meal, and on the in-flight TV, a panel of Christians are talking about the recent execution by lethal injection of a man on death row in Texas.

'He was a Christian,' says a woman holding a crucifix.

'For his last meal he requested a banana, a peach and a salad with either ranch or Italian dressing,' says a man with a beard.

'He should rot in hell,' says another.

I lift the foil from the white plastic dish on my tray, but I cannot eat.

I don't know how the old woman sitting next to me can stuff warm chicken into a bread roll and eat it, while right in front of her there's a picture of a gurney covered in leather straps in an execution chamber.

Now there's a picture of death row. Men wearing orange shirts and trousers are holding onto the bars of their cells, or lying on their narrow beds staring at the ceiling.

The old woman looks at the screen and drinks her drink.

Now there's a man being interviewed, his eyes covered with a black strip to protect his identity.

'Many years ago,' he says, 'I worked for a certain state

penitentiary. I was the guy who pulled the switch.'

The interviewer asks him if he was always certain of the guilt of the men he helped to kill. The man looks away from the interviewer. 'Pretty sure. As sure as you can be, I guess.' And then, after a confused pause, 'Yeah, I was sure. Most of the time.'

The old woman finishes her chicken roll. 'Good riddance to bad rubbish,' she says. 'An eye for an eye.'

To stop myself from screaming, I count the uneaten peas on her tray and start to give each of them a name.

'What do you do with bad eggs in your country?' she asks.

'We put them in the bin.'

Paula, Patrick, Patricia, Penelope, Paul, Pilar.

'Huh?'

'The *trash*,' I say. 'The *garbage*. We put them in the garbage for the cats and birds to eat.'

She says 'Oh' and then is quiet. I know she would gladly watch an execution, stare through the glass as the needle is plunged into somebody's arm.

'Have you come to America to study?' she asks.

'Yes,' I say. 'I'm an exchange student.'

I look away.

'That sounds like fun,' she says.

I turn back to her, just in case she's a plant from the Organisation, sent to check on my civility. This is just the kind of thing the Organisation would do.

'What city are you from?' she asks. She has green sleep in the corners of her eyes.

'Sydney,' I say. 'I can see the harbour and the opera house from my bedroom window.'

'How wonderful.'

'Yeah,' I say. 'It is.'

I can't see the harbour, or the opera house, from the

4

bedroom window of the high-rise commission flat where I live. All I can see is the edge of the city; the lights spread out in rows like a circuit board.

'Well, you won't have views like that in Chicago. And it won't be sunny all year round, either.'

'I hate the sun anyway,' I say. 'I prefer cold weather.'

'Oh my,' she says, folding her arms for emphasis. 'You won't be saying *that* in a few months.'

'Maybe not,' I say. 'Do you want my chicken?'

'Oh, no,' she says, disgusted.

When the plane begins its descent, I look down at the edges of Chicago and wonder why I'm only happy when I'm looking forward to something, and why when something happens it's never as good as I have imagined it will be. I'd like to know whether I'm the only person in the world who feels this way. Right now I should be happier than ever. Being on this flight is something I've been looking forward to for a long time.

I keep thinking this way, chewing it over like a cud, so that ten minutes before landing I am so nervous about meeting my host-parents, I can hardly breathe. My teeth feel metallic. I get up and lock myself in the bathroom and coat the palms of my hands with talcum powder.

The seatbelt light comes on and the bell rings. I stay where I am. An air hostess knocks on the door. I open it.

'Please return to your seat,' she says.

I follow her down the aisle to my seat. She smells nice.

'Excuse me?' I say. 'Could I possibly borrow some of your perfume?' She puts her hand on the small of my back and her zombie face does not move.

'Sorry,' she says, 'you'll have to return to your seat now.'

When I sit down the old lady grabs my arm, digging into

me with her sharp yellow nails. Compared to the air hostess, she smells like stale vase water.

'Are you afraid of landing?' I ask.

'I think I'm going to die,' she says.

'You won't die,' I say, and immediately blush to crimson at the stupidity of my words.

The aeroplane lands and the passengers rush into O'Hare's domestic arrivals area. It's noisier than a turkey farm, and the hot lights, orange as incubator lamps, beat down on the back of my head.

A man in a dark suit holds a sign with my name on it. I know that he is Henry Harding, my host-father. I know that the woman standing next to him, also wearing a dark suit, is my host-mother, Margaret Harding.

No member of my family has ever been overseas. My mum (Sandra), my dad (Mick), and my two teenage sisters, (Erin and Leona), live squashed together in our three-bedroom flat (four bedrooms, if you count the box-room) and the few places I have ever been with them did not involve visas, suitcases or aeroplanes.

I wave at my host-parents. Henry is the first to step forward.

'You must be Louise Connor,' he says, holding out his hand.

'Yes,' I say, as I offer my hand. 'It's great to meet you.'

'The feeling's mutual,' says Margaret, smiling. 'Welcome to our family.'

'We hope that the year you spend with us will be a very happy one,' says Henry.

'Me too,' I say.

'Let's get you home,' says Margaret. She steps towards me and takes my hand between both of hers.

This sudden intimacy makes me acutely aware of my teeth and the way they don't sit properly in my jaw. My mouth has lost its hold on my face. Nobody has ever held my hand before, except when I was a small child, of course, and except for the first boy I kissed, who held my hand when we were roller-skating. I couldn't stand it then, and I can't stand it now. Nothing makes me feel more uncomfortable.

I let go and she keeps smiling.

'Wait,' I say. 'We can't leave until somebody from the Organisation fills in some forms.'

'Why don't we sit down, then?'

'Good idea,' says Henry, who is fair of skin and hair. His eyelashes and eyebrows are barely visible. Henry is an almost-albino.

We sit in moulded plastic seats and watch the other exchange students meet their host-families.

'I love flying,' I say. 'I love how on the wing of the plane there's writing that says, *Do not walk past this point.*'

'That's funny,' says Margaret to Henry. 'Don't you think that's funny?'

'No,' says Henry softly. 'I mean, I hadn't thought of that before.' He frowns.

'Well,' says Margaret to Henry, 'isn't it just a great treat to meet Louise at last?'

'It really is,' says Henry, putting his hand on his wife's leg.

'I agree,' I say and put my hand on my jeans to soak up the claggy paste made out of my sweat and too much talcum powder.

The Organisation's regional president comes over. Her name is Florence Bapes and she was my team leader during the week-long orientation camp in Los Angeles.

'I'm Florence Bapes,' she says, 'That's *apes* with a "B".'

'Hello,' says Henry. 'Great to meet you.'

Florence shakes Margaret's hand.

'I'll be Louise's mentor this year,' she says. 'You can call me Flo.'

During the flight, Flo paced up and down the aisle and checked on me four times. She said 'How ya doin'?' each time, and I don't think I want to hear her say it again.

'Hi, Flo,' I say. 'How are you?'

Flo has abnormally small brown eyes, tiny and dark, with no discernible pupils.

'I'm fantastic and getting better,' she says.

This is Flo's catchphrase; she says it every time somebody asks her how she is, as though she is the host of a game show.

Margaret smiles at me, then licks her top lip with a tongue that's surprisingly wide and fat.

'Well,' says Flo, 'make sure you ring Lou's parents and let them know she's safe and sound.' She drapes her arm over my shoulder and squeezes me. 'This young girl needs a lot of TLC.'

Flo threatens to hug me, so I move away from her. She thinks I need help because I'm here on a scholarship for disadvantaged students, and because she found out I've never eaten salmon before. At the camp she came into my dormitory, and sat on the end of my bed, so I felt compelled to tell her things. When she found out that I used to eat tinned soup donated by the Salvation Army, she nearly cried.

'Yes, of course,' says Margaret, reaching out to put her hand on my shoulder. 'We'll call tonight. I'm looking forward to talking to Louise's parents.'

'You can't,' I say.

Flo looks at her watch. 'Why not?'

'I've just remembered,' I say. 'My whole family's gone to Spain for a month.'

'Oh,' says Flo, not as sceptical as she should be. 'Well make sure and call as soon as they're back from their holiday. And don't forget tonight's meeting at my place.'

'That'll be great,' I say. 'Let's go to luggage-claim and get my suitcases.'

'I'll be going then,' says Flo, as though we should be sad that she has to leave. 'See you tonight. Seven-thirty sharp.'

'We look forward to it,' says Margaret.

'Terrific,' I say. 'Fantastic.'

Henry looks at me, and frowns.

It's true that my mum and dad won't be home to answer the phone. They're staying with my mum's eldest sister who has broken her hip. But Erin and her twenty-five-year-old boyfriend Steve will be at home, fouling my bedroom with dope fumes from their shampoo-bottle bong. Leona will also be there, probably getting drunk and using my mum and dad's bed to make a baby with her fiancé, Greg, a mechanic, who has eczema on his oil-stained fingers.

If Henry or Margaret were to ring the flat tonight, Steve would probably answer the phone the way he always does, with some supernaturally unamusing comment. It was Steve – who works as a bouncer at the pub on the corner of our street – who made me realise that I never want to live with my family again.

Three weeks before leaving home, I took the day off school so that I could have the flat to myself. My mum and dad – who are unemployed and collect fortnightly pensions – spent the whole day lounging together on the couch, smoking and watching chat shows. Erin came home at lunchtime with Steve and three of his mates, each carrying a six-pack of beer.

I was sitting at the kitchen table, reading anonymous lyrics of fifteenth-century poets. Steve stood over me while the pizza rotated and unfroze itself in the microwave.

'Ha!' he said, pointing over my shoulder at the page. '*I have a gentle cock.*'

I closed the book and stood up. 'It's a poem about a *bird*,' I said.

'Yeah,' he said, 'a bird on my cock!'

I kicked him in the shin, and one of his mates said, 'Whaddya wanna do with her, Steve?'

Steve clipped the back of my head and said, 'She'll keep.'

I tried to spit at Steve's friend, but the spit landed on my shoe.

'Hey,' said Steve, excited at how much I was blushing, coming towards me with pizza in his hand. 'Does miss scholarship smartypants wanna go down to the car park for some spitting lessons?'

'Yeah, all right,' I said, and went downstairs with Steve and his mates to spit at the washing on the clothes line and drink some beer. I was saying goodbye.

'I'll carry your suitcases,' says Henry.

'They have wheels,' I say, but when he tries to pull my suitcases along behind him, a wheel falls off. I pick it up and turn red.

'It always does that.'

'Never mind,' says Margaret. 'We'll carry one each.'

As Margaret and Henry walk on ahead, I stop and look back. The other exchange students are saying goodbye to each other, hugging and exchanging addresses as though they are lifelong friends.

'Wait for me!' I call out, in a voice that's not really mine, and run towards Henry and Margaret, towards their tall bodies and the backs of their clean, dark suits.

Henry reaches out with his free arm and drapes it over my shoulder. I take a deep breath, and then, at last, it happens. I smell my future in Henry's aftershave.

It is easy for smells to remind people of the past: the smell of a cake eaten at the seaside, a ham sandwich, rosary beads or an orange. But I can smell my future in just the same way, and the smell of Henry tells me that, from now on, I will sleep on cleaner sheets.

2

Henry drives us home. The Mercedes smells as though it has just come out of its plastic packet.

'Is this a new car?'

'Yes,' says Margaret. 'Do you like it?'

'It's lovely,' I say.

'It's a pretty long drive,' says Margaret. 'We hope you enjoy the scenery.'

'I will,' I say, but all I can see so far are cars and billboards – just like Sydney.

Henry and Margaret take it in turns to ask me polite questions. What food do I like? What sports do I play? How hot does it get in Sydney? Do I like the beach? Have I ever seen a kangaroo?

I sit in the back and wish I did not have to talk. I feel too nervous and can't help lying. I say I play lots of sport. I say I like the beach. I say I once had a pet kangaroo called Skippy. They like these stories and so I tell more of them. I feel dirty. They have such white teeth and mine are so rotten.

'Do you agree with capital punishment?' I ask.

Margaret turns around to look at me. It's the first time she's looked at me without smiling.

'Me?'

'Yeah, and Henry.'

She looks at Henry.

'No, I most certainly do not,' she says, as though I've accused her of something.

Henry looks at me in the rear-vision mirror.

'No, I don't either. Definitely not.'

Margaret faces the road.

'Why do you ask?'

'I just wondered,' I say.

Nobody speaks.

'I think I'll lie down for a minute,' I say.

'If you like,' says Margaret. 'But keep yourself strapped in.'

Henry wakes me as we enter town.

'We're here,' he says, pointing at the sign that says 'Welcome to B——' and tells you the population, which is 480,320. The sign says B—— is 'A Great Town to Be In'.

Margaret tells me about the national parks, the new shopping centre and about the teacher-to-student ratio in the high school I'll be going to, and then we pull into the wide drive of the Harding house.

My new home is a suburban mansion: two storeys, wide, tall and white, with six big white columns on the front porch and curtains clean as milk in the windows. The middle attic-style window at the top has one pale-blue shutter open, one closed. I want this to be my room.

The quiet street, lined with identical trees, has the cropped symmetry of a street in an elaborate model village or train set, freshly painted, no dirt.

'What a magnificent house!' I say. 'I love it.'

Henry pushes the front door open with his back. He goes up the staircase, dragging my two suitcases behind him. Another wheel falls off.

'Come with me,' says Margaret. 'I'll take you on the grand tour.'

There are stained-glass windows on either side of the front door. In the entrance hall, red and blue spots, cast by the glass on the sun-soaked floor, look like spilt paint.

'Oh, look!' I say, as though I've just seen a cat use a sewing machine.

Margaret smiles. 'Isn't it pretty?'

'Yeah,' I say.

When I say 'yeah' I think I have already picked up an American accent.

Margaret shows me some of the fifteen-room house: dining-room, kitchen and family room. The air is fresh for the inside of a house. It's a dewy, clean air, easy to breathe, as though the leaves of the giant trees are inside as well as out.

Where I used to live there is carpet so threadbare you can see through to its veins, and the couch and armchairs are made of vinyl that peels away like sunburnt skin. But here there are polished wood floors, heavy, solid furniture, oil paintings and ceiling-high bookshelves.

I point to the panels of wood that reach half-way up the walls.

'What's that called?'

'Wainscoting. Do you like it?'

'It must be like living inside an enormous tree house.'

'I'd never thought of it like that. What a sweet idea.'

She sounds like she has a cold. So does Henry, but I like their accents. Not too strong, not too distracting.

Margaret leads me up the stairs. I am just thinking how I will probably like her and Henry, and how I hope they like me, when she puts her arm through mine. My arm feels like a sick snake, allergic to something, hot and poisoned. My face

grows hotter. My ears and my neck burn red. I try not to let
her see my face. Henry comes out of a door at the top of the
landing.

'We'll meet you downstairs,' says Margaret.

'Good idea,' he says with a smile so tight and wide it must
be hurting his face. I know how he feels. When the pressure to
be happy is this strong, it feels like somebody is strangling
you.

Margaret takes my hand and leads me along the hallway.

'This is mine and Henry's room.'

This room is yellow, has a four-poster bed and an ensuite.

'This is Bridget's room.'

Bridget's room is pink and neat.

'This is James' room.'

James' room is blue and messy.

She leads me back the way we came, and we stop at the top
of the landing. 'And this room is yours.'

Margaret opens the door and I see the clean, white, tiny
room with the attic window; one pale-blue shutter open, one
pale-blue shutter closed.

'This is your bed.'

'What a beautiful room,' I say. Life would be perfect if she
wasn't holding my hand. 'It's great.' I let go of her hand.

The quilt is as white as a new stick of chalk and hangs
down to the dustless floorboards. There is a stack of pillows
on the bed, white, pink and cream, like marshmallows spilled
fresh from a bag. All I want to do is sleep.

Here is my walk-in cupboard and here is my redwood desk
with its set of drawers. Here are the keys to the drawers.

'Do you like it?'

At home, the room I share with Erin has buckled posters
of stupid pop stars all over the walls, and ugly, smutty photographs of my sisters stuck on the back of the door; photographs

from the day they paid a hundred dollars at the shopping mall for a makeover and slut-like portraits. There are always stinking ashtrays full of butts next to Erin's bed and knickers drying on the doorknob.

'It's perfect,' I say.

'Good,' says Margaret, suddenly standing between me and the bed, her eyes flickering blue and delighted. I feel dirty and don't know what to do.

Her hair is shiny and tied in a neat bun on her round head. I am like a small, rotten boat with a leak, bobbing in the water under the hulk of a luxury liner.

I think she wants me to hug her and I think I want to; at least I wish I were the kind of person who knew how to hug somebody.

Margaret moves around me to get to the other side of the bed. She pulls the quilt back and fluffs the pillows.

In place of physical affection, I say, 'This is a *really* beautiful room. Thank you so much.'

'Good,' she says, standing close to me again, in a way I thought only people in films did. Is she waiting for me to get undressed in front of her?

'We were worried it would be too white,' she says. 'You don't think it's too much like a hospital room?'

I happen to like hospitals and hospital wards and especially hospital beds. I like to have the doctor call on me in the dead of night with a white coat and leather case and I like it when I'm taken to hospital. Nothing compares to the comfort I feel in a hospital bed when a doctor or nurse comes towards me with a stethoscope or a clipboard, and the promise of pills.

The cleaner and whiter the room, the better, as far as I'm concerned. I like hospital gowns too; modesty gowns made of blue tissue paper, the ones that tie up at the back like shoelaces, flimsy, small, disposable and sterilised, cold and nude around the back.

'No,' I say, 'I really love it.' I yawn, and look around the room for something to hang onto.

Margaret stays still. Her hands hang by her sides without the need to fidget, fold or point. It is as though her body does not exist in the way mine does. Her body is no obstacle, no hindrance. It's as it should be: a thing for carrying thought, and for converting thought into action.

'Do you want me to help you to unpack?' she asks. She wants to see what I own.

'Thanks,' I say, so afraid of being touched again, my tin-foil teeth have begun to rattle.

'You just sit,' she says. 'I'll hang your clothes.'

Why don't you let me sleep? I want to say. *Why don't you pull back the covers, tuck me in, bring me tea and toast, draw the curtains and make it dark? Don't you know how difficult it is for me even to stand up straight?*

Margaret works slowly, and to put my nervous misery in perspective, I do this thing.

I think of Mawson, the Australian Antarctic explorer. I read a book about him once, about how he had to eat a jelly made from the boiled bones of his sledge dogs so that he wouldn't starve to death. He ate so much dog liver that he got vitamin A poisoning, which causes desquamation, which in turn causes the skin to peel off in sheets, especially from the hands, feet and genitalia. Mawson had such a bad case of desquamation that the soles of his feet came away and he was forced to strap them back on to keep them from being lost forever.

I stand up, take a bundle of clothes from Margaret, open a drawer and dump them inside. She takes them straight back out from the drawer and rearranges them.

I step back and sit on the bed.

'Do you know what desquamation is?' I ask.

Margaret folds my pyjamas and puts them on the end of the bed.

'No. Why do you ask?'

'I read about it in a book about Antarctic explorers who sometimes perished in the snow. They suffered from desquamation. I just wondered if you knew what it was.'

'We have an encyclopaedia downstairs. Do you want me to show you?'

Margaret's a bank manager, but she sounds like a primary school teacher.

'Thank you,' I say. 'Maybe I'll look it up later. Maybe I should have a little nap now.'

'Oh,' she says. 'But don't you want to see the rest of the house and grab a bite to eat before resting?'

'Oh,' I say, my eyes burning. 'Yes.'

Henry sits at the table reading a newspaper and eating an apple. He is healthy and handsome, like Margaret. I don't know much about healthy people but they seem peculiarly clean and they smell brand new. It will be so much easier to eat in this clean kitchen. Maybe I'll even start eating breakfast.

'Do you like your room?' asks Henry. 'We were worried it might be a bit small.'

'No. It's fine.' I say. 'It's utterly perfect.'

My voice sounds posh, the way I've been practising. I like how it sounds, slipping itself into the house like a new piece of polished wood furniture across the polished wood floor.

'You look prettier in real life,' says Margaret as she opens the fridge and picks an apple from a big, see-through drawer.

There are many apples in this drawer. Carrots too.

Henry looks at me.

'It's true. Your photos don't do you justice.'

Margaret holds two apples.

'You have a very lively and pretty face,' says Margaret.

'That's good,' I say.

'We hardly recognised you at the airport you know,' says Henry, and it feels like they've had a meeting to discuss this.

Margaret stands behind Henry and now there are two faces looking at me.

'Would you like one?' asks Margaret, holding two apples aloft.

I hate apples. I haven't grown up with them. I haven't developed a technique with them and I'm worried about my teeth. I'm wary of hard food.

Within a week of one another, both my sisters lost adult teeth eating hard caramels at the movies. Erin brought her tooth home wrapped in tissue paper. The tooth was wedged in the caramel, bits of melted chocolate like dried blood around the edges, mixed with saliva. My mum said her favourite thing to say (which also happens to be one of my dad's favourite things to say): 'You made your bed and now you'd better lie in it.'

'But, Mum,' said Erin, 'I can't walk around with a big black hole in my mouth.'

'Why not?' I said. 'You walk around with a big black hole in your head.'

Erin grabbed hold of my hair, kneed me in the stomach, and left. I fell to the floor, and as I lay there, I could smell the dirty dishcloth Mum uses to wipe the lino.

'Enough of that,' said my dad, re-hooking the strap on his overalls which had come undone without him realising, probably hours earlier.

'Do yourself up, Mick,' said my mum.

'What do you think I'm doing?' said my dad. 'Dancing with a poodle?'

They laughed, and I got up off the stinking floor. My dad gave me a hard slap on the back and grinned at me.

'Good one,' he said.

'No thanks,' I say, 'I'm not hungry.'

Margaret puts the spare apple on the kitchen table next to Henry's newspaper and they kiss. They kiss on the lips in more than a perfunctory way and Henry says 'Mmmmm' with a deep voice that makes my stomach feel strange.

'Come on,' says Margaret, 'I'll show you through the rest of your new home.'

She shows me the piano room, a small library, two dens, the living-room, the two downstairs bathrooms, and as we walk, she chomps at her apple with large square teeth.

She tells me about the five years the family lived in Chicago, where she worked as the bank's state president.

'We moved here to get out of the rat-race,' she says, 'but I might as well still be the bank's president with all the hours I have to put in.'

'Do you hate work?' I ask. I'm tired and nervous but I know I must talk.

'No, but it's just that I used to do so many things. These days,' she says with a sigh, 'all I do is work.'

'What did you used to do?' I ask.

'I played the piano for many years and before the children were born, Henry and I lived in Paris and I taught piano and painted.'

'You could still play now, and paint,' I say.

'Not these days,' she says. 'You'll find out one day just how hard it is to do everything you want. Sooner or later you just have to get your priorities straightened out.'

I hate it when people say this kind of thing and I especially hate it when people use the expression 'these days'. When people have verbal ticks, or clichés they can't stop themselves from using, I sometimes have to count to ten to stop myself from screaming. When I walked out of the flat in Sydney I thought I'd never have to face another cheap platitude or homily again.

'Maybe you could go part time,' I say.

'Oh boy,' she says, 'don't *you* start!'

'Sorry,' I say, ' I just . . .'

'That's okay,' she says, 'it's an obvious solution.'

As we walk around the house, she tells me about Henry's work as an actuary. I don't ask what this means, even though I know I should. She tells me about her kids' plans to go to the best colleges in the country and how they both want to be doctors.

'Me too,' I say. 'I desperately want to be a doctor. Reconstructive plastic surgery and other —'

'Oh, like faces and — '

'No,' I say. 'Definitely not facelifts. Hand transplants, that kind of thing.'

'That's so great,' she says. 'I think the three of you will get along just great.'

She tells me what 'the kids' are studying and what sports they play. She tells me so many things it feels like every new fact is pushing an old one out of my brain. But I try hard to concentrate. I want to remember the details. Only selfish people don't listen to other people's details and the most selfish of all people never ask any questions. Like my sisters. They don't even ever ask anybody how they are. They just launch into puerile conversation about the sales on at the shops, or the way certain stockings ride up your arse.

When we are standing under the tree house in the enormous garden I say, 'This is the poshest house I've ever set foot in. You must be so rich.'

Margaret stops and grips my hand.

'I know this is a different world for you,' she says, 'but I don't want you to compare us to your family.'

'But this is like a castle compared . . .'

Margaret hugs me, without warning, holds me tight and pats my back, then lets go and looks right at me. Just like Flo Bapes, it's as though she is hoping I will cry.

'No comparing,' she says. 'Now, let's go to your room.'

'Great,' I say. 'I'm so tired.'

Alone at last. I draw the curtains, kick off my shoes and lie on the single bed with its chalk-white quilt. There's a breeze circling my bare feet and I'm desperate for sleep. But within minutes of closing my eyes, my brain springs open, like a flick-knife. It has been nine days since I slept for more than four or five hours. Although I've had insomnia for a long time, it has never been as bad as in these past few months. Every morning I wake just seconds before the birds do, as though my sudden waking is what causes them to start their chirping. Then I lie there, a dead weight, listening to the birds and hating them.

I open my suitcase, get the thesaurus out and look up synonyms. At the start of the year I made a promise that I would learn two new words every day, and so I lie on my back and say them over and over again: soupy, juicy, sappy, starchy, marshy, silty, lumpy, ropy, curdled, clotted, gelatinous, pulpy, viscid, grumous, gummy, clammy, sticky, treacly, gluey and glairy. I think, *I am counting slime instead of sheep* and this makes me smile, but I would rather sleep.

I am about to get down on my knees and pray for sleep when my host-brother and sister arrive home. I hear them coming up the stairs and their quick footsteps on the floorboards on the landing.

Margaret calls out, 'Louise, are you awake?'

I sit up. 'Come in,' I say, as though I am the important occupier of a big office.

I stand up when my host-sister and host-brother walk into the small white room. I have learned that this is what you should do when in somebody else's home. Margaret stands in the doorway with her arms around the shoulders of her children.

'Louise, this is Bridget and James.'

'Pleased to meet you,' I say, and shake hands with both of them, wishing I'd had time to re-talc my palms.

James' hand is dry and strangely small and soft; a hand-shaped cushion.

Margaret squeezes her children close to her side but they break away and come into the room. I sit on the pillows with my back to the wall.

'You look different in your photos,' says Bridget, looking smack into my eyes the way her mother does. I must have looked like a gargoyle in my photographs.

'Do I?'

Bridget is thirteen, but looks older. She is taller than both her brother and her mother. She sits on my bed and crosses her long, bare, brown legs then pulls them in to her chest, as though she has no joints. I cannot stop looking at her legs and her clean white shorts.

'Maybe it was the uniform that made you look different,' she says. 'We don't wear uniforms at our school.'

She too sounds as though she has a cold.

My school has no uniform. I borrowed a navy one with

burgundy pinstripes from Mrs Walsh, my English teacher, whose daughters go to private schools. She told me I looked a million dollars in that uniform and she took twenty-four photos of me standing next to her piano. I thought that these photos were the best to send because when somebody is in uniform you can't tell much about where they come from or what they're really like.

Bridget smiles, so at ease considering she is speaking for the first time to a stranger who will live with her, as a sister, for a whole year. She wants to know about the orientation camp in Los Angeles because I sent them a post-card from there every day.

I tell her all about the campus and the three swimming pools and the library with – I lie – more than seven million books.

'Do you like reading?' she asks.

'Yeah,' I say. 'Do you have many books?'

'Not seven million, but you wouldn't be able to read them all in just one year.'

But, I think, *what if I should stay much longer than that?*

James sits on the bed next to his sister as though to gang up on me. 'Did you know that I'm exactly one year younger than you?' he says. 'I'm fifteen and you're sixteen.'

'Wow,' I say, wishing the word hadn't been invented.

Bridget gets off the bed and stands next to Margaret. She is very tall.

'I need to take a shower,' she says. 'I'll see you soon.'

James stands and opens the drawers of my empty desk. He is chubby. His skin is pimply around the chin and there is a thin and patchy growth of hair above his top lip, the beginnings of a juvenile moustache.

He looks at Margaret. 'Is Louise going to do chores too?'

'Call me Lou,' I say.

Margaret smiles at me as though to tell me not to worry.

'But isn't Lou a boy's name?' says James.

'Don't tease,' says Margaret.

She sees that my face is red and puts her hand on James' shoulder. 'Okay. Let's leave Lou in peace for a little while before dinner.'

'That's no problem,' I say.

James continues to look at my face even though I'm blushing, and when I redden further still he looks down at my suitcases, then straight back up at me and says, 'Don't you think you should unpack all your presents and stuff?'

He's still staring at my face, fascinated, curious, wondering what will happen to it next.

'Come on,' says Margaret, pulling the door closed behind them. 'Let Lou have some peace.'

I lie down on my stomach and moments later James comes back. He leans over me, as though to whisper, but he does not whisper. His voice is loud, almost angry.

'What IQ did you need to score to get into that gifted school, or whatever it's called that you go to?'

I sense the danger in telling him, and the equal yet different danger in not telling him. I whisper the answer, and like everybody else, his reaction is a combination of impressed, depressed and disbelieving.

'Oh,' he says, 'that's pretty phenomenal.'

He leaves quickly without looking at me again. At least he didn't ask me whether I'm going to find a cure for cancer or why I don't work for the space program or why I don't play chess and win millions of dollars or something.

Finally, with the thesaurus opened on my chest, I drift into sleep, but Henry wakes me by rapping on my door. 'Time to hit the road!' When I don't answer, he opens the door and looks in.

'Sorry,' he says, his voice cracking. 'It's time to go.'

'Wait,' I say. He comes into my room. 'I just want to say thanks heaps for letting me come and live with you.'

Henry sits on the bed, the top three buttons of his shirt open now, almost-albino blond hair on his chest, rising and falling with his deep breaths. He leans awkwardly to put his hand on my knee. He is nervous, like me, and I feel calmer in his company than in Margaret's.

'I have a feeling,' he says, 'that having you in our house will be pure pleasure.'

The air is thick with our happiness. I hold my breath and look at the quilt.

'Thanks,' I say. 'Thanks a lot.'

Henry leaves the room, and for a moment I feel calm.

We climb into Margaret's black four-wheel drive, a high monster of a vehicle. I prefer the Mercedes. Maybe I could get a licence while I'm here and drive it fast on some open country roads.

We drive through the centre of B——, past the shopping strip and the town hall and the brand new civic centre, heading somewhere to have dinner. The sun is hot and bright.

'We drive the kids around a lot,' says Henry, whose invisible eyebrows are visible now, wet with sweat and shining.

'We're not *kids*,' says Bridget.

'Kids belong to goats,' says James.

Henry ignores this exchange and taps the windscreen. 'Bullet-proof,' he says. 'All the windows are bullet-proof.'

The business district is full of low-rise glassy buildings, tinted windows reflecting identical office buildings across the street. There isn't a single old car on the road and all the rubbish is where it should be. No police sirens, no car horns, no used syringes and no graffiti.

'It's such a peaceful town,' I say.

James laughs a sudden and ugly laugh, full of derision. He wants me to look at him and when I do, he smirks, his face and body agitated by an emotion so strong I can smell it.

Henry looks at me in the rear-vision mirror, smiling, as though worried I might have leapt out the window since he last checked on me. I know that the Hardings expect me to talk and so I try to think of something good or nice to say. I look around for inspiration in the streets.

We stop at traffic lights and a woman is wheeled across in a wheelchair, her young face contorted by involuntary grimaces.

As the wheelchair is lifted onto the kerb, I say, 'Do you know that witches who were burnt at the stake in the seventeenth century have descendants with Huntington's chorea? All that horrible grimacing might have been what caused people to think these women were witches in the first place.'

Nobody responds.

I wish I hadn't spoken at all. I don't like the sound of me. I'm an impostor. A fraud. James says something under his breath to Bridget, and she pushes the heel of her hand into his forehead.

Margaret points out the window. 'Your school is at the end of that street.'

'When does school start?'

'In about four weeks,' she says. She turns around in the front passenger seat. 'You'll have ages to settle in first.'

Henry looks at me in the rear-vision mirror. 'But before school starts, we're going on a two-week vacation.'

'A nice long road trip,' says Margaret, 'so we'll get to spend some quality time together. As a family.'

'That sounds great.'

'We're mainly going for you,' says Bridget. 'Mom never takes holidays.'

'That's really nice,' I say. 'I'll be able to see more of America.'

I don't care about scenery but maybe I'll find a college I can go to next year.

James laughs his ugly laugh again. 'What's so funny?' I ask.

He's staring at me and I stare back.

'I don't know,' he says. 'Just how you say things. You're weird.'

'Don't be nasty,' says Margaret and suddenly, from the front passenger seat, her hand reaches out for mine. I don't know what to do with it. I look out the window and put my hands under my legs. She turns around in her seat but I don't look at her. My hands are wet. She wouldn't really want to know about them. She reaches around and squeezes my knee instead.

'Everything okay?' she asks.

'Yes,' I say.

'Why are you all red then?' asks James.

Bridget hits him on the arm.

'Shut up, James!'

We pull into the car park of a large family restaurant, the kind that's probably part of a countrywide chain.

'It's enormous,' I say, to cover my disappointment.

Margaret opens the back door, 'Don't you have restaurants like this at home?'

'Nothing like this,' I lie.

It would disappoint them, perhaps, to know that around the corner from where I live, there are places just like this one; just as big, with dire food and disturbing décor. The kind of place my sisters rush to with their dole cheques after not having eaten properly for two days.

Henry is frowning at me again. Maybe he likes the way he looks when he frowns.

'We've never been before,' he says. 'But we thought you'd like it.'

'I will,' I say. 'I can already tell.'

I stand in the smorgasbord queue with Margaret. The others have rushed up ahead. Margaret stands close, just like she did in my bedroom, so that when I turn to look at her, I can smell her breath. It's like milky picnic tea poured from a flask.

She puts her hand on my shoulder. 'I'm so excited about having you stay with us. We've been really excited. Haven't you been excited?'

I redden as though I have been thinking – or have seen – something indecent. I go red now just as I do when somebody tells a dirty joke, or there's a sex scene on TV and my mum and dad are in the room.

'Yes,' I say. The real answer is that I am happy to be here. I want to tell her exactly why I am so happy to be away from my family, but if I do, all the hatred I feel for my sisters will rise up, bilious, like a putrid emotional burp.

We move a little further along the smorgasbord, and I try not to breathe in the smell of bacteria struggling to survive.

Margaret puts her hand on my arm. 'You haven't chosen much to eat. Isn't there anything you'd like?'

'No, no. I'm fine. I'm just tired and I can't eat much when I'm tired.'

Margaret spoons some potato salad onto her plate, next to a large chicken schnitzel, flat and thin, like a strip of human hide. I take nothing. She grabs my empty plate.

'Honey, are you *sure* you're all right?'

I am trying to think of something to say and then I notice Margaret has small breasts. Through her thin, white t-shirt, I can see brown, erect nodes for nipples, like the hard dark knots found on trees. She has become flesh. I can't help but think what it really is to be a human being; how perishable the body is, what goes on, and how it will end up.

'I'm fine.'

Margaret smiles. 'How about you try some re-fried beans? They're nicer than they look.'

They'd have to be.

'They look nice,' I say, afraid I might vomit.

When we get to our table, I have three chicken wings on my plate and they look like the elbows of that girl in the wheel-chair. When Bridget sees my plate she stands up.

'Mom, I'm going to get her something. Don't let her move.'

I hate it when people say 'her' or 'him' in place of a person's name.

Bridget goes away and comes back with more salad than my entire family (aunts and uncles and cousins included) have eaten in a lifetime.

'Thanks,' I say, with no clue how to manage a lettuce leaf. What are those little white crunchy cubes? Are they edible?

James goes back for three more helpings. As he chews his food, an especially red pimple close to the right corner of his mouth seems to grow. He touches it between mouthfuls, as though it were something worth taking care of.

It's growing dark when we arrive at Flo Bapes' house. We sit in a lounge room with eight other host-families and their exchange students. Flo stands before the gathering next to a whiteboard and writes up the rules of the Organisation. Along the back wall there are three bowls of punch, with pieces of pineapple floating around in them.

Each of the exchange students is asked to stand up the front and introduce themselves. I am last, and I say some stuff I've been rehearsing for a long time. In front of a crowd I'm not as nervous as I should be.

I talk about Sydney and I make people laugh. There's no greater pleasure as far as I'm concerned. When I sit down,

Henry pats my back and says, 'That was *very* well done.' James is staring at me sceptically and Bridget is plaiting her hair.

In small, barely legible handwriting, Flo writes the following on the whiteboard: *No drinking, No smoking, No driving, No drugs, and No hitchhiking!*

An exchange student in the middle of the room says, 'I can't read that.'

Flo frowns. 'Well, I have to write small so I can fit it all on!'

Flo is an example of a smudge: a person with no definition, no clear lines of personality; a dull, untidy mind containing bad copies of original thoughts. You could spend a year locked in an empty fridge with a smudge and learn nothing. But the worst thing of all about a smudge is that they talk all the time and never listen. My sisters are smudges.

It's too hot in Flo's house and I begin to have a vivid fantasy about the airport. I daydream that we stayed longer in O'Hare's airconditioned terminal and that Margaret and Henry took me into a duty-free shop and asked me to pick out a present. 'We'd like to buy you a welcoming gift,' I hear Margaret say. 'Pick anything you like from one of the shops,' says Henry. 'We'll come back and get you in a few hours.'

Suddenly my daydream is interrupted by a storm, and cracks of thunder that dent the sky. I stand up in the middle of one of Flo's never-ending sentences and go to the window. The storm is close and the room is transformed by it. There's crashing, war-like thunder and zigzag lightning. This is my favourite weather.

I wish I had taken the 'wake me for meals' eye mask from the aeroplane. I could lie on the floor, put the mask over my eyes and listen to the storm until somebody carried me home and put me to bed in my new clean white room.

Flo starts to stammer. 'Oh d-d-d-dear.' Her nostrils flare up like prawn crackers dropped in hot oil. 'I'll have to speak up,' she says, almost crying with frustration.

People shuffle to the back of the room and reach for corn chips. I can no longer hear Flo as she drones on under the storm's perfect music.

Margaret and Henry are standing with me by the window. We do not speak. Henry is standing close to me. We look out. There's another long and booming crack of thunder, which sounds like a keg of beer being dragged along the concrete outside the pub on the corner of my street in Sydney.

The lightning is so close it seems to strike the front yard of the house across the road. Margaret steps back from the window but Henry and I stay where we are.

'What a storm,' says Henry, with awe in his voice.

Heavy rain pelts down on the driveway.

'I love rain more than anything,' I say.

'It's so clean,' he says. 'Isn't it clean?'

'Yeah,' I say and it is as though our neurones have taken a shower. I look up at Henry and smile, and he smiles back.

'No spiders now,' I say.

I'm thinking of the nursery rhyme.

'Let's see,' says Henry as he opens the large window all the way. The room becomes quiet and still. People are looking at us, at Henry and me, for the rain is getting in and the sound of thunder drums against the walls.

'No. No spiders now,' he says, and he is close enough for me to notice that his voice smells like rain.

3

I have read that a sheep raised by dogs will eventually learn to chase cars. But how long does it take to learn the tricks of another animal? How long will I need to live with the Hardings before I unlearn the tricks of my own family?

It is my second day with the Hardings. We're sitting, after dinner, at the dining-room table, and I'm facing the opened doors of the piano room and library. I imagine the scene at home: Mum, Dad, Erin, Leona, Greg and Steve, all in the boxy lounge-room, all smoking; so much smoke you can hardly see, the burning ends of their cigarettes glowing, moving from lap to mouth, somebody waving at the smoke to see the TV screen. No windows open.

Margaret removes two small sheets of notepaper from the pocket of her jeans and puts them on the table.

'I think Flo said some interesting things about conflict management last night,' she says, as she turns a page and looks at Henry. 'I might be able to use some of this stuff at work.'

Bridget sighs. 'Work, work, work,' she says. Margaret pretends not to hear, or care.

Henry puts his hand on his neck and clears his throat.

'We should probably explain some of the house rules for Lou. Then we can get on with having some fun.'

James looks at me, to see what my face is doing.

'We have breakfast every morning at seven-thirty, as a family,' says Henry, 'and we'd like you to join us.'

'Bridget,' says Margaret, 'would you explain to Lou what happens on weekends?'

Bridget sighs again. 'Can't she just do what she wants? It makes no difference either way.'

Margaret looks at Bridget. 'We try to go to each other's games and concerts,' she says. 'Bridget has jazz ballet, basketball and French club and James has science club and debating. We hope you'll come along and support them in their extra-curricular activities and that they'll get along and support you.'

Henry puts his hand on Margaret's leg. 'And Margaret sings in the local choir . . .'

In the silence that follows, nobody bothers to speak for Henry. He stares at the table for a moment then takes his hand from Margaret's leg.

'We're a busy family. It might seem odd to you at first but we keep our schedule on the fridge.'

Margaret smiles as though this is happy news. 'You might like to have a look at it later. We've put your name on it so that you can add your own appointments.'

Bridget says, 'But you don't have to put stuff on the schedule. It's just so we know where everybody is. It doesn't really matter.'

James looks at me. 'Do you think you'll join the debating team?'

'I don't know.'

'Want some ice-cream?' asks Bridget.

'Yes please,' I say.

Margaret picks an apple from the fruit bowl and slams it down on her side plate as though to declare war on the idea of dessert.

'Not for me,' she says.

Bridget brings in the ice-cream and Henry and Margaret go on talking about meal times, the dishwashing roster, co-operation, teamwork and mutual respect. I look around at the spotless dining-room; the piano, the bookshelves in the library, the wainscotting and the framed family photos on every polished surface.

I realise I'm not speaking enough and look for something to talk about.

'Who do you think would win in a fight between an apple and an orange?' I ask.

'Don't be stupid,' says James.

Henry smiles at me. 'The orange,' he says.

'Yeah, because it has armour!' says Bridget.

We all laugh (except James) then nobody speaks again.

Margaret drinks the last of the iced tea then gets back to the business of the rules.

'There are really only a few other things that you should know,' she says. 'When school starts there's a two-hour limit on watching TV and the weekend curfew is ten o'clock.'

Bridget sighs. 'Don't call it a *curfew*, Mom. This isn't *apartheid*.'

Margaret smiles. 'I think Lou understands what a curfew means in this context.'

'Yes,' I say. 'I have the same curfew at home.'

In Sydney I stay out until the early hours of the morning playing cards, listening to music and drinking, without ever having to call home.

James grins at me.

'Hey! Why don't we have a sing-a-long and Lou can sing.'

James' only aim is to make me blush again, but his parents don't see it.

'What a good idea,' says Henry.

'Do *you* sing?' asks Bridget.

'Duh,' says James. 'It's only all over the information we got.'

'Not really,' I say.

James laughs. 'Yes you do,' he says. 'You wrote it down as your number two hobby after reading.'

Margaret is staring at the floor by my feet as though waiting to see what will fall off me.

James is right. I wrote everything on my application forms. I was in an altered state of super confidence when I was filling them out. I thought that being in America, surrounded by wealth, the new air, the very idea of a fresh start, would obliterate all my fears. I thought I could change identities like a double agent.

'I don't really sing in front of people,' I say.

James laughs again.

'That's pretty stupid. What's the point of singing if nobody ever hears you?'

Margaret doesn't stop him. I feel like a red walnut about to be cracked open by James' next sentence and I would do anything to make him stop. I start coughing. It's not real at first, but soon it is. Before I know it, I'm in the middle of a violent coughing fit.

Margaret goes to the kitchen to fetch some water, but when she returns, I have run up the stairs to the bathroom. I drink some water and the coughing stops. I need to use the toilet but there is no lock on the bathroom door. I take a chair from under the window and shove it under the door handle.

Margaret comes to see how I am. The door handle rattles. 'Are you all right in there?'

'I'm fine. I'll be out in a minute.'

'Okay,' she says.

I wait until I hear her footsteps on the staircase before I go outside.

According to the Organisation's rules, I'm supposed to tell Margaret or Henry where I'm going *whenever I leave the house* but

I need to be alone, urgently. I go right out the front door and start walking around the neighbourhood.

I like to walk around the streets at night and fantasise about being in other people's houses.

It started when I was nine and I wagged school one day. The night before, my sisters pulled my trousers down to my ankles in front of their boyfriends, because I used a big word. My mum just laughed, and I hated her.

I got on a train and travelled as far as I could on one ticket. It was a hot day and the sun curdled the asphalt, drugged the crows on their wires and made people smell of vinegar. The sun also made the day easy to remember.

I had my face pressed to the train's window and made curtains out of my hands. The train sped through green suburbs. I saw back yards and gardens filled with toys and sheds and swings and swimming pools. I wanted to get off the train and into one of the lives I could see from the window.

I got the idea then that I would one day live in somebody else's house and be adopted by somebody else's family. I had engaged in a great deal of adoption fantasy before this, but this was much more than daydreaming about who my real parents might be: famous writers, royalty or billionaires. This was about getting out for good. More exciting than my favourite book, *Papillon*, and more treacherous than *The Great Escape*.

I got off the train and walked until dark, in the silent lamp-lit streets and cul-de-sacs. I walked slowly past front yards filled with the homey blue lights of televisions flickering through lounge-room windows. I became hungry as I watched the shadows of people moving behind net curtains, their shadowy shapes slow and drowsy, as though they rolled and turned beneath heavy sheets.

I knocked at the front door of a two-storey house and said, 'Could I come in? I've run away from home.'

I wanted the woman who answered the door to acknowledge my craving without words or questions. I wanted her simply to get it.

In this big house, the family had been watching a movie together. The mother took me into the living room and told me to sit. The father turned off the TV and it hissed to a disappointing black. The small children — a girl and a boy — did not speak nor look at me. I said, 'This is a nice house.' The mother sent her children to their bedrooms. I wanted to follow them up the stairs and find a bed of my own. I wanted the mother to say, 'This is your bed. You can stay here tonight.' But the mother had a hard voice. She wanted to know why I was out on the street alone when it was so late.

I told her that I wanted to sleep in a bed in a nice big clean house. The father stood by the door. He had a nasty double chin and I didn't want to look at it.

'Has something happened to you at home? Are you in trouble?' he asked, the crease in his chin bobbing.

For a moment my body believed that something cruel and dreadful had happened to me at home. I considered acting out a lifetime of imagined torture.

'No,' I said, 'nothing has happened. I just wanted to see what it was like somewhere else.'

'I'd better call your parents,' said the mother, but I refused to give her the number and wished that I had cried or lied.

'Can't I just be a visitor for one night? Couldn't I just stay on the couch and watch the TV with you in front of the fireplace and then go to bed?'

The mother walked to the phone in the entrance hall. 'I'm calling the police,' she said. 'Your parents will be worried about you.'

I curled into the corner of the big leather couch and held onto my knees. I stared at the black TV screen.

I wanted a cushion behind my back and a cup of hot chocolate in my hand. I wanted to eat some of the bread and butter pudding and ice-cream the children had left on the table, but the mother called the police and told them that a runaway had come to her home.

When the receiver dropped into its black cradle the curtains ballooned suddenly with cold fat misery.

I ran into the hallway and picked up a small red coat that was lying on the floor. I held the coat – too small to wear – against my chest and ran to the train station.

Since then, I have fantasised so vividly that sometimes I believe I have spent the evening in the company of rich strangers. I go home after nights of walking the streets and looking into people's windows and I feel a distinct urge to ring them to thank them, or write them a letter to tell them how I am (perhaps enclosing a recent photograph of myself and my dog).

On my way to school each day I use the same laneway and pass a house whose kitchen window has no blinds and is always open. I crouch in the laneway and peer inside. I watch the family of four – mother, father and two young boys – as they eat their porridge and toast and drink their orange juice.

The smell of the scene haunts me. The way the father reads the paper, and the mother reads a serious magazine, makes my heart expand in my chest so much that I can barely breathe. I ache with wishing I could climb inside, or that they will see me one day and ask me to live with them.

Sometimes, as I walk the streets of neighbourhoods far from home, I get so hungry my mouth fills with water. Then I go home and deep-fry chips and shallow-fry eggs, cover them in tomato sauce and eat in my bedroom with my eyes closed while my mum and dad and sisters sit in the lounge-room, yelling 'Get fucked' or 'That's fucking stupid' at the eleven o'clock news.

As I walk up the drive of the Harding mansion, I can see my family again — all of them — chain-smoking in the lounge-room, the air thick with smoke, and I no longer care what happens to them.

Henry is sitting on the leather divan near the phone in the entrance hall, waiting for me.

'There you are,' he says, his face strained with the effort of concealing worry.

'Sorry,' I say. 'I just went around the block to get some air.'

'That's no problem,' he says. 'You're home now.'

4

It's Saturday morning. For most of last night, and the night before, I lay in my bed and turned from side to side, hoping that with the next turn, sleep would engulf me, but sleep came nowhere near.

The weather is milder today and there is a scent in the air of grass drying; the perfume of summer. The house is flooded with light and dust motes. Although I have slept for only three or four hours, my appetite is back and my breathing is less shallow.

I go to the kitchen and sit at the table with the Hardings even though I don't want breakfast. I never eat breakfast. Suddenly, Bridget and James leave and head for the family room where the TV is. Henry gets up from the table. 'It's my turn to do the dishes,' he says. He takes his cereal bowl and his hand touches mine. I feel weird and I wonder why they don't have a dishwasher and why they don't put the stereo or radio on during meals. It's too quiet.

'I'll do them,' says Margaret.

Henry leaves and Margaret and I are left alone.

'Come sit with me in the dining-room,' she says.

'Okay,' I say.

We sit at the dining-room table. She turns around in her chair to face me, her healthy skin glowing. 'Well, what do you think so far?'

She pulls her chair in closer and puts her arm around my

shoulder. I fall into a thick-throated silence. I need to cough. I need to urinate. And I cannot think. I am better in groups; terrible at being alone with just one confident and chirpy person, especially when they move in so close.

Margaret wants to play the role of confidante. The scene has been rehearsed not just in her mind, but also in the collective mind of the family. Or perhaps this is another of the Organisation's planned interviews.

'Great,' I say. 'It's great.'

My throat tickles and I start another coughing fit.

Margaret watches and doesn't offer to get me some water.

'Sorry,' I say when I've finished.

'Tell me about your singing,' she says. 'I'd like to hear you.'

I only sing when I'm home by myself, when the flat is empty and I can put a CD on. I don't think it's any great loss that nobody else will ever hear me.

'I really don't feel confident enough yet. I have to know people a bit better before I can sing for them.'

I tell this lie so that I might force myself to find the confidence. I'll go even further. I will trap myself into doing it.

'I'll sing for you next weekend,' I say. 'That's usually how long it takes me.'

'Only if you feel ready,' says Margaret, 'but it would be nice to hear a good voice in the house.'

She stands up. I stand up.

'But you sing, don't you?' I ask.

'Only in the choir. Hardly ever. I used to sing much more,' she says. 'In the old days. It's been a long time.'

'Maybe you could again. We could rehearse a song together and then surprise everybody.'

She takes my hand and kisses it on the knuckle. Then she holds it against her chest and stares at me.

44

'It's so great to have you here, Lou,' she says. 'You make me think.'

I follow her into the kitchen.

'How about some pancakes?' she says.

'Yum,' I say.

And I think: *What do I make you think? Why is it great to have me here? I haven't even been very interesting. I haven't been half as interesting as I planned to be. I just cough and blush and act half crazy.*

When I've finished eating, Margaret asks me to load the washing machine and Henry comes in and puts a tick next to my name on the washing schedule for this week. When he passes me, I look at him and I notice that his eyes are watery.

From my bedroom window I watch the wide, tree-lined street below; children ride tricycles and bicycles and skateboards. Lawns are mowed and cars are washed. People jog wearing bright clothes that seem to be made of plastic. A man practises tai chi on the wide median strip and looks as though he is under water. I hang my head out the window and the breeze on my face and the smells from a barbecue make me smile.

While I'm lying on the bed reading my favourite short story, 'The Overcoat', by Nikolai Gogol, Bridget comes to my door

'Do you want to come out with me and my friends?' she asks, the edges of her white t-shirt implausibly clean against her brown neck and arms.

'Where are you going?' I ask.

'Shopping,' she says.

'What kind of shopping?'

'For *clothes*,' she says. 'I haven't got any summer clothes yet. It's a nightmare! I'm wearing last year's fashions.'

This is the kind of ridiculous thing my sisters would

45

say. I frown at her. I do this without thinking. It's the kind of disdainful look my sisters like to beat me up for. I regret making a mean face, and try to smile.

'I don't really like clothes shopping,' I say.

Bridget sighs and puts one sneaker down hard on the other as though wishing she could kick me. '*Whatever.*'

'Wait,' I say, hating the idea that I am responsible for ending what could have been our first real conversation. 'Do you know what desquamation is?'

'What?' she says.

'Desquamation.'

She crosses her arms over her breasts. 'How do you spell it?'

'How it sounds.'

She shrugs.

'Why don't you just look it up in a dictionary or something?'

'I will,' I say, trying hard to smile. 'Thanks.'

'*Whatever,*' she says and leaves the room, the door wide open.

I am terrified of girls in groups; their gossip and treachery. Shopping malls, fashion magazines, change rooms and trying on clothes, they all make me feel angry and dirty. And shop assistants who barge in on you, and girls who like to shop; they always want to see what other girls' bodies look like.

I follow Bridget down the stairs, but she is out the door before I can explain. I go down to the basement, where James is playing table tennis with some friends. They stop playing their game of doubles and turn to look at me. Like James, they have oily skin and the beginnings of thin moustaches, conspicuous and patchy. James' facial hair is the least developed of the four, and he seems younger than them.

James comes towards me, but not to speak. He is picking up a six-pack of root beer, a big bottle of cola and two large bags of chips. His friends stand and watch.

'This is Lou, our exchange student,' says James, as though I were the new cat.

'Hi,' I say.

They look at me to see if I am gorgeous and decide that I am not. I am too much of an 'it'; neither boy nor girl. Short black hair, white skin, and thin, without shape. Only older women look at me for long, fascinated by what Mrs Walsh once called my 'androgyny'. My mum's best friend, Paula, always says, 'But with a bit of make-up, some peroxide and a dress, she could be a model like you used to be.'

My mum is dismayed by my tomboy clothes and leaves her old dresses on the end of my bed with strange notes, like, *You would look lovely in this.*

'You could be beautiful,' she says. 'You could really stand out.' According to my sisters, however, I have mean eyes. 'Dark and evil grey,' Erin says.

James' friends say nothing more than 'Hi' and get back to their game.

I go up the stairs, into the kitchen, and stand with the fridge door open, staring inside, waiting for my face to cool down, thinking about what James' friends will say to him: *'Bummer, James. She looks like a choir boy.'* I suppose I do.

I return to my room by the back stairs, passing Margaret in her den.

'Hi,' I say.

'Hi,' she says. 'Why don't you go help Henry in the garden?'

'Okay.'

Henry is dismantling the tree house.

'Hi,' I say.

'Hi,' he says, with a busy look on his face, hammer dangling from his hand.

47

I lie on my bed for a few hours. Henry comes to my room to ask me if I'd like to go for a drive with him to get some chicken for dinner. His eyes are weepy again and his bottom lashes are sticky. I want to ask him why his eyes are wet like that.

'No,' I say, 'I think I'll stay here.'

'If you like,' he says.

'I'm tired,' I say. I want to go with Henry, but I'm nervous about having to find enough to talk about, alone with him, in the car, especially if we were to get stuck in traffic.

We are having dinner at the dining-room table. The front door is open to let in the sounds of Saturday evening. James had a shower before sitting down to eat and his wet hair drips onto his place mat. Bridget takes two phone calls during the pumpkin soup and Margaret tells her not to get up while dinner is on the table.

Bridget sighs. 'It's no big deal, Mom.'

Henry removes the soup bowls and brings in the main course, a chicken casserole.

The pepper grinder is passed around the table and Henry coats his casserole in fine black powder.

I was once in a restaurant with my mum and dad. One of Dad's greyhounds had finally won a race and we were celebrating. A few tables away a waiter used a pepper grinder. My dad looked up suddenly from his steak and half stood to look out of the window. He was grinning.

'I think there's a horse and cart out there,' he said.

'Well go and have a look,' said my mum. I closed my eyes for a moment and listened to the sound of the pepper grinder and I got my dad's joke. The pepper grinder sounded a bit like hooves on cobblestones. I laughed and pointed out the big window behind me.

'Look,' I said, 'it's going around the corner.'

My dad squinted and looked. 'I can't see anything.'

I laughed. 'That's because they were going very fast. A big hansom cab with four high wheels.'

I liked my dad just then.

When we've finished eating, Margaret gives twenty dollars each to me and Bridget and James (in that order).

'It's your responsibility to make sure it lasts the week. Once it's finished, don't ask for another penny more.'

There is a conscious effort to include me in all that the family does: the good, the bad and the tedious. I wonder whether the Organisation has issued a handbook: *Your Guide to Being an Effective Host-Family* or *How to Make Your Host-Daughter (or Host-Son) Feel at Home*. I wonder if I would find such a book in Henry or Margaret's bedside drawer. I'll look later, when I'm alone in the house.

After dessert, I go with James to the lounge-room. I lie across one of the leather couches and James lies across the other. He is wearing basketball shorts and a singlet. For a moment we are silent. Suddenly he sits up and moves his body towards mine as though he has a secret to tell. I sit up too, but then he falls down again: a change of plan. He takes a pen from the coffee table and pretends to write something important in the margins of the TV guide; frowning, feigning worry, wanting me to look at him.

'You're left-handed,' I say.

'Congratulations,' he says, without looking up. 'I'm a south-paw.'

'Isn't that a boxer?'

'*Duh.* It just means a left-handed person.'

He looks even harder at me now, his light-blue eyes

narrowing on me, like a lizard suffering from too much sun trying to see what's trapped under its claw.

'I didn't know that,' I say, blushing.

I stare at his arms, his legs, his cheekbones. He knows that I'm watching and does everything he can to pretend he doesn't know. He changes the channel to a cop show. A team of FBI agents pounce on a bunch of drug runners in an alleyway. They are wearing yellow sweaters with FBI written boldly in red across the front.

'The FBI look just like a football team,' I say.

'No they don't,' he says without looking at me. 'They look nothing like a football team.'

I wonder how long it will be before I will be alone in this house. It'd be like being alone in a five-star hotel. I could sleep in each of the beds, snoop in the cupboards, sit in the spa in Margaret and Henry's ensuite, drink some alcohol, eat the whole box of chocolate liqueurs I saw in the piano room, smoke a cigar while on the phone and pull out the photo albums. I could roam around freely for a few days.

Perhaps something tragic could happen to the Hardings and the house would become mine.

It's almost dark outside and we haven't turned the lamps on. The room is blue. On the TV, two skinny, tattooed removalists are taking furniture out of somebody's house and loading it into a van.

I remember an old joke I made up that nobody ever gets.

'I'd like to start a furniture removal business called The Heimlich Removers,' I say.

James doesn't look at me, 'Congratulations,' he says. 'That's very funny. You should tell somebody who thinks it's as funny as you do.'

I am red again. James smiles, a twisted smile, and then he looks at me, long and hard. Our eyes connect for too long, my stomach lurches and I look away.

Margaret comes into the room and stands between the two couches.

'You've been watching that TV for hours,' she says.

'Really?' I wonder what the rule is on a Saturday.

'It's all crap,' says James, 'but there's been some witty distractions along the way.'

Margaret sits on the couch next to me, produces a small apple and starts to munch. These apples appear so frequently it is as though she is a tennis player producing balls from within the folds of her pleated skirt. She takes regular toothy bites and finishes quickly. She holds the apple core between her thumb and index finger. 'James, why don't you change out of those sweaty gym clothes?'

James ignores her.

She frowns. 'I don't know why you'd have a shower and then get right back into the same clothes.'

Margaret leaves the room and I say, 'I'm going to my room to read.'

James swings around. He sits up and rests his chin on the back of the couch so that he can watch me go.

'We have root beer,' he says. 'If you get me some you can watch whatever you want on TV.'

I am forced to look at him and he sees that I am blushing again.

'You're blushing.'

'Congratulations,' I say. 'How astute.'

He returns to a supine position, so that I can't see his face.

I go to my room, but feel lonely straight away. I decide to find Henry. I want to talk to somebody.

I knock on the door to Henry's den.

'Come in,' he says.

'Hi,' I say, 'I was wondering if I could come and sit with you for a while.'

I look at his armchair and the identical armchair opposite him. He has a newspaper on his lap and is smoking a pipe. I have always wanted to smoke a pipe. He looks at his watch.

'Sit down,' he says. 'Is there something you need to talk about?'

'Oh no,' I say, 'I just wanted to sit in here with you and maybe read a book or something, while you keep doing whatever you're doing.'

'Okay,' he says, 'if you'd like.'

'Oh.'

He puts his newspaper down and starts asking me questions; the kinds of questions he and Margaret asked me on the drive from O'Hare airport. What do I like to do on weekends? What are my favourite subjects at school? Have I seen many koalas? If I tell too many more lies, I'll have to write them down, to keep track.

I like talking to Henry. He is shy, yet calm. He makes me feel better. I think he's the kind of person I'd like to be. His shirt is loose, about three buttons undone. I feel like telling him something about my family, something that will make him realise I should never go back. Instead I say, 'Could I just read one of your books for a while?'

Henry tells me to help myself and I take a book off the shelf. We sit in silence then and it is good to sit and read in Henry's den like this. I look at him and his relaxed body and try to relax like him. I read five pages and then suddenly I start talking.

'Actually,' I say, 'my life at home is probably not what you think it is.'

Henry moves in his seat and sits up straighter.

'I know that your family isn't well off,' he says. 'Which must be hard sometimes.'

'It's not that,' I say. 'The trouble has more to do with my sisters and the bad characters they hang out with.' I pause to swallow, but not long enough to stop myself from telling this lie.

'My sister Erin's boyfriend Steve is in prison and before he went inside he was always hanging around with his mates in our flat and giving me a hard time. I'm not looking forward to him getting out.'

Henry rubs his neck.

'What is this Steve character in prison for?'

'Grievous bodily harm,' I say. 'He's a violent guy.'

Henry shifts in his seat and frowns.

'I don't know what I should say,' he says slowly. 'I would have thought the Organisation would have told us something as serious as this.'

Henry is suddenly standing. I don't know why. I stand too.

'Sorry,' I say, 'I didn't mean to shock you. It's really no big deal. My sister is going to break up with him anyway. I'll probably never see him again.'

I think Henry wants me to leave but he also looks like he wants to give me a hug. I think I want him to hug me.

'Well,' he says, standing back, looking almost angry. 'I hope that your sister has enough sense to get rid of Steve and that you'll keep out of his way.'

'Okay,' I say.

Henry closes the door and I stand in the hallway, my heart thumping. I don't know what to do next. I wish that I could start again.

I find Margaret. She's working on her laptop at the dining-room table. I ask her if I can have a bath.

'Of course you can,' she says. 'And you don't need to ask. You're part of the family now, Lou. Just go ahead and make yourself at home.'

She says all of this while typing, as though she were telling somebody where the pencils are kept.

'Thanks,' I say. 'Thanks a lot.'

I am feeling happy until I realise the chair that I've been using to stick under the handle has been taken away. I undress in my room and run to the bathroom wearing a robe. I leave the door open while I run the bath so that they will all know this is what I'm doing and so nobody will come in to use the upstairs toilet.

A few minutes later somebody knocks.

'I'm in the bath,' I say.

'It's only me,' says Margaret. 'I just need to get something from the cabinet.'

I want to say 'No' or 'Wait' but she is already inside. She's got a small towel wrapped around her torso. She's naked. I can see some of her pubic hair poking out, black against the pink of the towel. She looks straight at me — not for long — but still, she looks.

She's humming. She opens the cupboard over the sink and then turns to me.

'Scoot over,' she says. 'Make some room.'

I do not speak. I pull my legs into my chest. I think I say 'There you go' or 'Okay then' but I can't be sure.

'Only kidding,' she says. 'I'm taking a spa in the ensuite. It's all yours.'

I pretend to laugh but my face, neck, ears and throat are burning with shame and my throat feels like someone's fist is stuck inside it.

After my bath, I lie on my bed and read a letter from my mum. Here is some of it:

Dear Yankie Daughter,

. . . Your cousin Paul is two and a half years old now. Your auntie Marys all worried because he doesnt speak at all and can't walk properly and he cries all the time and bangs his head against the wall. But I tell her that Einstein didn't even talk until he was three and was a bad baby and he was a world genius and that shes not to worry. I tell her he's probably real special and she should keep him away from those crazy doctors. You know what doctors are like? They used to say you had that disease and keep you in hospital all the time and they used to say they could do an operation to stop you going red. What do any of them know about children my love? Look at you now!

. . . Your auntie Sallys hip is all fixed and . . .

. . . Your dad won the cricket last weekend and is happy as Larry. He shoved the trophy in the TV cabinet so we can all see it all night long but I'm going to stash it away in his sock drawer.

. . . Erin is happy because shes thinking of doing a nursing course. It only takes one year and then she'll be able to work and move into a house with Steve. She said shes thinking of moving inter-state because the nurses are always going on strike there and she'll get more holidays!

Etc, etc . . .

Love,

Your one and only mum

p.s: Leona wanted to add a note without me seeing it. She insists on seeling this letter herself. So dont blame me if its really rude. It probably will be!

Dear Sisko Kid!

Greg thought up the best joke the other day about Catholics. He said theres one thing about Catholic girls. . .half of them take it in

55

the hand and half of them in the mouth! Pretty bloody clever dont
you think? It'll take you a while to work it out. A hint — remember
when we used to take holy communion when we were kids?

    Farewell,
    The Hand Maiden

To recover from this obscene letter, I write seven pages of
promises, pacts and undertakings.

I write that I will learn a language and take up the piano.
Margaret can teach me. This might help her get back to what
she misses and loves to do. I write a promise that I will do
extremely well at school, sleep well and write for the school
newspaper. I will swim in the mornings before school to get fit
and develop legs like Bridget's. I will fulfil my enormous poten-
tial, learn a new word every day, read a novel every week and
become the world's most impressive autodidact and polymath.
I will go to university and live in student digs.

This is only the first page.

When I finish, I lie down and look at the light coming in
under the door and I am convinced that everything will be
better from now on.

5

The Harding vacation is about to begin. Bridget and James are packing their bags and Henry is whistling in the bathroom. I want to stay here. It's hot out there and my eyes are stinging.

Last night I couldn't get to sleep. I got up and walked around the house in my socks. I drank some milk at the kitchen table and then I stood outside James' bedroom and looked at him sleeping. Henry and Margaret's door was ajar, so I opened it and looked inside. Henry snored. I walked up and down the landing and wished that I could wake somebody. I thought about it. I thought about making noise and waking them just to have somebody to talk to. The longer I paced the angrier I got with them for being able to sleep. I thought about emptying the pots and pans from the kitchen cupboards or pushing a bookshelf over in the library then running back to my bed.

We could sit up together and talk about whether there had been a burglar and whether or not to call the police. But when the excitement faded, they would return to their pillows to sleep and I would still be awake.

I sat against the banister and fantasised about throwing myself down the stairs and lying there at the bottom. Henry would find me first. I would lie there with my eyes closed and they would think I had sleep-walked and fallen from the top of the landing. I could do this five or six times, get myself covered in bruises and then they'd send me to a sleep clinic. I wanted not to be awake and alone.

Margaret comes into my room without knocking.

'Are you ready?' she asks, her mouth red with lipstick, her long hair out of its bun and in two thick plaits. She is wearing shorts and long socks.

'Yep,' I say. 'When are we leaving?'

I wonder if I might have time to snooze for ten minutes.

'Now!' she says, grabbing me playfully by the hand. 'Let's hit the road.'

'I'll just pack some books,' I say.

'If you think you'll need them, go right ahead.'

What?

'But you might want to take a break from the books and take in some scenery.'

'Okay,' I say and we leave my room together.

The vacation will last fourteen days and take us through three states. The mini-van (the Hardings' third vehicle) is packed to the gills with blankets, pillows, games, a first-aid kit and junk food. But I have only one book packed, and I feel uneasy about all the time I'll have to fill.

It is our second day on the road. James and Bridget and I lie on our stomachs and stare out the back window at the broken white lines oozing out from under the van. I am sick from the heat and doze fitfully, having eaten my way through several bags, buckets and cartons of food made mostly from salt and sugar.

I open my eyes after a foul-mouthed sleep and catch James staring at me. I look out the back window and discover that we are travelling through completely new scenery, steep mountains and deep, green valleys, but I am too palsied by the immense heat and over-eating to think any of it beautiful.

Margaret turns around in her seat. 'How are you getting on back there?' she asks. 'Fine,' we say, or 'Great.'

When Bridget and James fight, Henry threatens to pull over and when they stop he says *tsk tsk*. I am surprised to hear him say *tsk tsk*. My mum does this. It drives me mad.

Bridget plucks her eyebrows, plays solitaire and talks about her best friend, Sonia, whose mom and dad – she tells us several times – have bought a yacht and gone sailing. She doesn't say she wishes she could have gone with them, but it's obvious that's what she's getting at.

'Can I use your cellphone, Mom?' asks Bridget every time we stop to get gas.

'Just one call,' says Margaret.

James reads comics and waits until Henry and Margaret are out of earshot so that he can make sarcastic remarks using words he has obviously picked up from the cartoonists. He tells me I'm weird about ten times a day.

'Why?' I say.

'Because you are,' he says. Or, 'Because you can't help it.'

I read a few pages of my book at a time, until I feel car sick and need to lie down and doze. I want to be back in the air-conditioned house. I want to be alone so that my heart can slow down.

Four days pass in this way and the only relief from the tedium of driving comes when we stop to eat at roadside diners or to picnic in a forest. At first, I liked the tacky roadside truck-stops; each one of them different and yet all of them the same, with their salmon or peach coloured plastic chairs, cigarette burns on the toilet seats, striped or floral curtains gathered up with greasy ribbons.

But like the motel rooms we stay in, these truck-stops are only satisfying for a little while. The first sight of a motel room gives me a thrill of newness and surprise, but by the morning it has closed in on me and I feel dirty.

At first I took an inventory of peculiar American brand names and slang words. But this novelty has already worn off and I have to force a kind of traveller's awe. It's not really very interesting that things are called something else.

The only entry in my diary is a long one about fast food and the neon signs and billboards advertising giant-size portions of everything. The food in the ads is so big that by the time you unwrap your burger it looks like a flea. I want more. I want something different. I've never felt this hungry before. I've never felt like I needed to put so much in my mouth. Maybe the ads produce saliva. Suddenly I expect food to give me an emotion, the one I *saw*, the one I've seen on the billboards of beautiful people.

After years of exposure to this advertising frenzy, people must start to despise each other for being ugly, for having so much as a birthmark on their chin with hair growing out of it.

Yesterday, when we got our photos developed, I hardly seemed real to myself: teeth not white, hair not shiny and arms not lithe. I felt like ripping my face off my skull.

That's the only thing I've written about in my diary.

Whenever we stop somewhere, Henry spends a long time taking our rubbish to the bin.

'There's a trash can right here,' says Margaret, but Henry wants to walk with the rubbish bags.

'I feel like stretching my legs,' he says and it's clear he wants to be alone.

Bridget always has her basketball with her and she runs up ahead and dribbles the ball, sometimes circling us and throwing the ball at us when we aren't ready.

'Catch!' she says, and the ball hits one of us in the chest or head.

Whenever we get stuck in traffic, Margaret suggests we play a word or memory game and James always refuses to play.

'You've got some competition now,' says Henry, winking at me in the rear-vision mirror. 'You'd better get used to it.'

Wherever we go, James wants a new pair of expensive gym shoes or a new comic book.

'You have plenty already,' says Margaret. 'Why do you always want more?

'Call it boredom,' says James, 'call it the materialist age. Just let me be free, man. Just let me be free.'

In the roadside diners, we sit with our fries and our burgers and above us slow fans turn, covered in grime. Henry orders the same thing at most meals: a piece of steak, rare or medium rare, which he covers in maple syrup. I feel dirty and dishevelled and wish I could have a cold shower and lie down in the shade. I wonder how it is that the Hardings always look clean; how even when they say they find the weather hot, they do not seem to sweat.

Perhaps it is a question of having lived cleaner lives, a cumulative thing. The brand-new clothes they have bought already look filthy on me, and I've worn them only once.

In the back of the van I try to read in spite of the heat and car sickness, but there is always a fly or two harassing me, and one big fly, in particular, who seems to be staying with me all the way. He edges his way across the page, reading one word at a time. When I shoo him, he comes right back, and crawls sideways from the start of the page as though I have made him lose his place.

Henry asks me whether I'm okay whenever we are alone.

When I say I'm fine, he frowns, so I say, 'Do I not seem okay?' and he always answers in the same way, 'No, you seem fine.'

It's like an argument with no subject. It stops all conversation – this checking up on me – so I tend to ask him back, 'Are you okay?' and he says, 'Of course I'm okay.' And that's that.

We don't get much further even though it's clear we both want to. Sometimes we talk some more, but if Margaret is near, his sentences become shorter and he slips away.

I want to be back in the house. Henry and I alone in Henry's den, at night, each in our own matching armchair, him smoking his pipe and me reading. It would be best of all to go back in time, to my first or second night, or forward in time, to winter, so we could be wearing woolly jumpers. That would be best, with the open fire burning. We could start again.

It is our sixth day on the road and Margaret and Bridget and I are sitting on a bench in a small-town shopping mall while Henry takes James to look at colleges.

Nearby, a woman beats her child. She is screaming at him, smacking his bottom. The woman says, 'Bad boy! Bad boy!' over and over, while the child cowers between her legs, and when she whacks him hard across the head, he runs behind a pot plant and howls, with guttural disbelief.

I walk towards the woman. I hope that when she sees I am watching, she will stop beating her boy. Margaret rushes after me, takes my arm and says, 'Come and sit down. There's nothing we can do.'

I take Margaret's hand off my arm and say, 'What's the point of just standing here and watching a woman beat the living crap out of her child!'

Margaret pulls harder on my arm.

'Lou,' she whispers. 'Don't ever speak to me like that.'

'Why the fuck not?' I say, using the word fuck as though it were capable of inflicting pain.

Margaret walks away and the woman drags the boy into the bathroom.

I sit down on the bench next to Bridget and put my head in my hands. 'That was *stupid*,' she says. I am too angry to speak, so I look at the floor. A few minutes later Margaret returns holding three ice-creams, one flavoured scoop on top of another; three brightly coloured *Sesame Street* scoops each.

We eat our ice-creams and nobody speaks until I say to Margaret, 'This is the biggest mall I have ever seen.' Bridget is still furious with me and she narrows her eyes.

Margaret smiles. 'This is nothing. Some malls are so big, joggers use them in winter for doing laps.'

Bridget drops her half-eaten ice-cream into a bin. She looks at me as though I were something the cat dragged in.

'Let's find some new clothes for Lou.'

'Thanks,' I say. 'But there's really no need.'

The next day, Henry, Bridget and I go to a basketball game. Margaret stays in the motel room, because she has a bad back and James is staying with her, in case she needs help.

It's hot. This kind of intense heat pins you to the ground and, sooner or later, you feel like crying.

Henry stares hard at the game and when I talk he doesn't want to look at me.

I take out a tissue and wipe the sweat that is crawling along the back of my neck. I want this vacation to be over; to go back to the airconditioned house.

'I'm boiling,' I say. 'It's too hot.'

'Hum?' he says.

For the next hour I sit quietly and Henry looks sideways at me every few minutes. He's probably wishing that Margaret could be here too, instead of having to go to bed with lumbago.

That's how Henry said it: *She's gone to bed with lumbago.*

I want to tell him that 'going to bed with lumbago' makes it sound like Margaret has gone to bed with another man, probably a Spanish man with lumps, but I change my mind.

Henry presses his finger into the side of his face and chews at the flesh on the inside of his mouth.

I try to distract myself by concentrating on Bridget's legs. Her brown skin is like a stocking and you can see the muscles shudder as she extends her legs, strong and animal. Although she has fair skin on her face, like her father, she doesn't redden and, unlike James, her skin is never damp.

The game finishes and Henry rushes towards the exit. We go to the car park and Henry is holding Bridget's hand. He buys her a drink from a man with a fridge on wheels. The man has a flat, squashed nose.

'That man,' I say as we get into the car, 'looked like somebody would look if they wore a stocking over their face.'

'How cruel and mean,' says Bridget.

Henry is silent.

I don't want to point out to either of them that every one of Bridget's friends looks like a model, that none of them are black, Asian or Hispanic, and that most of her conversation is about clothes and who looks good wearing what. I don't want to explain how hypocritical Bridget is, even though it might help Henry to know.

My insomnia is getting worse, and as we drive for hours and hours in the hot sun, I daydream about a world full of rental beds where insomniacs could sleep. These beds would be in small, neat, clean rooms. You could drop a coin into a box and obtain a half-hour of guaranteed sleep. Perhaps these special rooms could fill with a benevolent sleeping gas, or include a bottle of something to drink to help you along. It would not matter, so long as these beds were everywhere you needed them, and so long as they were comfortable and the sleep was guaranteed.

These special rooms for insomniacs would be found in shopping malls, in restaurants, in libraries, in cinemas and in schools; the beds tucked away behind discreet, sound-proofed walls with lockable doors, in small, temperature-controlled rooms with music if you wanted it and a toaster and a kettle (and a basket of plastic-wrapped biscuits).

Yesterday morning James bought a flick-comb: a fake flick-knife that opens out into a hair comb. He uses it constantly. He flicks it open now at an old lady who is looking at us from across the diner.

'Stop that!' says Margaret, but James continues.

Henry gulps an enormous lump of meat too quickly.

'What's *wrong* with you, James?' he asks.

James flicks his flick-comb at my face.

'Nothing's wrong,' he says, his baby moustache like a scribble above his lip.

'Please stop it, James!' says Henry. 'I don't know what's wrong with you. You've been acting very strangely ever since . . .'

Henry realises what he is about to say and turns away, awkward, shifting in his seat, ashamed. *But who are you ashamed of?* I want to ask. *Are you ashamed of your son or of me? What have I done wrong?*

It is our ninth day on the road and we stop at a roadside cafeteria because I say I need to go to the toilet.

'The *bathroom*,' says Bridget. 'You need to use the *bathroom*.'

Margaret follows me into the cramped cubicle. It smells foul; a mixture of human waste and 'Pine Forest' air freshener.

The smell forces me to breathe through my mouth.

There is one small sink in the cubicle, a room so small that when the door opens it comes close to hitting the toilet bowl.

When Margaret follows me I think she must be coming in to use the sink while I urinate. I expect that when she realises both sink and toilet are in the same tiny room, she'll leave and come back when I'm finished. But when I open the cubicle door she is right up behind me, and I can feel her bosom on my back.

'You go first,' she says.

I am paralysed by this idea. I know that I should say something smooth and easy like, 'Okay. You wait outside and I'll yell when I'm finished.' I rehearse this sentence but can't speak.

She stands in front of the locked cubicle door, and is staring, in her phlegmatic way, at the lower half of my body. She strikes me as being emotionless, a person who would never blush or burst into tears over anything. She is too normal, too relaxed, as she stares right at me and talks loudly at me about the heat.

I am skinless.

'Sorry,' I say. 'I don't need to go after all.'

'Okay,' she says. 'I'll go then.'

And so I stand and stare at the wall, red-faced, while Margaret slowly unbuttons the metal studs on her jeans.

Back in the van, while James and Bridget sleep, I remember saying goodbye to my mum at the airport.

'Okay, I'm going now,' I said.

My mum looked down at the brand-new camera hanging around her neck. 'But there's an hour and a half till boarding.'

'I just want to go,' I said.

She wanted happy pictures of us together. She wanted something good to happen, so that one day it would be possible to say, 'Remember when I saw you off at the airport when you were going to the States?'

She looked over her shoulder at a group of exchange students sitting with their families in the cafeteria. She wanted to ask one of them to take a photo of us, our arms around each other, smiling.

'All right,' she said.

She lifted the camera up over her head and put it carefully back in her bag, making a comfortable nest for it and checking to see if it was secure, as though it was a miniature me she was stashing away. My mum wore her cardigan wrapped around her waist, the other mothers wore theirs draped around their shoulders.

'Gimme a hug,' she said. So, with my backpack on my back and my shoulder bag swinging heavily down to my elbow, I hugged her and my breasts made awkward contact with the top of hers. Her breasts, flattened against mine, repulsed me. They were too large and warm, eager to maintain contact, mine small and cold.

I let go, adjusted my bags and said, 'Rent out my room if you want. You could probably get thirty dollars a week for it.'

I turned away from her and started walking, my throat fat with grief, my jaw shaking and my teeth grinding. Even at a distance of a few metres I could hear her crying. I adjusted my bags again, felt for my passport and rushed towards the boarding gate. My throat cleared.

Her sadness didn't matter. If my new family could afford a sleep clinic or good doctor to help me, I'd take them; I'd take two dozen of whatever I could lay my hands on.

A few hours later, James sits up close to me and stares. His once thin and scrawny moustache is thicker now, more like

those being grown by the friends he takes down to the basement. We are under his black sheet and his leg is rubbing
against mine.

'Hey there, weirdo,' he says, his voice a deep, low whisper.

'Piss off, loser,' I say, and to stop myself from turning red,
I think of myself as a disused telephone, its plug wrenched
from the wall, the cord dangling, no longer capable of being
startled.

'Weirdo,' he says.

6

It's our eleventh night on the road, and I'm sitting cross-legged, looking out the back window, riding the bumps in the road, letting myself sail. At times the road is so quiet that we seem to hover like a spacecraft under the bright stars, taking off when the road climbs up a hill and landing when it glides down the other side.

I like the open country road at night. It is one of my favourite things, along with the sound car tyres make on a wet road, and road signs with knives and forks on them to signify food, and beds to signify sleep, and the sight of an aeroplane at night, with its landing lights on. Everything that is stupid by day seems intelligent and meaningful by night. I love to look out the wide back window and pretend that I am alone.

I love how the road lights burn holes in the dark. The damp air, and the darkness, inside and out, remind me of my first game of murder in the dark. The shock of pitch black, of hands reaching out for hands, exaggerated cries, an odd weightlessness in my legs as I ran fast to hide in a cupboard at the end of the hallway. I was nine or ten and my sisters' boyfriends were much older, adults compared to us.

When we drive at night, I feel that same weightlessness and speed in my blood. And when we drive at night something happens to James. During the daylight hours his conversation is quick and sharp, defensive, like verbal kung fu.

But at night there is a change. James' big face, his tufty, immature sideburns, his pimply skin, his oiliness, are all covered up. He looks better, but more than that, the fact that his flaws can no longer be seen in the dark seems to cause in him a psychic transformation, and his words are kinder.

Bridget and Margaret are sleeping and Henry drives. All is quiet and smooth and peaceful. James sits close to me, and copies my cross-legged pose. In the darkness his face looks good and it occurs to me that mine might too. I look at him, much longer than I could bear to look at him with the light on us.

James' eyes rearrange me when he stares back. My body shudders; a tiny, sharp, quick pulse travels through me, and my face, rather than rising to a blush, feels warm as though I were sitting before an open fire. My palms, rather than sweating, crave the sensation of skin and so I rub my own hands, one over the other softly, deliberately, to feel flesh. James' eyes have narrowed but they do not look away. He continues to gaze into my eyes and his chest rises violently; a deep, sudden breath. We have become something else in the darkness and it feels more like the truth.

A car overtakes us, going too quickly, and Henry beeps hard and clicks his tongue on the roof of his mouth, *tsk, tsk.*

I look away from James, excited, and afraid. We have nearly kissed each other's shadow and now we pull away. We lie down, facing out the back window, close enough to each other for it to take a long time for the stirring to go away.

One of us has to speak. I ask him, 'Do you know what desquamation is?'

James does not look at me.

'I don't know. It's clearly a noun. Probably some kind of illness. Am I right?'

'If I knew what it was I wouldn't have asked you,' I say,

staring out of the window. This disappointing bit of conversation ends, and what had seemed to be the truth suddenly looks like a dangerous lie the darkness told.

We are eating in a hotel restaurant to celebrate Bridget's fourteenth birthday. Bridget opens her presents. Margaret and Henry give her a gold bracelet with a diamond in it and her grandparents have given her a gold pen. Henry orders champagne and my stomach churns at the sight of it. For the past few days I've been craving alcohol. I miss the way it makes me feel: soft, nerveless and edgeless. Most of all I miss how it helps me sleep.

'Let's toast to Lou. Our newest family member.'

My glass is empty but I don't refill it. When we toast, I use both hands to hold on, and drink the air from the glass.

I look at Henry. 'Since it's a special occasion, could we drink some champagne?'

Henry looks at Margaret and Margaret looks at Bridget.

'I'm sorry,' says Margaret, 'but the legal age for the consumption of alcohol is twenty-one.'

After our fancy dinner we go to the movies in a decayed old movie house in a small country town. Bridget gets to pick the film. We shove our hands into boxes of greasy popcorn and the almost-fluorescent white pieces bounce like tiny erasers from our knees and litter the carpet.

The movie is boring and it reminds me of Steve and his habit of deliberately disturbing innocent people in cinemas.

Steve and his best friend, Ryan, find a romantic, feel-good movie and sit next to a woman, preferably an old woman. Then Steve turns to Ryan during the pre-movie advertisements and confesses to a murder or some other violent crime he pretends to have committed only a few hours earlier.

In a loud voice he'll say something like, 'Look, I didn't mean for the knife to go right through her lungs,' or, 'She wasn't meant to fucking die!'

Then he waits for the woman to get scared and move seats or leave the cinema.

Steve has an unnerving and convincing imagination when it comes to making up crimes. I pointed this out to Erin once and she spat in my hair. 'It's only *fun*,' she said. 'But *you* wouldn't even know what that is!'

Bridget is holding her mum's hand while watching the boring movie and Henry has fallen asleep. After all the popcorn has been eaten, James moves in his seat so that his shoulder touches mine. I move away but he moves closer. His knee presses up against me and then he pretends to scratch so that he can rub his hand on my leg.

I feel as though I've swallowed fast-acting poison. I'm sweating, not just a light prickling sweat, but a pouring sweat from the palms of my hands. I need to leave the movie theatre.

I make my way over the outstretched legs of Bridget and Henry and Margaret

'I'll be back in a minute,' I whisper.

I sit in the foyer for about twenty minutes and then decide to find something to drink. A drink will help the panic and maybe help me sleep when we get back to the motel. What I need to do is buy a small bottle of gin and drink some now and some later, but not too much.

I take my wallet out of my pocket and check for the twenty dollars Margaret gave me.

I walk a few blocks and find a licensed grocer. The woman behind the counter bothers me. There's no doubt I look older than I am, but older women are better at knowing the difference between sixteen and twenty-one.

72

The shop is dark and there is a group of teenage boys getting ready to shoplift in the back corner.

'Can I have a small bottle of gin, please?'

The shopkeeper is trying to keep one eye on the shop-lifters and one on me. She puts her pen in her mouth and looks me up and down.

There's a Guatemalan worry-doll stuck to the cash register with sticky tape – a thick wad of tape wrapped round the head and feet – a sad, desperate and superstitious presence in this bleak, grimly-lit place. I decide to speak a little more; perhaps my accent will help convince her that I'm old enough.

I say, 'If you don't have any gin I'll have that vodka instead.'

'We have gin,' she says with tired resignation, putting her pen down on the counter. 'The big bottle is on special if you want that.'

I realise that this is a gift horse.

'How much is off the usual price?' I ask.

'Two dollar twenty,' she says. I am surprised she hasn't asked me what part of England I'm from. Everybody else does.

'Okay,' I say, 'that's a terrific bargain. I'd better take two.'

Suddenly she is suspicious and she squints at my face. I get ready to leave, worried that I might collapse or vomit.

There is a menacing burst of laughter from the corner full of boys.

'Damned kids,' says the shopkeeper.

She looks back at me one last time then swings around. With her back to me, and one hand reaching up for the bottle of gin, she says, 'One bottle per customer only.'

I say, 'One bottle's fine.'

I sit in a nearby park and drink enough gin to feel soft. I stand once or twice to see how I am on my feet and I am fine. I wrap the bottle inside a jacket in my backpack and head back to the cinema. I buy a bottle of water and wait in the foyer.

Margaret comes out of the cinema looking angry. 'It's bad manners to walk out of a film. It makes the other people feel awkward. Where did you go?'

'Nowhere,' I say. 'I just didn't like the film and I thought I'd go for a walk around the block a few times.'

Margaret has strong feelings about this, which is rather strange. I walk out of films all the time, especially when actors continually don't know what to do with their hands and have only got parts because they're handsome or pretty.

'You should always finish what's on your plate,' she says. 'When you start something you should finish it.'

All along I expected her to be cross about me being on my own in the dark, in a strange town, but this doesn't seem to be her concern.

'You should apologise to Bridget,' she says as we walk out.

'Let's hit the road,' says Henry when he catches up with us a few minutes later. For once, he isn't trying to hide the fact that he's having a boring time. I wink at him, but he doesn't wink back.

In the back of the van I tell Bridget I'm sorry. 'What for?' she says.

'For walking out of the film.'

She rolls her eyes and looks away from me. '*Whatever*. I don't care. You can do whatever you want.'

Our motel for the night is down-market; neon sign busted, a skip of overflowing garbage near the manager's door and brickwork the colour of shit.

Margaret comes back from the manager's office with only one key. I notice this right away. James and Bridget are swimming in the pool.

'There's only one room left,' she says.

'Couldn't we go somewhere else?' I say.

'It won't kill you,' she says.

Henry gives her a look, as though he'd like to argue with her, but can't find the courage. She always gets her own way.

'I'll walk up to the motel further back that way,' I say. 'I'll ask if they have three rooms.'

Henry shakes his head and makes his favourite *tsk, tsk* sound.

'It's not the end of the world,' he says. 'Just relax.'

There's no airconditioning in the small room, not even a kettle or small basket of plastic-wrapped biscuits. Worse still, there is only one double bed and that's where Margaret and Henry will sleep. There's no other room or beds and I am desperate for some privacy.

James, Bridget and I collapse on the couch and sulk about the prospect of having to sleep on the floor. Margaret puts her hands on her hips and says, 'It won't *kill* any of you.'

Bridget keeps on protesting, and saying that it isn't fair, and when she looks at me I'm suddenly aware that this is my punishment for trying to intervene when that woman was beating her child, or for walking out of the film; or both. It's obviously not an economic necessity.

We put our blankets on the floor and lie down under sheets with two pillows each under our heads.

Bridget and I are in the middle of the room, and James lies away from us, nearer to the wall. We have agreed that none of us will sleep on the couch, for the sake of fairness, but I wonder if James plans to move there once Bridget and I are asleep.

The window is open but there is no breeze. For several hours I lie awake listening to cars arriving, people spilling out and making their identical arrangements. I watch the motel room wall on which car headlights cast sudden beams of light, and I imagine this is what it must be like crouching under the searchlights of the enemy. One beam of light scans from left to

75

right and then holds to the ceiling for too long, and I think the enemy has no intention of giving up. Another beam swipes quickly across the wall and disappears and I know that the enemy is leaving. I wonder if the enemy, whose beam has just been doused outside my door, will stay up all night drinking, the TV turned up too loud.

I'm not sure how long I've been sleeping when it happens; when I am woken by James, whose hand is in my underpants. I think that I am dreaming at first, and move to shake it off.

I have my back to him and move away, in case he is sleeping and doesn't know what he's doing. But he moves in closer, and I decide to pretend to sleep. If I am asleep, then how can it matter? It will be as though nothing has happened.

I close my eyes, to remove myself from this strange thing. I am woozy at first then something else. It's a surprise, the slow release of a pleasant poison, drip by drip. I should want him to stop, remove his searching hand, but if we are asleep, what can it matter?

I lie still. His hand is moving and I don't block its path. I'm curious. I'm curious as hell about what happens next.

His hand makes its way — as though it belongs to somebody else — into the front of my pants. I clench up. I want the feeling, but don't want James to be at the other end of it. I clench still more, then relax. His finger starts to rub.

Tomorrow it will be as though nothing has happened. I don't want to touch him and I don't have to. How can somebody who is asleep touch somebody? His finger continues in its fast, silent, and tireless way and the better I feel the more I wonder how it is he knows what to do and what it is that he's getting out of it.

He stops and we both play dead.

In the morning, Margaret opens the curtains and the room becomes too bright, too soon.

'Time to get up,' she says. 'Time to hit the road.'

7

I have read somewhere that one is not permitted to think of the Torah whilst on the toilet. I have also read that when Tolstoy was a child, his older brother would torment the young writer by telling him to stand in a corner and *not* think of a white bear. Consequently, a white bear was all that Tolstoy could think about.

This morning – the morning of our last day – all I can think about is sleep. Breakfast has finished. The others have gone to buy some more soft drinks and Margaret and I are sitting in the airconditioned fast-food restaurant where we had our breakfast.

I decide to tell her about my problems with sleep.

'Margaret, I think I have insomnia.'

She raises her eyebrows.

'You just need to relax. Try not to think of sleep. You're probably thinking about it too much.'

'That's funny,' I say. 'I was thinking that maybe that's my exact problem but the point is that because I can't sleep it's impossible not to think about it all the time. Like Tolstoy and the white bear.'

'What?'

'It doesn't matter. I just think maybe it's a treatable condition. Maybe if I went to see a specialist in a good hospital or something.'

'Just relax. Breathe deeply through your nose and out of your mouth like this.'

Margaret demonstrates how to breathe. She even makes me put my hand on her diaphragm so I know how it all works.

But I already know all about breathing and relaxation techniques. I know about the importance of being calm and doing exercise, and drinking hot milk and all that crap. Mrs Walsh is an expert.

I wish I had told Henry instead.

'It'll come,' she says. 'It'll come.'

I want to tell her that as a member of that class of slack-minded, unimaginative, easy-sleeping snorers who do not understand insomnia and never will, she has no right to tell me how to sleep. I want to tell her that not only can I not sleep most nights, when I do sleep, my dreams are awful.

Instead I say, 'I'll try that. Thanks.'

She hugs me for too long and says, 'It's only a phase. It'll pass.'

'What if it doesn't?' I say. 'It's been happening for a long time. Maybe I should see a doctor or something? Some kind of specialist?'

Margaret's hair is back in its bun and she reaches to adjust it. This means she is either annoyed or bored. She says, 'You just need to relax your mind. Stop worrying. It's all a question of serenity. Peace of mind. Just don't worry so much. You're too young to worry so much.'

I want to kick her in the shins. That's where I always want to kick somebody when they're being stupid. Right on the bone.

I also want to tell her that my insomnia and my blushing are closely connected – the less I sleep, the more I blush – and that perhaps I have a treatable condition, but she is standing up, looking for her purse.

'Okay,' I say. 'I'll try relaxing a bit more.'

'That's the spirit,' Margaret says and we start walking towards the door.

Now she's using her loud voice, the voice she uses when it seems she wants everybody to enjoy the benefits of her wisdom.

'You know, at your age you really shouldn't be so uptight. When I was your age I slept like a baby. Maybe you could try some more exercise. That'll fix you. Wait till you're my age and working all hours, then you can lie awake all night thinking about what to do with the world.'

I feel annihilated but I smile.

'Thanks,' I say.

After breakfast we stop at an amusement park called 'Old Mac-Donald's', somewhere in a field on the outskirts of a country town. The whole fair is based on the nursery rhyme, with rides made out of plastic sheep and cows and chickens. It's my fault we've stopped here at all. I pointed to it as we drove by and when Henry asked me if I'd like to have a look I said 'Yeah, that'd be great fun' because I thought, for once, I should sound enthusiastic about something other than visiting bookstores or playing word games in airconditioned motel rooms.

It's another hot day. The clouds sit low and are full and bulging, like egg whites whisked into stiffness; a benign blanket above. Usually this kind of cloud cheers me up.

We walk up and down the Barnyard of Games, the tune of Old MacDonald tinny and insistent, the smell of manure forcing me to breathe through my mouth.

We don't play any of the games and ignore the prospect of shooting ducks, gagging geese with ping-pong balls or throwing balls at bales of hay.

There is something depressing about a small and dirty fairground; the cheapness of the stuffed-animal prizes, the smell of frying fat, the way the games are rigged, and this one is the worst I've ever seen.

Everything is automated. There are no carnies to take tickets for rides. Instead, machines into which coins are fed and from which tickets spew out, operate the rides. The gates open to let people through only when enough tickets are taken, and then the rides begin.

The whole thing depresses me in the same way that bathroom vending machines do; those machines that issue condoms, polo mints and headache tablets all at once. It makes me gloomy to think that, one day, vending machines will issue books and music and shoes and wigs and underpants and goldfish and death certificates.

And so we walk up and down the same avenue of farm-yard-themed arcade games listening to the metallic sound of Old MacDonald Had A Farm, Eeee Eye Eeeee Eye Oh. There's nobody to explain the rules, nobody to grab at a soft toy from the back wall with a comical hook.

I catch up with Henry.

'Could I talk to you?'

'Sure,' he says.

He slows down and we let the others go on ahead.

'I have insomnia,' I say. 'Most nights it takes me hours and hours to get to sleep, or I wake too early, and then I feel tired all day. I think it's a treatable condition.'

Henry looks at my hands while I speak, a habit that is driving me crazy. It's as though he's some kind of body language expert trying to catch me out, and his habit forces me to put my hands in my pockets and then I feel like I'm going to fall over.

'How long have you had trouble sleeping?'

'A long time,' I say. 'Maybe since I was nine or ten.'

'That's a pretty serious problem then. Have your parents ever taken you to a doctor?'

My parents? It sounds like such a strange and out of place word, *parents*, a word referring to a concept I'm not exactly familiar with.

'Not really,' I say. 'They know about it but they just keep telling me it'll go away.'

'Well,' says Henry, 'why don't I talk to Margaret about it and we'll work something out. Maybe you could see our family doctor. He's very good. We met him on the flight coming back from Paris. About eighteen years ago.'

Henry looks at the pavement in front of his shoes.

'Eighteen years,' he says. 'Could it really be that long?'

'I couldn't tell you,' I say, sarcastically.

Henry's voice has become flat, like my dad's is most of the time. I wonder if Henry is disappointed with his life. I remember what my dad said a few weeks before I left, late at night, when Erin and Leona and my mum had gone to bed.

He was sitting forward in his chair and, quite unexpectedly, he turned the TV off and stood up, and he looked down at me and said, 'When I got to the age of thirty-three, the age they say Jesus was when he died, I started to panic because I hadn't done all the things I'd planned to do.'

He started to open the door to the hall and then he turned around and let me see that his eyes were wet and he said, 'Don't let time run out on you.'

8

We've been back for two days. It's Saturday night and Henry and Margaret arrive home late, after dinner with friends, their teeth blackened by red wine. They look oddly beautiful, deranged, and somehow more real. They come into the living room to chat before going to bed.

'Did you have a nice night?' asks Bridget.

James, who is sitting on the floor, close to the TV, turns up the volume and does not look around to greet his parents, perhaps because this would involve looking at me, which he hasn't done since we got back from our vacation.

'Yes,' says Henry, smiling broadly. 'We had a wonderful time. But there's something wrong with your Uncle Pete.'

'What?' says Bridget.

'Well, he might have gone a bit mad.'

'Mad*der*,' says James without turning around.

Henry laughs hard and I stare at him. His face is flushed and he looks handsome, his eyes have lost their weepiness and seem brighter. He sits on the arm of the couch, grinning and swaying, as though he is sitting deck-side on a cruise ship, moved gently by the waves, pleased with his lunch, keeping an eye out for whales or seagulls.

'Wait till you hear this,' says Margaret, and Henry continues.

'Early in the night, while everybody was drinking wine, he asked for some milk and after he drank it, he said, "This milk is really weird. The cows must have been eating unusual things. I think I better pour the rest down the sink."'

'And did he?' I ask.

'The whole lot,' says Margaret, 'and we had none for our coffee after dinner.'

I laugh and so does Bridget.

'That's *stupid*,' says James, looking at me.

Henry and Margaret are in great form, quite drunk. Henry is less polite. When he can no longer hold himself up on the arm of the couch, he rolls off and lands next to me.

'Shit. Sorry,' he says. 'The couch must have the hiccups.'

I move across to give him more room, but we are still close; close enough for my knee to knock his whenever he moves.

Margaret is lying across the other couch with her legs on Bridget's lap. Her hair is down and it is long enough to reach the belt of her trousers. Henry reaches across and strokes Margaret's head and this makes her laugh for no apparent reason. It is as though they are celebrating some secret and wicked deed, and the fact that we have no idea what it might be makes them even jollier, and adds a perverse and pleasing angle to their smiles.

Without saying what he is going to do, Henry leaves and returns with a bottle of port and pours half a glass for everybody.

'Just this once,' he says, splitting his sides with loud laughter.

'Never again,' says Margaret, her teeth so black she seems to have lost them all in a street brawl.

James turns the TV up.

'James, turn that off!'

'I'm watching something,' he says, like a baby.

'Just turn it off!' shouts Margaret. 'Or I'll come and sit on your head!!'

Then Margaret says something in French and Henry laughs

so hard it's contagious, and we are all laughing. For the next few hours we take it in turns to tell stories about strange people we've known. Margaret and Henry tell more stories about Uncle Pete and other crazed relatives, like the aunt who wears aviator sunglasses and a red scarf when she drives, and Margaret's great-grandmother who wore corsets so tight she flew to Switzerland each year to have her lungs reinflated.

While everybody is laughing I stand and turn off the only lamp in the room. Nobody asks me to turn it back on. I often wish that all conversation could take place in the dark; that it were always night and that the redness of my skin could never be seen. In this dark room, I feel no inhibition. I sit close to Henry on the couch; Margaret sits on the other couch with Bridget. James sits at his mother's feet. I feel the beautiful warmth of the port around my heart.

Henry pours more port into my glass and winks at me. I wink back. James massages his mother's feet and for a long time I can't keep my eyes off his hands; the way that he takes each of his mother's toes in turn, squeezing each of them equally so that none miss out.

I am finally and completely at home; in this dark room, with the slightly drunk Hardings.

'Well,' says Margaret when the birds begin to sing, 'I think we'd all better hit the hay.'

What a nice change it is for me not to be alone, awake in bed, when the birds start to sing.

'Yes, we'd better,' says Henry and both he and Margaret begin to laugh, perhaps at the surprise of having completely shattered their usual routine. Perhaps laughing at Margaret who has pulled the phone plug out and who is trying to walk away with the plug still in her hand, trailing the phone behind her, or perhaps they are laughing at James, who has fallen asleep and is snoring.

The following day we get out of bed late, and, as though we have signed a solemn agreement, no one mentions last night. Breakfast is made and eaten with less talk than usual. It seems the Hardings have all been made coy by last night's late-night laughter and drinking. I have slept well for the first time in months. I feel good and wish that every night were like last night and that every morning I could wake from a night of rest instead of sleepless misery.

At the end of breakfast, when it is nearly time to go our separate ways into the day, I say, 'Last night was great fun! We should do it again.'

I understand at once, from the look on Henry's face, that I have said the wrong thing.

'Lou,' says Margaret, her lips tight and angry, 'last night was not something we intend to make a habit of. Henry and I were a little drunk, and more than a little irresponsible. It will most certainly not be happening again.'

James and Bridget gaze into their bowls of cereal shaped like space-craft and say nothing. Nothing. The room is stuffed with righteousness and dented morals and I am left to look like the only fool who thought last night was a good idea, that drinking together made us happy and free.

I go to my room, grab my bag and head out to the supermarket parking lot for a smoke. I wonder whether there are just some people who need to live a different kind of life. I buy a small bottle of gin with what's left of my pocket money and go home to watch the first movie I have rented for myself, to watch by myself. Nobody bothers me all day. I lie on the couch and remind myself that I am better off here than at home with my slutty sisters who can beat me up whenever they feel like it and never get punished.

I eat three packets of Oreos and re-read a book by a famous forensic pathologist who specialises in the study of serial killers. He says that serial killers often have one thing in common: a history of being treated randomly as children. Being treated randomly, he explains, means that no matter what these psychopaths did as children, whether their behaviour was good or bad, their parents treated them randomly. Willy nilly, without warning, they might be punished one day for doing something that the day before they had been rewarded for. Therefore, the serial killer, as a child, can never know which way the parent is going to turn: hot or cold. But the forensic pathologist doesn't say anything about the effects of being treated with embarrassing consistency.

Whenever my dad has a few too many beers he makes a point of embarrassing me by telling the same story. 'I broke a man's knee caps by pointing at them. I pointed at his knee caps and he fell off the earth-mover the next day and landed right on the road and broke both his knees.'

If somebody says, 'But you can't injure a man just by willing it to happen!' my dad replies with one of three responses, the worst of which is, 'Well, if you think that's something, I made the first woman I had sex with levitate right off the bed.'

The next few days are peaceful, yet ominous. Nobody in the Harding family is the same as they were before, and when people are not precisely who you expect them to be, not exactly the people you have grown accustomed to, you cannot trust the world, even a dreaded world, in quite the same way.

Henry and Margaret work longer hours than usual, come home, cook and eat a healthy dinner and retire to their dens for more work or reading. Bridget comes home most days just minutes before dinner – as though she has been hiding behind a small bush outside, waiting for the smell of food – after spending all day in the sun, swimming, rowing or water skiing.

James spends all day at the mall, or down in the basement playing loud music, or table tennis with his three moustached friends.

I spend a lot of time lying on my bed reading books for school. I memorise the names of every U.S. president and all the states, the rivers and the lakes. I read five novels and two plays. I learn seventy-nine new words. Margaret asks me if I've called my mum again (I've called only once since arriving) and when I tell her I haven't, she tells me to do it 'right away'.

I call her and we have a short conversation. When she finishes telling me about her volunteer Meals on Wheels job and who's having a baby, I tell her that Margaret needs to use the phone and then I hang up.

Three days a week, my mum and dad drive a dirty van around the streets near our flat, delivering trays of sloppy, tepid food to the old and infirm.

Before the Meals on Wheels job my dad had two other real jobs. Once he worked at the dogs, the greyhound races, as a Tic Tac man and wore white gloves and communicated race results by gesticulating in a special hand-code. Before that, he worked on the roads, using a jackhammer to smash concrete all day long. From the roadwork job he developed 'vibration white finger', a vascular problem caused by gripping vibrating tools, which cut off his circulation, causing a blanching of his fingers.

Then one day my mum said to him, 'Why don't you sue your old boss for compensation and then deliver meals to the old folks with me?' a sentence which my dad likes to quote and re-quote to friends, as a way, I suppose, of showing his gratitude for what he still regards as a stroke of genius on my mum's part.

Now there are two of them collecting trashy hand-me-downs from the elderly who seem fond of saying 'thank you' by giving away egg-stained doilies, ornamental dogs without heads and hot-water bottles with teeth marks in them. Sometimes, I'm fairly sure, my parents even steal the odd object, such as kettles and toasters. Whenever we have something break down or explode in the flat, they seem to replace it as soon as they come home from work.

My mum used to work as a beautician and tells everybody she is an ex-model, but has no photographs to prove it (they were all stolen, she says). She has a decent sense of humour, though, except when she's making bad-taste jokes about my dad's 'vibration white finger', which I don't wish to repeat.

Sometimes, when I feel lonely, I go outside, to the side of the house, to the window of Henry's study. I creep up to the window and look inside. I crouch low to the ground and look through the blinds and watch him as he smokes his pipe. His eyes are worse then ever, and he wipes at them with a handkerchief to soak up whatever it is that's coming out. His face is much older in repose, when nobody is around, much older without Margaret, with nothing to do but wait for what might happen next.

9

It's another Saturday, and the last weekend before school starts. Margaret wakes me at eight o'clock by bursting through the door without knocking.

'Hey, lazybones,' she says. 'Get up! We're leaving for the game in ten minutes.' Her voice is harsh.

I pull the sheet over my head and wonder what to do. I have spent the night in a terrible state of fear. Woken suddenly at three a.m. after a violent dream, and unable to sleep again, I spent the next five hours in a mood so black it was as though I was at the mouth of a dark cave, a cliff beneath my feet, a small gust of wind playing at my back, pushing me forward, pulling me back.

When Margaret pulls the curtains open and stands over the bed, I remember the dream that woke me.

A man is lying across a table and another man has cut him down the middle with a pair of scissors; a deep but bloodless cut from neck to groin. The man stands on the table, undoes his zip and urinates into the other man's wound. Both men are versions of my dad.

Margaret tugs at the sheet and I wrench it back.

'I feel sick,' I say. Her voice is sharp and I would like to know why. It is as though she has seen inside my mind.

'Are you sure you're not just being lazy?'

'No,' I say, 'I want to go to the game. I've always wanted to go to a real baseball game.'

She doesn't believe me.

'Let me have a look at you,' she says.

I drop the sheet and squint into the harsh white light.

'I'll get the thermometer,' she says.

Margaret's voice, and the way she wants to tear the covers from my body, reminds me of a nurse who pressed her knuckles hard into my skull because I asked for more pills.

It was about two years ago and I had been taken to the emergency room in a taxi, suffering from another bout of mysterious and terrible headaches. I called the nurse back three times because she wouldn't give me anything for the pain. The third time, instead of using the red buzzer at the end of the wire, I screamed out for her.

'What's wrong with you?' she snapped. 'You'd think somebody was trying to murder you.'

'Please,' I said. 'I'm in a lot of pain.'

The nurse made a fist of her hand and rammed her knuckles into my skull, a kind of surrogate punch, the closest she could get to hitting me without being accused of assault. She left the room then and came back with the pills.

It was a public hospital, full of poor people without private health insurance and plenty of teenage junkies looking for pills in place of heroin.

My sisters were sitting on the end of my bed watching daytime TV. Both of them scrawny and slutty, wearing jeans so tight that when they walked into the room you could see the outlines of their fannies.

Margaret takes my temperature and it turns out that I do have one. Only a slight one, but enough to change the tone of her voice.

'Can I get you anything?' she asks, the back of her hand pressed lightly against my forehead.

'Maybe a few pain-killers,' I say. 'Some pethidine, maybe?'

She takes her hand away, frowns at me, then leaves the room, which radiates with unfriendly light.

A little later Henry comes in carrying a breakfast tray with eggs, toast, cereal and coffee and after he puts it down on my bedside table, he turns off the light and closes the curtains. It is a struggle not to clap my hands together with delight. The nightmare's residue has long worn off and I feel calm. Sitting up in bed in the dark like this, with Margaret and Henry standing over me, I feel the opposite of skinless, the opposite of my usual nervous state. I feel quite wonderful, in fact, especially when Margaret tidies my blankets, tucking them in around my hips, her firm hands jutting in quickly under my thighs.

'We think you should eat something,' says Henry.

'Do you want one of us to stay home?' asks Margaret, her voice so kind I nearly change my mind about not going.

'No, no,' I say. 'You've been looking forward to this game for ages.'

Henry looks at his watch.

'Oh well,' he says, looking at Margaret, 'sometimes you catch fish, and sometimes you don't. If you're sick and need looking after, that's just how it is.'

'No,' I say. 'Don't stay home.'

I want them to leave immediately so that I can drink the coffee from the perfect white cup on the perfect lacquered tray.

Henry closes the door and Margaret sits on the bed.

'Lou,' she says, 'I know you don't feel well, but we've been wanting to talk to you and we had been hoping to do it today.'

'Yes,' I say, my stomach dipping.

'We need to know whether there's anything troubling you. You've been acting a little strangely.'

'You seem a bit on edge,' says Henry. 'Is there anything you'd like to talk about?'

95

I am desperate for Margaret to go back to where she was only a few moments ago, straightening my blankets, her hands under my thighs, smiling, running her hand just once along the soft down on the side of my face, lifting a glass of water to my lips. I redden suddenly with desire and memory: part pleasure, part confusion, a taste in my mouth of a bad ham sandwich. I wish that right at this moment I could be treated with the kind of unreserved love dished out by intelligent and warm parents to a beautiful first child.

'No,' I say. 'What do you mean?'

Henry leans against the door like a security guard, and at once my usually airy white room feels dank and stingy, robbed of breath, like a gloomy locker room.

'We've been noticing that since we returned from the trip you've seemed quite withdrawn.'

'Oh,' I say, relieved that this is all it is. I had worried they might know about the cigarettes or the gin. I want to drink my coffee but also want to look too sick to drink it.

'Maybe I'm just tired. When the weather isn't so hot I'll be better.'

Margaret puts her hand on my knee and when I flinch, she moves her hand to the bun of hair coiled on her head, as though to stop it from leaping off.

'James says you've been very rude to him since we got back. He says you don't speak to him in a civil way.'

'Really?' I say.

Henry brings a chair over to the bed and sits in it. He seems not to want to say what he has to say. He looks at Margaret before he begins, like an actor looking to his prompt.

My food is going cold.

'Lou, it's going to become a serious problem if you can't get along with our children, especially James. It was his idea . . .'

'Well, *and* ours,' says Margaret quickly, 'but James was particularly looking forward to you coming to live with us. He has wanted us to get an exchange student for a long time.'

What happens next happens without any forethought; as though my body, injured by Margaret and Henry's words, has taken over my mind.

'I bet he was,' I say, 'I bet the fucking creep was looking forward to me coming.'

I take the cup of coffee and throw it against the wall behind Henry's head. I realise that this is what I have done only when I see brown liquid running down the wall. The idea of grin-faced, oily James; the idea that he has spoken in hard-done-by tones about me, that he has complained, that he has made trouble, makes my arms burn with rage.

Margaret gets off the bed and moves backwards towards the door. Henry gets up out of his seat, slowly, and stands, mute. I know I should apologise, take it back, but when Margaret and Henry simply stare at me and then at each other as though I am a lunatic, I cannot stop myself from making things worse.

'Don't look so shocked,' I say. 'You must know it's true.'

Margaret is suddenly crying and I feel absolutely nothing but curiosity. It's interesting how people cry – I think – interesting how when something awful happens it doesn't feel real.

Henry wants the scene to end immediately. He has no interest whatsoever in more information, or any kind of resolution, good or bad; no interest in any confession or apology. He puts his hand into the small of Margaret's back and guides her out the door and onto the landing. They talk in whispers for a while and Margaret is no longer crying. I cannot hear what they are saying. I wait for them to come back but they don't.

About ten minutes later the Mercedes pulls out of the driveway and the Hardings are gone. I have the house to myself for the whole day.

I take a shower in the ensuite in Henry and Margaret's bedroom, use some of Margaret's perfume, try some make-up and stand naked in front of the full-length oval mirror in their beautiful bedroom. I give myself the creeps by imagining Margaret and Henry changing their mind about the baseball game, coming home and bursting into the room. They would see my bare back and my reflection in the mirror and I would turn and face them, or not turn to face them, and do what I can never do – stare at them through the mirror – the way some women do in bathrooms when they hold comfortable conversations with each other, about nothing.

I wear Henry's dressing gown untied and lie on the bed. I sleep for a while, in a way that I can never sleep in a bed that's my own. I look at the books they each have by the side of the bed, read a few pages of each, but cannot concentrate. I go to my room and get my collection of Gogol short stories and read some of them. I stand by the open window, daring myself to lean out bare-breasted. I change my mind. This is not my idea, but an idea Erin and Leona have planted in me. I close the dressing gown and look at the clouds: three dimensional, yet flat, hard yet empty, capable of dissolving in an instant.

Next I go to James' room. I lie on his bed and smell his unabashed smell. I don't sleep there and the blue walls make me uneasy. I go through his drawers and find a birthday card from somebody called Isabella, which says, 'Dear James, You are such a great friend. I hope I know you forever, Love Isabella, with lots of kisses.' There's no date on the card, but I suspect that it is a few years old. It makes me cringe.

Bridget's room is pink and has photographs stuck all over the walls; neat, in frames. Many are pictures of her standing in gangs of beautiful girls and boys. In every group photograph, she is the only girl without a boy's arm wrapped around her middle or draped over her shoulder. I sit at her dressing table and open a tube of pink lip-gloss.

Bridget has a make-up mirror with three facets labelled Day/Evening/Office, which swivel so that you can pull one to the front and allow the others to slip behind. Each mirror is lit for a different setting: bright and natural for Day, subdued and pink for Evening and dully fluorescent for Office. I don't understand what she cares about at all.

When I have been alone in the house for several hours, the only thing I can think to do is lie on the couch. I'm not in the mood to drink, so I take some gin from a bottle in the liquor cabinet and put it in a picnic flask for later.

I go to the supermarket and buy some cigarettes and smoke in the garden until my chest burns and I feel dizzy. I fall asleep on the couch and wake with an ear so squashed and sore that I wonder for a moment if somebody has belted me up while I was sleeping.

I make two cheese and mayonnaise sandwiches, go to my room and read some more books for school.

At seven o'clock, when I hear a car pull up outside, I close my curtains and undress for bed. I spend the next few hours listening to the sounds a family makes in a large and beautiful house; the noises of a family as they must have been before I arrived: the unselfconscious and peaceful sounds of doors opening and closing, chairs scraping on polished boards, a microwave beeping, names being called out and answered, a TV turned up too loud then turned down, a fridge door opened and closed, bathroom taps running and toilets flushed. I listen to all this with great concentration and remote sadness, as though it were a radio play.

I don't leave my room, except to use the bathroom.

It's Sunday morning and time for the Harding family breakfast. I have slept badly and worry about facing Margaret and Henry. My head is full of sour, persistent thoughts.

Last night I read a letter from Erin. She writes, amongst other things:

Dear Louisville (ha ha!)

Mum and Dad say Hi or howdy or something like that. They bought a new car and are driving all over the place like motor-heads

Etc . . .

Guess what? I've decided to study nursing. Remember Michelle from school? She only had to study for one year and now she has the most grouse job except for one bit. Do you know what she has to do? She administers consolations for old men who are dying. Know what that means, clever clogs?

Etc . . .

Mum and Dad say they'll write soon when they've finished burning rubber. I went to the show last week with . . .

Etc . . .

Lots of lurv,
Erin

I don't reply to Erin's letters. I don't reply to any of their letters: Mum's, Dad's or Leona's. They have all become shreds. I have written only one letter, a special letter – full of lies – to my English teacher, Mrs Walsh.

One day – a winter's Sunday – Mrs Walsh was in the same train carriage as me. I was surprised to see her using public transport and didn't want her to see me at all. I was with Leona and Erin and three of their male friends; all three of them dirty with tattoos, and drinking stubbies of beer.

We were making noise, shouting obscenities. Mrs Walsh made a special detour half way up the carriage to say hello to me.

I was sitting apart from the others with an unlit cigarette between my lips, flicking it up and down with my teeth. She asked me how I was and congratulated me on my most recent assignment, for which I'd received ninety-six per cent. Then she looked at Erin and said, *sotto voce*, 'Your intelligence is useless to you. You are clearly destined to fly economy class for the rest of your life.'

The train stopped and she got off.

I have written Mrs Walsh a tremendous letter; my only letter. I described an approximation of the contents of the colour brochures I saw advertising the benefits of this international exchange-student program: boys and girls in canoes on sparkling rivers, boys and girls rehearsing in full costume for a Chekhov play, families sitting together on a bleacher eating hot dogs at a baseball game, and a happy party of exchange students wrapped in the flags of their respective countries singing and dancing in the park.

Bridget comes into my room and sits on the end of my bed with a towel wrapped around her head, the skin on her face tight and dry from too much soap and water. 'How are you?' she asks.

'Fine,' I say.

I notice for the first time that Bridget has a wart on her right knee, a small one, but still a wart. I think about the question on my passport application form, which asked whether I had any distinguishing marks. I didn't, but felt a strong impulse to write that I have a blue wart on the back of my right knee.

'Look,' says Bridget. 'Just don't worry about James. You take him too seriously and you shouldn't. He lives inside some stupid comic strip.'

She is pleased with the adultness of her tone. Only fourteen and she is giving a sixteen-year-old advice about her older brother.

My sternum aches. 'Have Margaret and Henry told you what I said to them?'

Bridget pulls the tail of the towel around to the front of her shoulder as though it were a veil.

'They said you are upset about James being a bit of a pain.'

'Were they angry?' I ask.

'They just want you to get along with him, that's all.'

'I want to get along too,' I say, as though everything were simple.

She squeezes my foot just like her mother does to her, and just like James does to his mother. I want to talk more, I want more information, but she gets up to leave.

'Just don't take the bait,' she says. 'You *always* take the bait.'

'Thanks.'

She stops in the doorway. 'Have you been smoking in here?'

I haven't brushed my teeth.

'No,' I say, quite incredulous.

'It smells a bit like smoke in here. Anyway, see you later.'

At breakfast Henry and Margaret sit at opposite ends of the table, as usual, and seem calm, cheerful. The difference is that they don't pass me anything. There's usually a lot of 'Have some more eggs, Lou' or 'Would you like some orange juice?' and 'What a beautiful day'.

Perhaps the only difference is that Henry doesn't look at James. But then I wonder if Henry ever *did* look at James.

I might assume he did because there's usually an awful lot of eye contact going on in this family. A lot more than I think I could ever get used to.

James scoffs his food, but just as he is about to leave the room he turns to face me.

'Hey, Lou, I was wondering if you want to see a movie tonight. I'm being picked up at six o'clock, if you're interested.'

At least at the movies there's always the darkness and always the chance it will be good and even if the film's bad you can pretty much not exist for two hours and not feel too gloomy, unless the film is so bad that you are forced to walk out.

'That'd be great,' I say.

James smiles and I smile back.

Henry stands.

'Everything's okay?' he says, not quite a question and not quite a statement.

'Everything's great,' I say, but Margaret says nothing and I know it isn't great.

In the car on the way to the movies, James makes a point of telling his friends (one of whom is Isabella) that I can play chess better than Todd (whoever Todd is) and that I can get most crosswords out in less than ten minutes.

'Shit,' says just about everybody. 'You must be pretty smart.'

James makes the moment brighter by not leaving me to have to answer this myself.

'Sure is,' he says. 'Lou makes my sister look like one of the seven dwarfs.'

James and I sit next to each other in the cinema and even though I am mostly repulsed by him, in the dark it is simply as though I am sitting next to a friend, which isn't something I even know a great deal about but that's what it feels like, and

I wonder if we might be able to sort each other out.

The movie isn't especially sad but right at the end when a couple who are maybe somewhere in their thirties are behaving happily together, my eyes get hot and I think that it would be pleasant to cry. I reach out for James' hand and hold it. We stay still like this and when the movie ends I let go and we walk out side by side and even in the bright lights of the foyer I am not afraid to see him.

Part Two

10

It's my first day in high school. Margaret drops us at the front gates on her way to work. Today she looks like an air hostess, ready to serve passengers in first class; a pristine white scarf around her throat and a gold brooch on her navy-blue lapel.

'Good luck, Lou,' she says. 'And don't forget to introduce yourself to the principal.'

'I won't,' I say. 'Thanks for the lift.'

James walks on ahead then turns to say, 'You don't have to say *thanks* for everything, you know. It's not like she gave you her *kidney* or anything.'

Bridget sighs. '*Whatever*,' she says, and we walk together in silence through the gates.

The building is large and square, dirty white, and surrounded by a wire fence; like a former gulag with an empty, well-mown lawn in front and a limp American flag hanging from a pole near the enormous front doors.

We are early and there are only a dozen or so students hanging around the front steps in their brand new clothes. Some of them are brandishing their first set of car keys, eyeing off their new cars which are parked beyond the fence, clean and shiny in the distance.

The corridors are wide and long and lined with metal lockers and dozens of red, blue and white doors, all snapped shut and freshly painted. The building is hushed, still emerging from hibernation, stale and sleeping; lights out, eyes shut, stuffed full of things that happened last year, scarred by the scuff marks, graffiti and smells of those who have moved on.

We see James rushing on ahead, turning a corner, almost running.

Bridget says, 'Well, this is me.' She opens a locker, puts her bag inside and takes out a notepad and some pens. 'I'll take you to your locker and then show you where your first class is. Mom collected your locker key last week.'

I take the key. 'Thanks.'

Taped to the inside of her locker is a photograph, a portrait, cut into a heart shape, of a red-haired boy; rufous and sleek, like a certain kind of fox. 'Who's that?' I ask.

'Nobody,' she says and slams the metal door.

My locker is in the basement; a dark, hollow, subterranean place without windows, away from classrooms. This suits me fine. It's cooler down here and there is a bathroom nearby, but the smell is dreadful: a mixture of eggs and donuts, coming from the basement's cavernous, over-lit cafeteria.

'Show me your program,' says Bridget. I take the crumpled sheet out of my backpack and she grabs at it.

'American History,' she says. 'Let's go.'

I haven't finished unloading my bag when she starts up the wide stairs, two steps at a time. I close my locker and follow.

I stare at her. The cartilages at the back of her fine brown knees splay like miniature cathedral buttresses. I stare at the clean white edges of her short skirt. She doesn't look back to see if I'm following.

The corridors begin to fill with students. Bridget greets her many friends along the way, dozens of them. She stops to talk to a few, mostly quick conversations about who's got a new car and who's dumped whom over summer. All of the people she stops to speak to are handsome or pretty. She introduces me to no one and no one asks her to.

I had been ready to swallow my nerves, had rehearsed some clever things to say, had expected to be the centre of considerable and awkward attention, but Bridget's friends barely look at me. I wonder what it would be like to be one of them: tanned, healthy and brave.

She takes me into a small classroom crammed with graffiti-scarred desks and tells me to pick one, 'You better choose one you like now,' she says, 'you'll be stuck with it all year.' Her tone is censorious.

'Thanks, boss,' I say, trying to assert myself. 'It's hardly a big deal.'

There is nobody else in the room and it smells of suffocated paint.

'Whatever,' she says. 'I'll leave you alone now.' As though I should want it that way.

'Thanks,' I say.

I sit next to the farthest wall under a portrait of Abraham Lincoln. His skin is dark and sagging under black eyes and he has thick dark sideburns which look as though they have been glued on, like an ape from *Planet of the Apes*.

The bell rings, but no one appears, not even the teacher. It's ten past nine. I take out my new notebook and a red pen.

In primary school I was good at ruling up the pages in fresh exercise books. I liked to write my name and classroom number neatly in the box provided, open the front cover and press it down, take out my new ruler and favourite red ballpoint pen and begin to rule every page in the book.

I performed this painstaking task with immense pleasure. What a tremendous feeling to be at the start of a clean and promising new exercise book. Perfect ruling, and lots of straight neat lines signified that I would never make another mistake. But if the ruling went wrong, I would fly into a rage of self-disgust. I'd tear out the page and then, disappointed with the torn edges left behind – this crinkly proof of failure – I'd tear out the corresponding page to even things out.

A few crooked lines later and I had torn out every page until there was no exercise book left. I did this countless times, in every school year, and hid the piles of waste paper in my cupboard. To support this habit, I stole dozens of fresh red and white exercise books from the local newsagent.

The room is still empty. Although I know something is wrong I sit and wait, inert and stubborn, feeling lonely. I pinch my thigh hard so that it hurts. I talk to myself. *This is another fresh start and I'm going to get it all perfect. No more blushing. Act really confident. Say lots of funny things. Look at people when you speak to them. Answer lots of questions. Meet the smartest people in the class.*

I hear singing: the American national anthem. I leave the classroom and wander the corridors but by the time I find the assembly hall I am red and the back of my neck is crawling with perspiration. The singing ends and a row of students move onto the stage where they are presented with awards.

Somebody says, 'God bless this year's seniors' and there's a speech by last year's prom queen about senior year being the most significant year in a student's life. She must have taken the day off from her new job as the receptionist at the local mega dental clinic. Behind her, as she speaks, her yearbook photograph is displayed, a Vaseline haze around the edges as though she is a movie star.

I go to the bathroom near my locker, sit on the cold cubicle floor and wrap my arms around my legs. Will it be the same now? One crooked line and I turf the whole thing out? *No*, I say, *it won't be the same.* I stand up and go back outside, desperate for friendship and complete change.

The basement dwellers are at their lockers, talking and

laughing. I look around. At a locker near mine there's a pretty girl with long black hair and a broken and blackened front tooth. I like that she has this flaw in an otherwise dolly-perfect face. I stare at her and she says, 'Hi' and I say 'Hi' and then she walks briskly away, leaving for her first class which also happens to be the same as mine: American History.

All the desks in the classroom are taken, but one. A tall boy, good looking and blond, is sitting at the desk I chose earlier and I realise with a swoop in my stomach that I have left my notebook behind. He is flicking through it, as though trying to decide whether it's worth pawning.

I take a deep breath and walk over to him, my heart kicking. I hope he'll notice my accent. I hope he'll want to talk to me.

'Hello,' I say. 'I think I left my notebook on this desk.'

He looks up at me, slowly, calmly, and I wonder what it would be like to move so smoothly, instead of like a scared field mouse.

'Did you?' he asks, already in possession of the answer. 'Does it have your name in it?'

'I don't know,' I say.

He tucks my notebook under his history textbook. I realise we are being watched by a corner full of girls, their long blow-dried hair stiff with spray. *Vainglorious pig*, I think. *Probably a footballer.*

I begin to blush as he speaks. 'How do I know it's yours then?'

'Don't worry about it,' I say.

He laughs, 'No worries, mate.' The stiff-haired girls laugh with him.

I take the desk near the door and watch the other students. They are almost manic with enthusiasm for this first day, hugging and saying 'Hi' to each other and catching up on their summer holidays. A boy and girl in the corner hold hands between their desks and do not speak nor move their faces into any kind of expression.

She is fat and so is he, like two people destined to become identical. They stare to the front, lost in the summery and secret world of their romance, smug yet terrified; their fingers gripping as though to say to each other — *don't let go of me or this is what you'll face again.*

The vainglorious pig-boy looks across at me and runs his fingers through his perfectly coiffed hair; hair like a golden field of something breakfast cereal is made of. The three girls stare at him from across the room like low-IQ witches.

The teacher — three-quarters bald and skinny — walks in, stands for a moment and starts the lesson by taking off his glasses and unbuttoning his jacket and putting them both, slowly, carefully, on the table.

'That's my cue for starting class,' he says. 'I hope you can remember it.' Everybody falls silent.

My neck tightens. I have nothing to write in, or with, and my desk is empty.

'For those of you who don't already know . . . and God forbid, I've been around long enough . . .' says the teacher, pacing behind his desk, wearied and wrathful like a zoo animal, 'my name's Mr Caldwell and I've been taking this class for seven years.'

Then, as though having a private joke, he snickers, and scratches an itch at the top of his left thigh.

After writing some notes on the board, Mr Caldwell acknowledges me with a perfunctory smile, then, as though I've given him a brilliant idea for a novel form of cruelty, says to the class, 'I know what I'm in the mood for. I'm in the mood for a quiz. We have some new people and I want to know who, and what, I'm dealing with.'

I don't like him. He has a jagged black hairline near the

front of his skull that makes him look like a shiny egg cracked open by a small and furious hatchling.

The topic of the quiz is the American Civil War. The questions are about Ulysses S. Grant and Robert E. Lee and thinning Confederate lines at Petersberg and the ruins of Richmond, and John Wilkes Booth. I know all the answers. There isn't a single one I don't know.

I rehearse the answers in my head and prepare my voice by clearing my throat, but when the time comes to put my hand up, my face reddens and my stomach collapses. My heart pounds so hard it fills my chest and there's no room to breathe.

And so, like the intellectually effete girls with long sticky hair and pink lipstick, I remain mute. The clever ones, including the vainglorious pig-boy, not only answer the questions, but offer elaborate embellishments; the exact numbers of remaining soldiers in the Union and Confederate armies at the time of Lee's surrender.

By the end of the day I feel exhausted by my shame and I want to get home, lie on my bed, write a few pages of new pacts and promises, take a bath then sleep for ten hours.

Margaret has left work early and prepared a special 'back-to-school' dinner. We eat it at the dining-room table, where linen napkins, crystal glasses and the best silver are all laid out as in a museum exhibition. James is late and the boy who has driven him home comes inside to say hello.

'You're late,' says Margaret.

'Sorry,' says James. 'It's just that we all went for a Coke . . .'

I'm sick of hearing about Coke. Henry stands. 'Is your friend staying for dinner?'

James' friend walks up to the table and stares at me.

'I wouldn't want to put you out,' he says. He has the greenest eyes I have ever seen. They can't be real. He is tall and dressed in a loose woollen jumper even though it's a warm afternoon.

'Sit down,' says Margaret, no longer angry with James, but curious, wondering, as we all are, how it is that James has made a new friend, and an older friend, so quickly, on his first day back at school.

'Hadn't you better introduce your friend?' asks Henry, still standing, wondering whether or not he should go to the kitchen to fetch more food. He is as bewildered as I have ever seen him.

I am obviously not the only one unsettled by this boy's pre-posterous good looks. It is impossible to look at him and not feel your limbs fill with shivering.

'Oh,' says James, 'this is Tom. He's just moved here. But he's Scottish, originally.'

'Well,' says Tom, looking at me again, 'I'm *still* Scottish.'

Tom stands with his arms by his sides. Like Margaret, he doesn't need to lean on something to occupy a room, doen't need to fold his arms, or fidget, or gesture gratuitously to fill the space around him.

'Nice to meet you,' says Margaret, who stands to shake his hand, so charmed that her entire manner is altered. Instead of her usual ease, she rubs her fingers across her neck and as soon as she sits down again, drinks half a glass of cold water and leaves her lips wetted.

Tom is a senior, and so, like me, this will be his last year of high school.

Henry returns with an extra plate and serves Tom's food while Tom explains that he spent most of last year in Europe with his mother after she was diagnosed with terminal cancer.

'It started in her breast,' he says, like a young doctor, almost comfortable with the word *breast* and yet aware of its impact and meaning. He stares at me and continues, 'And then it spread greedily to several of her internal organs.'

I cannot eat.

'Oh, how awful,' says Margaret, behaving as though there is a camera in the room, self-conscious, her chin held high. Perhaps this is always the effect of the presence of somebody extravagantly beautiful.

Tom hasn't begun to eat. Bridget is beside me, playing with her food on the end of a heavy silver fork. James is silent, busy wolfing his food as though nothing has happened or is about to happen.

'Well,' says Tom, looking at Henry so as not to leave him out, 'it was horrible, but then she went into complete remission. She's still alive and doing extremely well.'

Anybody else would have described this as a miracle. My mum would have said it was 'the work of God'. My dad would have said 'it was meant to be'. But Tom lets the facts speak for themselves.

I swallow some potato and look at him.

'You must have been relieved,' I say, and he smiles as though I have been his friend through it all.

'Yes,' he says, taking me in, 'but then, like everything, you get used to it and everything's taken for granted again. My father and I tried not to forget what might have happened to us, but we have. We go on as though nothing ever happened.'

I stare at Tom and he stares back at me, as though we are alone in the room. His hands rest loosely in his lap, one jumper sleeve rolled up, his long white fingers like little people wearing glass helmets.

I feel good just from looking at him.

Margaret clears her throat and puts her knife and fork across her plate to show that she is finished.

'Aren't you going to eat anything, Tom?'

Tom looks away from me and pushes his plate towards the middle of the table. 'Oh,' he says, 'I don't really feel like eating after all.'

Margaret is cross. I can tell by the way she fidgets with her wedding ring.

'It's really easy to lose your appetite,' I say, 'when you have been talking about your mother nearly dying of cancer.'

James reaches across the table, 'I'll eat it,' he says and takes this extra plate of food into the living-room; something normally forbidden in the Harding home, but under the circumstances, completely ignored.

'See you later,' says James to Tom as he leaves the room. 'Thanks for the ride home.'

Tom stays for an hour, talking about his trip around Europe. Margaret clears the table and Tom doesn't offer to help. This reminds me of my first weeks here and how often I forgot to offer to help, too nervous to speak, too nervous to say please or thank you.

Margaret is still angry with him for leaving his food uneaten. Henry wants to know about Spain and asks if Tom will come back one day and show us the photographs.

Margaret stands. 'Well, it's getting late,' she says untruthfully. 'I suppose you'll be wanting to get home to your family.'

As Margaret shows Tom out, she says, 'It was a pleasure to meet you.'

Bridget goes to the living-room without saying goodbye.

I do not go to the door, but stand near the hallway bookshelf.

'Bye,' I say, and think what a dull house it suddenly seems now that Tom is leaving it.

Tom looks at me. 'I hope I'll see you at school,' he says, and then he winks.

As we watch him get into his flash red car, Margaret stands by the window and grips the curtain.

'What an interesting person,' I say.

'What a rude young man, more like it,' she says, anger bulging around her chin and making her face ugly. 'Can you believe he took a meal and just left it there?'

Henry agrees even though he probably thought Tom was interesting too.

'Yes,' he says, 'I've seen better manners.'

I follow them into the kitchen. I want to hear what she will say. Henry starts washing the dishes and says nothing while Margaret continues to complain.

'Don't you think he was very arrogant?' she asks him.

'I guess he seemed a wee bit over confident,' says Henry, doing a pretty good job of a Scottish accent, 'but that might be a cultural thing.'

Margaret turns sharply and takes a plate out of Henry's hand.

'Why is that your excuse for everybody's bad behaviour?'

Henry frowns and tries to will me out of the room, but I stay where I am.

I lift a plate from the table and drop it. It hits the floor and breaks neatly in half. From where Margaret stands, it is impossible for her to tell whether it has been thrown or whether it has merely slipped. But Henry knows, and he frowns at me.

Margaret turns on me. 'Tell James I would rather not see that boy in my house again.'

Henry stops what he's doing and follows his wife upstairs. I know – without knowing how I know – that he will go along with her and Tom will never be allowed back in the house.

I I

It's the end of my second week at school. Last night I had trouble getting to sleep and when I did finally sleep, I dreamed about Leona and her fiancé, Greg.

Greg was sitting up in bed, naked, scratching his leg with oil-stained, eczema-scarred fingers. The bed was covered in a cheap red satin sheet, and his knees were up against his chest, his testicles squeezed between the tops of his thighs, purple and blackened with thick dark hairs. Leona sat in a chair in the corner of the room, sobbing without noise, staring at him. I was in the bed next to him, curled up against his awful arm. He whispered, 'Treat 'em mean, keep 'em keen. That's my motto.'

I go red whenever I think of him. He's in my mind like a word I use in company when I don't know its exact meaning and yet it just pops out of my mouth. I know I'm about to be caught out but I can't help saying it.

I go to the cafeteria at lunchtime hoping that I might sit at a table and have somebody come and sit with me. But as I walk into the brightly lit room — its awful smells, its terrible scraping of dishes and clicking of bottles in crates, its exaggerated laughter and squealing of hordes of students funnelling food into their throats as though they have no teeth to chew with — I see a boy with only one arm, sitting alone near the entrance, spreading tomato sauce with a spoon onto white bread. I walk away.

I spend the lunch hour without food, walking around the enormous campus pretending I'm running late for an appointment.

I have now explored every corner: the indoor swimming pool, two gymnasiums, four tennis courts, a theatre and three basketball courts with retractable bleachers.

There are students everywhere carrying sports bags and racquets, their hair wet, the armpits of their t-shirts lightly damp. There are so many healthy, good-looking teenagers, that a few crooked teeth, or short, fat fingers, suddenly take on the proportions of deformities. Everywhere there are bare limbs: well shaped, hairless, perfect. An end of summer gaiety, a sporting spirit. I cannot wait for winter.

The Organisation has held several parties for exchange students. I went to the first one, but was bored witless. Flo Bapes was there – my alleged mentor – and she wanted to know why I hadn't been at the assembly on the first day of school. 'Didn't the Hardings tell you?' They didn't. Henry told Bridget to tell me, but Bridget forgot. At least, that's her story. In any case, I don't like the way the other exchange students constantly complained about their difficulties with study and I'd rather avoid Flo Bapes – and her pestering and voyeuristic interest in my impoverished background – if that's at all possible.

Sometimes I sit in the mezzanine of the library and look down at the tennis courts and wonder what it would be like to wear a pair of shorts and sit with my knees apart opposite somebody who is also wearing shorts sitting with their knees apart.

I have seen many teenagers wearing shorts sitting with their knees apart and I have wanted to stare at the extra-white soft loose flesh of the inner thigh because it looks so surprised by the world, so apart from the rest of the body.

It is time to go home and I am at my locker. The corridor is nearly empty and the only sound is the hellish scraping coming from the cafeteria where white-coated staff pile orange plastic chairs too noisily onto blue plastic tables. It sounds like war in Lego-land. I gag at the smell of frying fat being poured through funnels into enormous vats.

Tom emerges from the bathroom, his hair damp.

'Lou?' he says.

'Hi,' I say.

'It's great to see you again,' he says. 'Is this your locker?'

'Yes.'

'Stupid me,' he says. 'If it wasn't your locker you wouldn't be rummaging around in it, would you?'

'I might,' I say, 'if there was something I really wanted to rummage for.'

'Fair play,' he says and offers to hold my things so I can keep looking with free hands.

He takes a camera out of his bag.

'Hey,' he says, 'you'll think I'm really vain, but I need a good picture for an audition. Would you mind coming outside with me and taking a few?'

He leans against his locker and smiles, aware of his beauty. I don't like actors. But I am feeling too happy to really mind. I wonder at the way it is that I can be a different version of myself around different people. For no apparent reason, I am not a blusher around Tom. My skin started out liking him and, so far, it still does.

'Sure,' I say.

'Thanks,' he says. 'Do you know that the person who had your locker before you died in a car crash and now there's a plaque for her on the bridge at the river? It says *Blithe Spirit*. It always makes me sad when I see it.'

I don't know exactly what blithe means. It's one of those words whose actual meaning never convinces me; whose actual meaning doesn't seem to suit the word, and I think, therefore, that it must mean something else; usually something quite opposite. In this case, I decide that *blithe* means ill, or vile, or diseased.

'Was she your friend?' I ask.

'No. I didn't even know her really. A cheerleader. Too bouncy,' he says, peering into my locker.

I search for something clever to say.

'I don't think cheerleaders are my type either,' I say. 'They're always climbing up on each other's backs and making human pyramids.'

'Exactly,' he says, thrilled to pieces, obviously glad to have me to talk to, one half of his face smiling.

We start walking up the stairs together.

I suddenly remember that I have to meet Bridget after her basketball practice if I want a lift home. Otherwise it's a long walk in the sun. Tom follows me, his steel caps clicking on the floorboards.

'I'm an exchange student,' I say, as though this explains everything.

'I know that, of course,' he says, checking for the cigarette packet in his top shirt pocket. 'James told me. Plus all the exchange students were introduced at assembly and you weren't there, but they showed your picture on a slide with all the others and gave, like, a synopsis of where you're from and everything.'

He is staring at my profile so I stare back at him. The thing about Tom's beauty is that it is not the perfect, symmetrical, blue-eyed blondness that's supposed to signify superiority. It's more that his bright green eyes deliver sharp and beautiful electric shocks every time you look at him. It happened to Margaret too, and Bridget and probably even Henry.

'You look better in real life,' he says, delivering a few quick shocks to my stomach. 'Anyway, there are seven exchange students in total, if you don't already know. They all got to say something about themselves. This school seems to absolutely adore exchange students. Practically treats them like royalty.'

'What did they say about me?' I ask and feel my insides curdle. I imagine what it would have been like if I'd gone up on that stage in front of hundreds of students, stuttering and stammering and sweating like a moron.

My face heats up as though I am reliving something horrible. I see myself as naked and wet as a peeled tomato, being led from the stage by the pig-boy, and I feel as though there is salt under my skin. I hide my face from Tom by looking at the ground.

He puts a cigarette behind his ear.

'I can't remember exactly what they said. Something really good though.'

I know that he remembers nothing and I don't care.

Tom and I walk through the school and onto the field. I take a few photographs of him sitting on the grass.

He sits cross-legged with a cigarette in his hand and looks up at the sky, not at the camera. I wonder if I should be directing him to tilt his head, lie on his stomach, put his chin in his hands. We are silent as I move from left to right, crouch down, then stand up again and all the while he is just looking at me as though he is falling in love or something.

'I better go,' I say. 'I have to get a lift home.'

We walk across the field and when it is time to say goodbye and we are standing at the gate, the breeze is blowing our hair across our faces. We stare at each other; we don't speak or move. Then he smiles, a quick, easy smile, especially on his left side, which rises up when he's amused.

'Which way do you have to go?' he asks.

'That way,' I say.

'I'm the other way,' he says, 'Well, I'm not *really* the other way, if you know what I mean!'

This is a stupid pun, a lame joke, and smarmy too, but he laughs like a person should, and when he finishes his eyes are swimming with water and his cheeks are red.

'Yes,' I say, 'I know exactly what you mean. Oh, here's your camera.'

Tom puts his hand on my arm and says, 'I have an idea. There's about ten pictures left. Why don't you take some and then when I get the film developed there'll be some of me and some of you and I'll get a great surprise and you get to keep your pictures if you like them.'

'That's a great idea,' I say. I don't care that I know he made the audition up. I don't care that he is vain and pretentious. I don't want to go home. I want to keep feeling good. So, I give him a playful shove in the chest and walk away. I turn back and he is still standing there, looking at me.

12

Two weeks later, a Saturday, and James and I are in the kitchen. I hand him a freshly laundered tea towel. It smells of the backyard autumn sun.

'Thanks,' he says. 'I hate washing.'

'Good,' I say, 'I hate drying.'

'How's school?' he asks.

His thin, juvenile moustache has been shaved off, his skin is almost clear of pimples and, except for a raised smear of dried blood on his chin, he looks quite handsome. We are alone together in the house for the first time since the vacation.

'Okay,' I say.

He stands close to me and twists the tea towel through his hands, 'You have Mr Caldwell for history,' he says. 'He probably *loves* you. Does he *love* you?'

I run my tongue across my teeth and watch James' fingers squeeze the tight rope he has made from the tea towel.

'Shut up,' I say.

'Okay,' he says.

We are silent, but James is looking hard at my face.

'How about you?' I ask. 'How's the old southpaw coping with advanced everything?'

James lunges and puts the tea towel around my neck.

'Argh,' he says, as he pretends to choke me.

His face is close and laughing. I do nothing, my hands dead, limp by my sides.

'Argh,' he says again, which is the sound I am supposed to make; a gurgling protest.

I lift my hands and put them on top of his hands but I make no sound and I do not look into his face.

He wraps the tea towel tighter around my throat, to see my face bulge and redden. My fear is suddenly real. James is pulling too tight, desperate for a sound from me, dying for me to scream, or to touch him.

I put my hands between the tea towel and my neck.

'Don't!' I say.

I break away and run around the kitchen table. He comes after me and grabs hold of my waist. He pulls my chest against his, his heart pumping. I put my face next to his, my cheek against his cheek. I do not want to see his eyes.

'Argh,' he says, pressing himself against me and rubbing sideways.

I am stronger than he is. Much stronger. I resist every push and pull and so we do not move. He stops pushing me, just holds me. My arms are limp but they want to touch him. I count to ten. I want to touch him because he is a boy and I am a girl, but he is the wrong person to touch.

Still, I want to let everything happen. I count to ten again and listen to his breathing in my ear. I am staring at the fridge and wonder what he is staring at. He has an erection. His eyes are probably closed and I am in there somewhere. I want to see what would happen next if I let it. I count to ten one last time. He has put his hand into his trousers. I wait for him to finish what he has to do. I am not a part of this any more.

When he's finished, he holds onto me as though I might slip through a hole in the floor, and as he holds me, he makes a muffled noise, a soft snort and then a groan. I groan softly back, then pull away.

The front door slams. Somebody is home.

'See you later,' says James.

'Yep,' I say, 'see you later.'

James is taller than when I first arrived.

I decide to borrow Bridget's bike and ride into town. I want to find an old Catholic church like the one around the corner from my high school at home; a church with a tabernacle, a refectory and a nave, a church that's at least one hundred and fifty years old.

I want a church where people genuflect and whisper their prayers. A church with the Stations of the Cross around the walls. I want to find a church and see what the stations are. I've forgotten them. I want to pay more attention to the detail this time.

I want to light a smooth white candle, one the size and shape of a finger, with a wick where the fingernail should be, and squeeze it tightly into the slot; line it up with all the other candles, each of them signifying a prayer.

I'd like to put coins in the collections box the way that you're supposed to; to pay a debt for all those candles I've lit without giving any money.

I wonder how much I owe; perhaps, at five cents a candle, I owe God about thirty dollars. That's not much. Maybe I should pay some interest.

I find a Catholic church and go straight to the candles and light four of them. I don't exactly pray when I light these candles, or say a novena. I merely sit and stare at Mary's statue and watch a lady move in and out of the confession box.

I like it when people climb inside the confessional and

shut the door as though they are climbing into a pantry to be with jars of jam and boxes of cereal. I like knowing that the priest will whisper behind the red curtain. It makes no difference to me that the Catholic church is shot to pieces with sleaze and sex scandals. Once I'm inside a church I feel calm.

I especially like the church near my school back in Sydney. I like that it has passages and alcoves and places you can't see when you are standing in the middle.

I sit and wonder if I should pray for something or someone. Maybe the woman who works at the school crossing opposite the church near my school at home.

She's one of my favourite people: a 'lollipop lady' who wears a white waterproof jacket with a fat orange diagonal stripe through her middle and a matching white waterproof hat with orange stripe around the brim.

We used to talk together and she'd ask me why I wasn't at school but she didn't ever get officious about it.

She took time out from working the crossing and hid behind a Moreton Bay fig tree so that she could jam her face with packets of chips and hot dogs she'd bought from the 7-Eleven around the corner.

As I crossed the road, I could see her white waterproof jacket bulging out from behind the tree, equal slices of white jacket on either side of the dark grey trunk, and I'd watch her fat white arm moving up and down to her mouth like an earth mover.

I should have told her that nobody would mind if she sat on the bench outside the church, where she could have eaten openly and without rushing. I wish I could say this to her now, so I close my eyes and talk to her as though she is dead and I am talking to her in her grave.

After dinner I go to my room to study but can't concentrate on reading and am desperate for a cigarette. I have developed the habit of taking a break from study at about eight o'clock and going for a walk around the block, finding a place in the supermarket parking lot and having a few cigarettes crouched behind the shopping carts.

If I had the right kind of friend, I'd ask them to push me around the car park in a shopping cart and we'd ride around like this for hours. If I had Tom's phone number, I'd give him a call.

I go to Henry's study to ask him if I can borrow some money. The door is open and he is hunched over the desk.

'Hi,' I say.

I look at Henry's face and I wish that I had come for another purpose. I want to act like a nice person. Maybe I should say I just stopped by for a chat; ask him if he feels like a break, a cup of tea or a game of chess.

'Hi,' he says, a smile so big it looks like he thinks I'm going to give him a present.

I don't know what to do with my hands, so I put them on my hips.

'Margaret forgot to give me any pocket money this week,' I say.

Henry points to a seat, as though he is a doctor and I his patient.

'I thought she might have spoken to you about that.'

'No,' I say. 'Is there something wrong?'

'Well, maybe we should discuss it when Margaret is here.'

I do not show my panic.

'Can't you tell me?'

Henry puts the lid on his pen and thinks for a moment.

The telephone rings but he doesn't lift the receiver. He waits for somebody else to pick it up on the other line. It's probably Bridget talking to the same mysterious person she speaks to every night in her bedroom for exactly fourteen minutes. The Harding phone-call limit on school nights is fifteen minutes.

'Margaret will want to clear this up herself, but she thinks that since you have all the clothes you need, and there's always plenty of food in the house for lunches, and since you rarely go out, it's probably better if you ask for money as you need it, or on special occasions.'

I've cried only once since turning thirteen. Now, to my astonishment, is the second time. The last time I cried was when Steve told me he'd seen a tomcat rape my kitten. I knew it wasn't true. It was the fact he was lying, and that he had waited until I was alone with him in the laundry, that made me cry.

This time I'm crying because I can't have what I want, when the whole point of my being here is to get everything I want and I'm standing in a big house where everything should not only be possible, but easy to get.

'Oh,' I say, turning away from Henry.

'Are you okay?'

The tears hit me in the jaw and I know that if I speak I will not be able to stop myself from gasping. I also feel the sad rush of pleasure that comes with the heat and uncontrollable nature of tears. I head for the door and as I do, Margaret comes in.

'That was your father on the phone,' she says to Henry. 'Your mother's had a fall. We need to get over to the hospital right away.'

There is something peculiar about the way Margaret speaks. It's as though she is enjoying the drama; as though she relishes the gravity and urgency of being suddenly needed in this way.

Henry does not speak. His eyes swell and redden and his

mouth goes slack. He takes his cardigan from the back of the chair.

Margaret does not look at me and appears not to have noticed that I'm here.

'Get Bridget and James,' she says to Henry. 'We'll take the van in case we bring your father back here with us.'

I walk towards her. 'Should I come too?' I ask.

She seems surprised by the question.

'No, I think it's important that you stay here and look after the house.'

Margaret plays with the rings on her left hand. I still have tears rolling down my cheeks and I want her to notice. Some people look good when they cry.

Bridget and James hurtle down the stairs, ready to leave in an instant.

'What's wrong with Granny?' asks Bridget, already crying.

'She's had a bad fall and she's in the emergency room at the hospital,' says Margaret with maximum *gravitas*, enjoying the suspense her voice creates when she could so easily tell Bridget and James that their granny is going to be just fine.

Henry's mum is sure to have broken her hip getting out of the shower or running to the phone, like my Aunty Sally, and be back on her feet, with a new hip, in a few weeks.

James is angry and grabs his father by the elbow. 'Come on! Let's get moving.'

I walk with them to the door and catch Margaret as she fumbles around in the key basket for the right keys.

I want her to see my face still wet with tears, one of them so plump and full it is running all the way down my neck like an animal.

'Is it true that I can't have any more money?' I ask.

She stops rummaging. 'I beg your pardon?'

'I know it's not a good time . . .' My tears have dried up and my voice is too calm, no longer sodden with water or constricted by a pleasant and awful misery in the chest and throat. 'But I need some tonight,' I say. 'I'm going out with a friend to the movies.'

Margaret is red around the neck, something I've never seen happen to her before.

'I don't understand you,' she says. 'I just don't understand you.'

She turns away from me, reaches into the basket and finds the right keys while I adjust to the shock. I'm wondering what she means and whether I should speak again.

'You're not going anywhere tonight,' she says. 'And if we're not home by ten o'clock, please go straight to bed and if you must smoke, please never, *ever* do it in my house again.'

She is happier in this particular moment than she has been for a long time. Bridget is standing behind Margaret and she, too, looks satisfied.

'What about Henry?' I say. 'He smokes!'

It never occurred to me that I'd be found out, caught like this, and I can't bring myself to apologise.

Margaret opens her mouth to show her bottom teeth: a shocked snarl.

'Henry is an adult and you're not. End of story.'

'Fine,' I say, instead of sorry.

I go to my room as soon as they have left and lie on my bed feeling lousy and guilty. Although the light is on, I fall asleep and do not wake until James stands in the doorway and softly calls my name.

'Lou?' he says.

'Hi,' I say through my drowsiness.

'Do you want the light off?'

'What time is it?' I don't need to know the time; I just want to speak to him. He is better than nobody.

'It's nearly midnight.'

The light goes off and I turn on my side to look at him, but he has gone.

Although I have slept easily with the light on, waiting for the Hardings to get home – just as I can sleep on the couch in front of the TV, especially when Henry is in the room – I cannot get back to sleep now that it is time.

It must be two hours later when I stand outside Margaret and Henry's room. The door is ajar and when my eyes adjust to the darkness I can see their shapes in the bed. I can also see Margaret's slippers and Henry's jug of water.

I want to go inside and sleep at the end of their bed or on the floor near the central heating duct. I fantasise about being there on the floor when they wake up, lying on the carpet without pillows or a blanket.

I imagine them finding me there and lifting me up from the floor. I would say, 'I couldn't get to sleep on my own.' And Margaret would say, 'You poor dear thing. Here, get into our bed. Sleep for a while. You can go to school late today.'

I would sleep in their bed while they showered together in the ensuite and I would drink the coffee Henry leaves for me on the bedside table in a perfect white coffee cup.

Henry moves, so I leave their room and go to James' room. His door is wide open. I have no intention of going in at first, but then I see him move and I wonder if he is awake.

'James?' I say. He groans straight away and I am sure he is awake.

'Hi.' I wonder if he can tell my voice apart from Bridget's.

'Good morning, Lou,' he says with affection so deep I want to touch him. He must love me, I think.

He moves to the edge of the bed, and pulls the blankets back, so that a large white triangle is formed, neat and white and empty. But when I see his grinning face, I remember just who he is, change my mind and want to keep things as they are. I do not climb into his bed. I get down on my haunches by the bed so that he can see my face, so he can remember who I am.

'I just wondered if you wanted to talk about your granny,' I say. 'I was too sleepy to talk before. Now I'm wide awake.'

He brings his hand out from under the covers and hangs it over the edge of the bed so that it touches my arm.

He groans.

'She's okay,' he says. 'Aren't you cold?'

'No,' I say, 'I'm fine.'

He moves across in the bed so that he is pressed up against the wall and pats the space next to him.

'I'll be good,' he says.

I climb in and lie on my back.

We lie shoulder to shoulder, the backs of our hands touching, but not holding, and talk until the dawn; until the birds start up and it is becoming too light and I worry about seeing his face, about him seeing mine. I worry about the light and the way that it will make us conscious again.

'I better go back to my room,' I say.

James rolls onto his side so that he has his back to me.

'Goodnight, Lou,' he says, in that same affectionate voice.

I look at the clock and see that it is not yet six o'clock.

'Sleep for an hour,' I say. 'I'll see you at breakfast.'

It's Monday. American History class. The fat girl is sitting alone. The fat boy she has been holding hands with every day is sitting away from her; has swapped desks with somebody. I stare at her and try to tell her telepathically that I am sorry for her and that I hope she and her boyfriend can make it up.

I want somebody to talk to in this place.

At the end of class I decide to follow her. She goes to the cafeteria and eats some breakfast: scrambled eggs and bacon. I sit near the entrance where the one-armed boy eats his tomato sauce on white bread. I watch as she eats. She finishes every mouthful. She walks to the library and I follow her.

She goes to the large-books collection and pulls out a hardback volume about Jim Henson and the Muppets. She takes the book to a study room. The study room is small and brightly lit with three walls of glass. She sits down to read and look at the pictures.

I wish I had met Jim Henson. Ask me who I would bring back to the earth if I only had one choice, and it would be him. I'd ask him if he could take me to his muppet studio and I'd watch him work. If he liked me, and we got along, he might give me a muppet that I could be the voice for. He would teach me to work and he would give me a job on 'The New Muppet Show: A Revival' looking after some of the smaller muppets, thinking of story lines and song lyrics.

The only problem is, I'm not that good on voices, but I could think of muppet scenarios. I'd love that. Maybe I should write to Brian Henson. Maybe he'd be interested in some of my muppet scenarios for whatever muppet programs he's putting together.

I open the door and go inside.

'Hi,' I say.

She is not surprised.

'Hi.'

'Are you a Jim Henson fan?'

'Does the pope shit in the woods?' she says.

We laugh loudly and the librarian taps on the glass.

We talk in a whisper for a while. 'Do you want to go somewhere and have a coffee or something?' she asks.

'Is the bear a Catholic?' I say.

The librarian returns. She opens the door and one of her breasts presses against the glass like a balloon filled with water, ready to burst if she presses any harder, 'Should you two be in class?'

'Journalism project,' says the girl, whose name is Yvonne.

When the librarian leaves, I say, 'Did you see her boob pressed up against the glass? It looked like a balloon about to burst.'

'Yeah,' says Yvonne, 'I noticed that too.'

Maybe I could talk to Yvonne about my obsession with breasts and how I'm worried that mine look like pork-buns.

We leave school and walk to the end of Main Street and go to a dark and dingy café where I drink coffee some weekends and where they don't care if you smoke. I light a cigarette and Yvonne looks at me as though I have taken out a gun or a knife, but she says, 'Oh, God! You'd better give me one of those.'

We smoke and talk and laugh.

'I'm a Mormon.'

'You don't look like a Mormon,' I say.

'I don't taste like one either,' she says.

I laugh loudly, a kind of ecstatic choking, almost exactly the way she laughs and I wonder if there's something wrong with me; a style of laughter is something you have for yourself, a highly personal trade-mark, it's not supposed to be contagious like a 'flu. But I continue to laugh hard and long for no good reason.

Yvonne puts her hand over my mouth to stop me.

'No, seriously,' she says, 'you should know that if my mom or dad were to walk in here now you'd have smoked your last, and your ass would be grass if Bishop Burpcrumb found out.'

Yvonne doesn't look nervous; doesn't look like somebody pretending to be tough or brave. She's not the biddable type; not trying to impress me because she needs a friend. I like her.

'Do you have to go to church and stuff?' I ask.

'Yep. Until I leave home. No sport, or anything else for that matter on Sundays. No caffeine, no alcohol, no sex before marriage, no anything much at all.'

'No masturbation?' I say.

'What's that?' she says grinning, and we laugh.

Next time we see each other I'm going to ask her if she's ever masturbated. I've done it about thirty times, and I want to know when other girls start doing it and whether I'm the only one or whether I'm in some kind of minority group.

Yvonne and I eat lunch. She tells me all about Mormonism.

'We baptise the dead you know.'

'Why?'

'To save their souls, so they can go to heaven. So far two hundred million dead people have been baptised, including Buddha, Shakespeare, Einstein and Elvis Presley.'

'What's heaven like?'

'I'll show you.'

She pulls a piece of cardboard out of her bag; it's a picture of Mormon heaven. It's all pink bunny rabbits, fairy-floss, soft white clouds, green meadows and fields of daisies with what looks like hundreds of six-year-old, blonde-haired, multiple twins, holding hands.

We laugh and I don't want Yvonne to go home and I want to tell her this, but instead I look at my watch.

'Do you have to leave?' she asks.

'No, not yet,' I say.

I think about what I am about to say next for some time. I try to weigh up the pros and cons. I lean across the table and whisper, 'Do you want to have a drink? I have some here.' I tap my bag. 'We could have some gin. I could order some orange juice and we could mix it?'

'God, I'd love that,' she says and I am immensely relieved

that I haven't persuaded her; that I haven't talked her into something she isn't ready to do. It could have been such a filthy thing to do, enticing a Mormon to drink. It could have been such a horrible thing to do.

At six o'clock Yvonne looks at her watch and for the first time I see dread in her eyes.

'I better run,' she says.

I don't want to move from the table in case my mood moves with it.

'I might stay a while,' I say. 'See you on Thursday?'

She fiddles with the straps of her backpack.

'I won't be at school on Thursday. I have to do something at home. But we'll meet again, for sure.'

'For sure,' I say. I want to tell her how funny she is. I want to tell her that I like her face.

'For sure,' I say again and watch her go.

Margaret is standing in the hallway when I get home.

'We've been waiting for you,' she says.

'Sorry,' I say, but cannot remember why I was supposed to be home early.

'You've forgotten, haven't you?'

'Yes,' I say, the base of my spine shivering, telling me I need to clench or I'll urinate right where I'm standing. Everything seems to collapse with something my body has realised before my mind.

'Tonight is James' first heat for the national debating championships. They've gone on ahead.'

Nobody has told me this.

'I didn't know,' I say.

Margaret is angrier than I have ever seen her; her mouth tightens, her chest heaves and she has to fold her arms across her chest so that I won't see her hands shaking.

'Bridget told you. I checked with her before she left. She said she told you after dinner and if you can't remember that far back then there's really something wrong with you.'

'Oh,' I say, paralysed, impotent, ready to cry for the second time in less than a week.

'Maybe I forgot because Henry's mum is in hospital.'

'I doubt it,' she says.

Margaret drives me to the auditorium in silence, but it is Henry who is most cross with me. During the last round of the debate, I lean over to ask him if he or Margaret would like anything to drink since I am going to the bathroom, and he turns on me, 'For God's sake, *please* just stay where you are.'

I stay in my seat and notice that Henry's eyes are watering badly, and that he uses his sleeve to dab them dry.

After the competition – which James' team wins – we go to a pizza restaurant. James is excited about his victory, but he's disappointed that Margaret has made what he calls a bank manager's decision not to go to the restaurant the rest of the team is going to.

'You were excellent,' I tell James, and he was.

As he stood on stage, waved his arms and walked into the aisles, he seemed much older, as though there are two versions of him.

'Thanks,' he says, blowing air on his knuckles and then rubbing them against his suit jacket lapel.

The mood is subdued. Margaret hardly eats and nor do I. She is distracted by every movement. When somebody walks in or out, she watches them; somebody scrapes their chair to get out from a table and she turns in her seat as though she is about to be arrested.

Henry does most of the talking, which is unusual, probably to make up for Margaret's silence and he conducts a thorough post-mortem of the flaws in the other debating team's performance.

'They were too greedy for laughs,' says Henry. 'Too worried about individual kudos to work as a team.'

'They were just too *retarded*,' says James, some stringy mozzarella dangling from his hungry mouth, and the other version of James, the better James — the one I saw up on stage, the one from last night — is obliterated.

I spend the dinner thinking about how I will make amends, how I will start again and how I will ask for help.

'I was wondering,' I say as we are walking through the front door, 'if everybody could meet me in the living room in five minutes.'

Not only am I going to turn over a new leaf but I'm going to ask for help and start behaving like a new and nice person. I smile at everybody, such a smile my whole face shakes.

'What for?' asks Bridget.

'I'll tell you when we're all together.'

Margaret drops the car keys into the basket and folds her arms.

'I think we're all too tired tonight, Lou,' she says. 'Why don't you just tell us now?'

James is unnerved by something he sees in my face and holds his bag in front of his chest like a shield.

All of Margaret's warmth towards me has been sucked dry, as though she was hooked up to a vacuum during the night.

Henry seems to harbour a deep suspicion, planted not by something he's seen, but by something someone has told him. Perhaps Margaret has persuaded him, at last, that I am no good or too much trouble.

Bridget is impatient; for her I am irrelevant. I think that perhaps only James will feel anything when I say what I'm about to say. 'It's hard to explain,' I say.

But that's as far as I get.

I am about to say sorry. I am about to tell them that I still can't sleep and that I want a doctor. I am about to apologise for everything and ask for help, but my nose begins to bleed.

James takes a box of tissues from the dining-room table and passes it to me. Margaret, who is normally so fond of any kind of action, especially action or drama involving the human body, takes a chair and places it behind me but does no more; not a single word is spoken before she leaves the room, followed obediently by Henry.

'They know you smoked in your room again last night,' says Bridget, and something tells me that she is the informant. 'They're really pissed about it too.'

James doesn't know I smoke.

'Fuck,' he says.

Bridget breaks into a smile, the kind that sometimes happens when somebody's nervous.

'Smoking is such a loser thing to do,' she says and storms out of the room, as though she needs to go away and fume in private.

I lie on my bed and take out four sheets of paper. I will write four apologies, starting with Henry.

Dear Henry,

I'm sorry about throwing that cup of coffee at the wall and for smoking in my room. I promise it will never happen again and I wish I had the courage to tell you how wonderful I think you are. If you were my real father I'm sure I'd be a hundred times better than I am. I've liked you since I saw you at the airport. I liked you when we were at Flo Bapes' house and there was a storm and you opened the windows to let the thunder and lightning get in.

I'll always like you and I'm very sorry.
Love,
Lou

I put this note in an airmail envelope and wait until three a.m. I go to Henry's bedside and stick the note in his shoe. Somehow I know that he'll read it privately; that he won't tell Margaret and that he'll think about what to do with me in a different light.

After breakfast, Henry calls me into the dining-room where he is stacking his briefcase.

'Thank you,' he says, a little nervously. 'But there's really no need.'

'That's okay,' I say.

He half clears his throat the way a person does when they don't want you to know that they need to clear their throat.

'You have a lot of sheer humanity,' he says awkwardly.

As these words roll over in my head, Henry stuffs a newspaper into his briefcase, looks nervously towards the kitchen door, shuts the lid heavily and locks the lock. He looks around at the kitchen door again and I know he is worried about Margaret.

He smiles with effort. 'That came out wrong,' he says.

'That's okay,' I say.

As he walks out the front door, I grab hold of the words and make them stand up: *sheer humanity.*

I can't let Henry leave without something lighter, something friendlier, passing between us.

He stands on the doorstep and I pull the door closed behind us.

'Henry,' I say. 'Do you know what desquamation is?'

He lifts his briefcase to his chest.

'Are there any clues?'

This is an interesting approach. I have to pretend to know less than I already do.

'All I know for certain is that Antarctic explorers suffered from it quite often before they died in the snow. From my reading, it seems desquamation was always around when Edwardian-era Antarctic explorers perished.'

Henry is glad of the change in tone and wants to employ his powers of deduction.

'Ah, well. I remember reading something about this. Is it what happened when a type of volatile fuel was used for portable cooking stoves? I think it refers to the effects of toxic fuel gases inhaled in close quarters, like in tents?'

Henry walks towards his car but is happy talking about this. I should ask him more encyclopaedia-style questions.

'Could be,' I say. 'That's sounds plausible to me.'

He opens the passenger door of his car and puts his briefcase on the seat. 'Anyhow, I could look it up for you at work. I have a good dictionary on my desktop.'

'No, don't do that. I want to find out for myself.'

'Bye, Lou,' he says, 'have a good day at school, and don't worry.'

'No?'

'No, I don't think you should.'

'Okay.'

As he is getting in the car, I walk around and stand next to him. He hugs me and I feel good. I know that I will start all over again; rewind this, and go back to the beginning.

13

The weather is colder, at last. At lunchtime, I lie on the lawn where I compose my apologies for Bridget, Margaret and James.

I feel a hand on the back of my head.

'Lou,' says Tom. 'I thought it was you.'

I look up and smile.

'It is me,' I say, 'and you must be you.'

I've been carrying Tom's camera around ever since he gave it to me and I've finished the roll of film, but haven't wanted to use my short supply of money to get it developed; nor have I known how to contact him without asking James. I've been hoping that Tom would find me.

'Did you take any pictures?' he asks.

'Yeah, they're in here.'

'Great. Any hints?'

'Oh, they're not that interesting. I hope you didn't miss any deadlines or anything?'

'What for?' he says.

'The audition,' I say.

'Oh,' he says, not a good liar, his eyes shooting out over my shoulder as though he's casual as anything. 'I decided not to worry about that. It wasn't a good play, anyway.'

Tom is crouching like a frog.

'Do you want to lie down?' I ask.

He lies down and we talk for a while. There is no explanation for this that I can think of, but in Tom's company, I am like a different person. For one thing, I still don't blush.

'What's your favourite film?' I ask.

'What's yours?' he asks back.

'I have a few,' I say. '*The Shawshank Redemption* is up there.'

'I love that film,' he says.

'Really? What's your favourite part? What's your favourite line?'

Tom isn't uncomfortable even when he's stuck or trapped.

'I dunno,' he says, 'I just love the whole thing.'

'What about when Morgan Freeman says "Get busy livin' or get busy dyin'." I love that line.'

'Isn't Morgan Freeman the greatest,' says Tom, like one great actor complimenting another.

'Yeah,' I say. 'But what about that line?'

'Sure,' he says. 'It's an awesome line.'

We are silent.

'What other films do you like?' he asks.

I half expect him to ask me what my favourite colour is, like the boy I held hands with at the roller-skating rink.

'*Down by Law*,' I say, 'and *Smoke*.'

'Never heard of them,' he says, as though he knows every other film and I just happened to have mentioned the only two he hasn't seen or as though these films are bad or don't count.

We are silent again.

'I like you,' he says, reaching for my hand and his eyes give me another shock. But still I do not blush.

I put my head on his leg and close my eyes.

'I was wondering,' he says. 'Do you want to escape with me? We could take the rest of the day off, go to one of those one-hour photo places together.'

'Why not,' I say, pretending to be casual just like him. 'Let's go.'

I move quickly to prove I'm keen, and to my amazement, I keep holding his hand.

'Maybe we could get a coffee,' he says.

'I was just about to think that,' I say, smiling, and watch as one side of his face lights up more than the other.

The photographs are developed and we go to a café to look at them. Tom is satisfied with the pictures I have taken of him.

'You're good at this,' he says.

'Thank you,' I say, worried about the photographs I have taken of myself, sitting up in bed, using the camera's self-timer.

'It's a photographic essay,' I say. 'It's called "Insomnia". I took them in the early hours of the morning when I couldn't sleep. I look like a corpse. Except, of course, not. 'Cos a corpse gets lots of sleep, and I don't.'

'You couldn't ever look awful,' he says, looking into my eyes.

I wish that people I want to like wouldn't say such stupid things and even though it's Tom that should be ashamed of this corny line, I blush for the first time since we met. Unlike James, he looks away to let me recover, and I do, quickly. For this I like him.

'I was going to do an essay called "A Day in the Life of a Tea Towel" but I would have needed high-speed film.'

'That's pretty funny,' he says.

'Then I was going to do an "Elegy for the Apple", but every time I tried to find an apple, Margaret beat me to it and devoured the poor thing before I could get started.'

I have used the word elegy in the wrong place. I meant something else but can't think what I meant.

'How bad's your insomnia?' he asks.

'Very,' I say. 'Sometimes I want to die just so I can shut down.'

'Me too,' he says, leaving his free hand resting prone on the table like it has fallen from a height.

'Really?' I ask. I hope like mad that he is a fellow sufferer but I also suspect he's lying, and that I might find him out.

'How bad? How many nights in a week, on average?'

'At the moment . . . about five out of six.'

'What about the seventh?' I ask.

'Then I don't so much sleep as knock myself out.'

'How?'

'With stuff,' he says. 'But you don't want to get into that. It's stuff my mum had to use when she was really sick.'

'Morphine?'

'Sort of, but you really don't want to get into that.'

Tom's face shows a mixture of not wanting to talk about it and wanting desperately for me to ask him more.

'Well, my friend,' I say, pretending to be very urbane and in some kind of cool movie, 'what shall we do now?'

'Go home?'

I'd love to be inside somebody else's house.

'Could I have a nap at your house, in a spare bed, or something, like in a guest room? I really like sleeping in spare beds, especially in box rooms,' I say.

'Me too. I love to nap in other people's beds.'

'Really?' I say. It's hard to believe that Tom shares yet another of my most personal obsessions.

'Yep. I used to get my mum to set up beds in all the guest rooms in the house until I was about fourteen . . .'

'But eventually even those beds lost their knack?' I say.

'Yeah,' he says and he lunges at me to kiss my cheek.

I am still not embarrassed, but when he finishes kissing me, I look down at the fleshy part of his thumb and think about the way it looks like a toddler's thigh, to stop myself from thinking too much about what is happening.

'I used to sleep on the fold-out bed in the lounge-room,' I say. 'I could always sleep this way.'

'It's a funny beast . . . insomnia,' he says.

'How many bedrooms do you have?' I ask.

'You'll see.'

'Is anybody home?'

'No, they're away.'

My heart kicks like a boot in my chest.

We arrive at Tom's house. It's so enormous it makes the Harding house look like a shack. He stops and grabs my arm.

'Shit,' he says. 'I forgot about the char.'

'The what?'

'Char. It's short for charwoman.'

'As in maid?' I say, incredulous. I think I know this word from Austen or Dickens, but I'm not quite sure. I just know it. 'How awful,' I say.

'It's a pretty big house to keep clean,' he says.

'I suppose,' I say. 'It's not exactly a cabin, is it?'

'The second-biggest house in town,' he says.

'Who has the biggest?'

'Actually,' he says, 'I think mine is the biggest.'

Leona and Erin would love to do over Tom's house, and kick him in the shins in a dark alley. They'd call him scum and say that it was disgusting that three people should take so much for themselves.

A few years ago my sisters brought me along as a kind of decoy when they burgled houses in wealthy suburbs. They thought nobody would suspect two teenage girls dragging their little sister around with them.

I wanted to explore these rich houses alone. It was my fantasy to discover that the owners would not be back for a few days and to stay there, so that I could treat the house as my own. I wanted desperately to find an oubliette, a secret passageway or a secret dungeon whose only entrance is a trap-door activated by removing a book from a bookshelf or moving a bar of soap from one part of the bath to another.

I craved being alone in these big rich houses the same way that I crave being alone in old Catholic churches.

Tom smiles. 'Tom's cabin . . .' he says. 'I just got it. That's why you said cabin.'

'Yes,' I say. 'Uncle Tom's cabin. You took a while.'

'I'm a bit slow sometimes,' he says. 'We'll have to come back another time,' he says. 'Sorry.'

'Oh,' I say. 'Doesn't matter. I think I might go back to class. I have Modern Literature. We're doing *Death of a Salesman*.'

'That's one of my favourite Arthur Miller's,' he says.

'I like it too,' I say.

I want to talk about Willy Loman and about Biff stealing the fountain pen, but somehow I don't want to talk to Tom about it.

'I might just go for a walk,' he says. 'Do you want me to walk you back?'

'Sure,' I say. 'That'd be great.'

We say goodbye at the school gate.

'Farewell, my fiend, until next time,' I say.

'Wait!' he yells. 'Do you want to meet tomorrow, the same place, same time and all that?'

I have no idea what I want. If Tom wasn't perfect looking, if he had an uglier face, I don't think I'd give him the time of day. That's what beautiful people can do.

'Sure,' I say. 'That'd be good.'

When Tom pushes his face forward to kiss me, I respond too slowly and our cheeks collide. He holds my shoulders and we try again and this time our lips meet, not for long, but long enough.

We stare at one another for an instant and my body is so alarmed I might as well have flung myself onto an electric fence.

'Oh my God,' he says, and this seems like the right thing to say.

I turn and walk away.

After dinner I write a note to Margaret.

Dear Margaret,

I have caused you too much pain and anxiety and I feel totally rotten for it. I am very sorry. This stupid note won't make up for anything, but maybe telling the truth can't hurt. I love living with you and I love the way you are. I love that you are so at peace with yourself and maybe you'd understand me better if you knew that I am not. You are an excellent, smart and humorous person and I'd be so sorry if you hated me.

I am sorry about smoking in my room. It will never happen again.

Your secret, apologetic and far too silent admirer,
Lou

In the morning, when James and Bridget are getting into the van, Margaret kisses me on the cheek. She's wearing one of five almost identical navy suits, all spick and span and creaseless and smelling as though soaked in perfume overnight; cleaner than any of my clothes could ever smell.

'Thank you,' she says.

'You're welcome,' I say.

'But you don't need to write me. You can talk to me anytime,' she says. 'I'm available for you at any time. If you want to talk.'

The thing is, I have lost the desire to talk to Margaret. I don't want her to put her hand soothingly on my arm, or sit too close to me and grab at my eyes with hers, or clean her reading glasses with a serious face and talk at me like a kindergarten teacher.

In American History class I find out that Yvonne has left to live in another state. It occurs to me that I haven't thought about her once since we met and it really makes no difference to me that she's not here any more. I've never really missed anybody and probably never will. It's not that I wouldn't like to miss somebody. I would. I'd like to miss somebody very much. I simply never have.

At lunchtime I write a note to Bridget in which I tell her that I dreamed she was a surgeon and that she won an extremely prestigious award for her work in a Third World country. I tell her that in this dream she gave such a beautiful speech that it was played on every TV station in the country. Although I didn't really have this dream, it sounds right.

Tom doesn't appear and I feel sorry for having spent the whole day feeling sick with nerves: sorry that I haven't eaten since we parted and that the saliva in my mouth has become flocculent and gluey with hunger and fear.

I stick the note in Bridget's locker five minutes before the end of lunchtime and she finds me at my locker at the end of the day.

'I just want to say thank you for the note,' she says. 'You're very sweet.'

'That's all right,' I say. 'My dream might be a sign about your future.'

'Maybe,' she says, blankly. 'Maybe not.'

Suddenly she leans across to kiss me on the cheek. But again, I move forward too quickly. Our faces collide and it feels as though my nose has poked her eye. She puts her hand over the left side of her face.

'Sorry,' I say.

'Don't be sorry,' she says. 'Anyway, I have to go to basketball practise now. I'll see you tonight.'

'Okay,' I say. 'See you.'

It's a ridiculous thing but I almost say *I love you*, as though the words are waiting — like a bee — to land on somebody.

After dinner, I write a note to James, borrowing heavily from the sentiment in the card to him from Isabella.

Dear Southpaw,

Do you remember our conversation about left-handed boxers? I haven't forgotten about that or anything else we've talked about and one day I'll find out why it's not 'Eastpaw'. You are one of the most interesting people I've ever met and I think you should write comedy or do something else that calls on a brilliant wit and fast mind. If I don't always laugh at your jokes, it's because I'm a bit jealous or too nervous. I'm very glad you're my host-brother. And I hope we'll always be friends.

Yours,
Lou

Several weeks pass. Instead of watching TV at night, I lie on my bed and compose notes. I am at peace doing this, in my lovely room, which seems to have friendly feelings towards me again.

Sometimes I draw pictures or compose stories for my letters; funny stories or detective stories in which Margaret, Henry, James and Bridget feature as characters. My notes are flying all over the house and although I have never received a written reply, I suspect that the Hardings are now sending notes of their own to each other. The house has become quieter; has a new atmosphere. We don't sit together at night, or borrow videos, or eat out at family restaurants or talk in the kitchen.

Margaret and Henry say they are reading more books. Margaret says she hasn't read a big book in years and might even try reading *War and Peace*. She and Henry go straight to their dens after dinner and James and Bridget go to their rooms to study.

At weekends, the Hardings are rarely in the house. When I go to the lounge-room, they are never there. I don't go with them to their concerts and charity fundraisers and picnics, not because I think they don't want me to, but because I prefer being alone in the house and want to give them some time to get on just the way they were before I came along.

14

It's lunchtime on Monday and Tom turns up. It's too cold now to sit outside, so I'm in a study room, reading a book.

'Hello,' I say.

'Sorry I haven't been around,' he says. 'My mum had to have some blood tests and I was feeling a bit blue.'

'That's okay,' I say, thinking he is the worst liar in the world. 'I guess sometimes a person just needs to be alone so they don't have to explain how they feel.'

'That's right,' he says, sitting down and putting his arm over my shoulder. 'You're really incredibly perceptive.'

I saw Tom two days ago with a girl, arm in arm, coming out of a Journalism class. She was his female equivalent, extremely good looking and tall, with a loud, sure voice.

'Thanks,' I say, and find myself wondering what I look like.

'Hey, wanna come to my place? I've just picked up my new guitar. I can sing you some of my songs.'

'Okay,' I say.

Tom shows me through the downstairs rooms of his mansion then takes his guitar out of its case. We sit cross-legged on the couch in the vast lounge room, and talk. The guitar leans against the wall, and I suspect that he doesn't know how to play.

'Are you hungry?' he asks.

'No, I'm too happy.'

'How come?'

I tell him how much I like to be in other people's houses. I tell him about the time my sisters and I broke into houses.

'Christ, how old were you?'

'About thirteen,' I say.

'Wow!' he says again, trying to hide his disapproval, trying to sound impressed.

'Anyway,' I tell him, 'one of the houses we broke into had a tennis court and swimming pool. It was during the summer holidays. I played the outgoing message on the answering machine while my sisters were upstairs looting the jewellery and the message said the exact date that the occupants were due back. Two weeks more. I told my sisters I wanted to stay in the house by myself for a few nights and to tell my mum and dad I was staying with a friend. They couldn't care less so they let me.

'I stayed for three nights, slept on all the beds, watched movies on the wall-mounted TV screen, read some books and ran up and down the spiral staircase with the stereo blaring through speakers that stuck out in the corners of all the rooms.

'But the best part was raiding the big double-door fridge, eating their food and using their microwave. One day I got a tub of chocolate ice-cream out of the freezer and ate all of it while lying on an inflatable bed in the swimming pool.'

None of this is true, but I have daydreamed the story so often and so vividly that its details are as known to me as if it happened, not once, but many times. My sisters, on the other hand, have robbed houses; I tell them I despise them for it, but sometimes wish that I could be part of it just to see inside the houses.

Tom stretches his arm out over the back of the couch.

'I feel a bit like that when my parents leave me alone in fancy hotels,' he says. 'Especially in Europe.'

Especially in Europe!

My heart folds up and puts itself away like a deckchair in winter. How dare he be that rich? How dare anybody be born so stinking rich.

I look at the top of his head: his shiny, clean curly hair. I look at his pure wool jumper and his clean blue jeans.

'I'd better get going back to class,' I say.

He has me by the hand and is staring hard, his eyes intensely focussed, a dart player eyeing the dartboard. I let him hold my hand because I'm not so good at hurting a boy's feelings when he wants to be affectionate. I'm usually too busy being surprised that he wants to touch me at all.

'Hey,' he says, 'it's not my fault my parents have money.'

I look at the home-entertainment unit, which takes up almost one half of a vast white wall, and say nothing. My hands are sweating a kind of depressed and sticky syrup. Tom lets go, puts his head down and rubs his forehead.

'Hey, man,' he says. 'There's no point walking around the rest of your life with a chip on your shoulder just because you're not rich.'

If he weren't so good looking I'd have hit him by now.

I look at the guitar, and wish people didn't have to speak at all. I wish that it were dark as pitch, and we, with only a candle to guide us, could have played the guitar and sung some songs.

I look at him, will him to say something better so that I can give myself an excuse for liking him.

'Sorry,' he says. 'Wanna hug?'

'I'd rather you played the guitar,' I say. 'That was the original plan, wasn't it?'

'Yeah,' he says, smiling his beautiful smile. 'I should keep my trap shut more often.'

'Maybe,' I say. 'Maybe not.' And then, just because he has an exquisite face and I want to be the boss, I kiss him. Then I put my hand on the back of his head and pull his hair.

'Ow!' he says, and for no real reason, this makes me feel better.

I laugh.

'You are the best kisser ever,' he says.

And because I feel better, I say, 'I could do that all day. All week. All year.'

We stare and stare, locking eyes to see what kind of feelings this conjures, and, surprisingly, it does conjure intensely good feelings.

'Guitar,' I say.

'Cool,' he says.

Tom stands and lifts me off the couch. There is something about being lifted that makes me sad and happy at the same time.

We go upstairs and Tom brings his guitar with him. He stops on the landing.

'There's a spare room just in here.'

'Show me,' I say.

The room is perfect. Huge windows open onto a balcony. A four-poster bed with blue curtains, tied at the corners. An ensuite and a walk-in wardrobe.

'This isn't a spare room.' I say. 'Spare rooms are dingy box rooms without a window.'

'It's for my dad's parents when they stay,' he says. 'Come on, I'll show you my parents' room.'

He holds my hand hard and tugs me along.

His parents' room is twice as big as the one we've been in, but too opulent. There's a bathroom attached to the bedroom with a spa so big that midgets could hold their Olympics in it. The taps are brass and the floor and bath are marble and the walls are mostly mirrored. It's a bit pornographic.

'God,' I say. 'What's your room like?'

Tom smiles, grabs my arms and pulls me towards him. We laugh, our eyes averted, nervous and unsteady on our feet. After a brief collision, we kiss.

Tom tastes of gum and tea and his lips feel soft and inflated like teething rings. We stop kissing for a moment and look at each other's faces. I wish that we were lying down; that it were night and that the curtains were closed.

Tom begins to walk backwards, pulling me with him.

It's darker in the hall and I want us to stay here. I don't want him to be in his own room; a boyhood world so utterly owned by him, smelling of him and everything he has done. I wish we were in a neutral, jointly discovered place.

I guide him towards the banister so that he leans there. He tries to make himself shorter so that I can reach his lips more easily, and in this position his neck seems to have grown long, his back so bent it is as though his excitement has broken him.

'Hi,' I say, to tell the silence who we are.

'Hi,' he says back, and we are even.

I am smiling because he is smiling.

We kiss for a long time. I push down on his shoulders until eventually we reach the floor. I hold myself up on my elbows and we kiss, then I let myself go onto him and I am lying between his thighs, and rocking, when he stops.

'Oh shit,' he says and I think I know what has happened.

'It's okay,' I say as I watch him unzip and reveal, momentarily, the slack-skinned, bruise-coloured thing.

'It's okay,' I say again as he runs to the nearest of five bathrooms.

A few minutes later Tom comes out of the bathroom carrying

a towel and he stares at me. His face is not as pleasant as it was before, but not unpleasant either. He looks worn out, as though recovering from an illness, and a little resentful.

He pulls me up to my feet, even though I want to stay where I am, and kisses me on the mouth for a long time. I feel drowsy and want to be unconscious.

'I want to go to sleep,' I say.

We walk lopsidedly towards the spare room with the four-poster bed, and when we get inside he pulls back the covers. I am too drugged to have a complete thought in my head. He will think that I have disappeared, and, in a way, I have.

'I'll tuck you in,' he says. 'Do you want some tea or something?'

His voice is nervous, shaky, smaller.

'Do you want me to go?'

'No,' he says. 'Stay here. I'll tuck you in.'

'Thanks,' I say.

In the doorway he stops and comes back, holds my foot and says, 'I lost my virginity a few months ago with a girl I've known all my life.'

He puts his hand limply and reassuringly on my thigh as though he hasn't the energy to lie.

'Then I had sex again about a week later with her cousin when we all got drunk at a party and then one more time with my old friend after that.'

Sure, I think, drifting off to sleep.

Tom wakes me with a cup of coffee. He sits on the end of the bed with his guitar, finally out of its box.

'How you doin'?' he asks.

'Good,' I say. 'What time is it?'

'Five o'clock.'

'Should I leave?'

'No. My parents won't be home till late, and even if they came home earlier, it wouldn't matter. They're completely relaxed.'

'Lucky you,' I say.

'Do you wanna hear some songs?'

His accent suddenly sounds a lot less Scottish and a lot more American.

'Sure,' I say.

Tom isn't quite the musical fraud I thought he was.

He plays classical and folk guitar, and sings well. He has a voice of his own, not a copy of somebody else's, just like his face. He plays some songs I know well, songs I know inside out, songs that pour out of me whenever I'm alone in the flat in Sydney and I've had a few drinks.

But I cannot join in. I barely manage to hum, and even then my throat feels like it's been rammed with a length of stiff rope.

'Do you have any requests?'

'Not really.'

There are some songs I'd love to hear; that I'd love to sing with him. My mind reels with instant fantasies of Tom and me singing duets in bars; dressed as sleek as otters, looking alike, passing knowing glances as though we share the secret language of the gifted and urbane.

'You must know this one,' he says. 'Everybody knows *this* one.'

He starts.

'You know it?'

'Yes.'

'Can you sing? I bet you can.'

'Yeah,' I say, 'but only when I'm in the right mood.'

'Come on, I'd love to sing with you. I've been wanting to sing with you since we first met.'

I sing, quietly at first and then, when he stops looking at me, a little louder.

But it's no good. We both know it's no good. I can hardly believe the transformation; mouth dried up and breathing desperate and shallow. I sound dreadful.

Tom is embarrassed for me and when the song's finished he leans the guitar against the bed and looks at it is though to say it is to blame for my terrible singing.

'That was fun,' he says flatly.

'That was shocking,' I say. 'I can't sing when I've just woken up.'

'That's okay,' he says, still feeling sorry for me for being a bad singer; the kind of pity only a good singer can feel. Probably also wishing I had complimented him some more.

'Don't stop,' I say, getting up out of the bed. 'Keep playing. Please. I need a quick shower to wake myself up and then a few glasses of water, then we'll sing some more.'

He starts to get up.

'Hey, now *there's* something I've always wanted to do.'

I kiss him on the nose. 'Maybe next time. I feel like showering by myself.'

There's a bar fridge in the ensuite in Tom's parents' room. I take four miniature bottles of gin and two of whisky — the kind you get on planes. I get under the shower. It's surprisingly easy to drink alcohol quickly with water running all over your body.

The water is probably too hot and when I get out, the doll's-house-size plastic bottles emptied, I need to crouch on the pink fluffy bath mat for a minute to regain my balance.

I brush my teeth and open the door, and just as I'd hoped, Tom is still playing. Not only that, but he's playing a song I know well. I sit on the bed and start to sing.

'Hey,' he says, his mouth, especially the left side, reaching up towards his happy, watery eyes, 'You sound great. You sound really great.'

He plays a dozen or more songs and I sing all of them. Sometimes I harmonise, even though I've never done it before.

'Wow!' he says.

'Thanks,' I say. 'Sorry about before. Like I said, I can never sing when I've just woken up. It's just one of those things.'

The guitar is on the floor and we are huddled together in the middle of the queen-size bed.

'Do you think we could pull the curtains around the bed?' I ask.

'Yeah,' he says, 'I was just about to think of that.'

Tom pulls the curtains around the bed and we are cast in a smoky blue light as though sitting in a chunk of trapped sky. The world seems utterly irrelevant, as though whatever we do next won't have happened at all.

I pull my top up over my head, slowly, so that for a good while I can't see out, my face covered, and the sense of Tom's eyes on my breasts ripples through me.

By the time I pull my top down and look at Tom my nipples are cold and hard.

'Jesus Christ, you're sexy,' he says.

This moment cannot be capsized.

'Let's see how long we can just stay like this,' I say. 'Let's see how long we can last.'

After dinner with the Hardings, I decide not to go straight to my room. I'm still softened by the alcohol and feel like talking to them; it's been a while since we had any kind of conversation.

I visit Margaret in her study. I put my head in the door, 'I'm going to bed early,' I say. 'But I just thought I should check in case there were any chores you'd like me to do.'

'Hi,' she says. She closes the lid on her laptop and moves forward as though getting ready for a long chat. 'How's school?'

I stay in the doorway even though she gestures for me to sit down.

'It's fine. The teachers are great and I think I've chosen the right subjects.'

Margaret rolls a pen across the desk. 'Who are your friends, Lou?'

My heart flickers. 'Just people in my classes,' I say.

'These days,' she says, 'it's important to make contacts as well as friends. It's a tough world out there. You won't survive on your brains alone.'

'Yeah,' I say, 'I know.'

She smiles. 'Well, it'll be getting much colder soon. We'll have to go shopping for some new clothes.' She looks me up and down.

'Thanks,' I say, bewildered by this intelligent woman's obsession with shopping and the clothes that people wear. I wonder if she and Henry ever had that discussion about me visiting their family doctor. I decide to ask her, in spite of my embarrassment, but she opens the lid of her laptop and clears her throat.

'Lou. Don't forget that you can hang out with Bridget if you'd like to. She's always there for you. You don't have to spend time with people who you don't really like.'

'Thanks.'

'Just don't forget that Bridget would like some of your company. Don't be a stranger to her. Okay?'

Bridget doesn't even like me. I don't even know how to talk

about any of the things she likes to talk about, and yet, I'm flattered.

'Okay,' I say. 'Bye.'

I poke my head inside the door of Henry's den. He's smoking his pipe and he looks as though the novelty of life has completely run out on him, and yet, as though, if somebody gave him a surprise, the novelty would come back.

Perhaps he looks sad because he is so fair and because his eyebrows are almost invisible – albino invisible.

'Hi,' I say. 'Could I maybe sit in here and just read for a while?'

Henry frowns. 'It's probably better if you read in your room tonight. I've got a bit to do here.'

'Okay,' I say and turn to leave.

'Everything okay?' he asks. I turn around. He takes the pipe out from between his lips.

'Excellent,' I say.

'Have you checked the schedule?' he asks.

'Yes,' I say. 'It's my turn to make dinner tomorrow night and I'll have to get home early.'

'That's the way,' he says, ending all hope of conversation.

'Goodnight,' I say.

'Goodnight.'

I go to Bridget's room and knock on the door. She's on the phone.

'I'm on the phone,' she says and I realise I've never been in her room with her in it.

I go to my room, still a bit tipsy, and sing just about every song I know. I sing at the top of my voice. My heart races when I hear noises outside my room, but I don't stop. My voice is working well and I want the Hardings to hear it.

It is nearly ten o'clock when James knocks on the door. 'Can I come in?'

'Yes. Of course.'

He sits in the chair by my desk. I'm sitting on the bed, cross-legged.

'You sound good,' he says.

'Thanks.'

He looks at the books on my desk; most of them are Russian and Norwegian novels that have nothing to do with school.

He smiles at me. 'I think those notes you've been sending are really weird . . .' He stops but I can tell there's more he wants to say.

'Oh,' I say, hangdog as hell. 'I thought everybody liked them.'

'Sorry,' he says, 'I don't mean weird in a bad way. They're really good. We were all just talking about them earlier.'

'Really?' I say.

'Yeah, but maybe you should stop now, you know. They're really good, but maybe there've been enough.'

'Oh,' I say, dumbfounded.

'So, anyway,' he says, 'I'm sorry about what happened, you know . . . that night ages ago.'

'Which night?' I say cruelly.

He stands up suddenly and moves towards the bed. 'You know?' he says.

'On the trip?'

'Yes.' He stands awkwardly, arms lost by his side. 'Can I give you a hug?'

'Okay,' I say, but when he presses too hard into my body and we both begin to lean backwards on the bed, I push him away.

'Let's stop,' I say. 'It's not a good idea.'

'You're such a tease,' he says. 'You're driving me insane. I wish you'd never come to this house.'

He walks to the door. 'And you *smell* funny,' he says.

'What?'

'Don't worry,' he says, about to start crying. 'I guess you can't help it.'

I look away. He recovers quickly and then in a low voice, his back against the door, he says, 'I came to say I'm sorry but now I want to sleep in your bed . . .'

Suddenly he's crying, snorting back snot.

I stand up and put out my hand. 'Let's just shake hands like you Americans all love to do so much and forget about all this.'

He starts to cry again. 'Oh fuck,' he says.

I hug him as carefully as I can, my groin held away from his, my right hand stroking his arm.

'I know what you mean,' I say, 'but we have to get on with things. We could both get in heaps of trouble and I could get sent home. We have to forget all about it.'

He hugs me hard and won't let go. 'Have you fallen in love with me too?' he asks, his wet nose on my neck.

'Yes,' I lie, 'but we can't do anything. We have to keep it all in our heads.'

'Okay,' he says, his hand gripping the door handle. 'I better go to bed, but if you ever can't sleep . . .'

I just nod.

James opens the door again. 'Oh,' he says, 'the auditions for the school musical are on Friday night. Bridget said maybe you should try out.'

I can't sleep. I think about auditioning and it terrifies me. I don't even like musicals. But if I can do this, maybe I can do other things. Maybe I can learn to be confident. Maybe I will change – if I do this. If I do this one thing – if I can do this one thing right – I'll change who I am forever.

15

The auditions are held in the school's dark basement, in the vast auditorium, where all assemblies and prize presentations take place. I take a few sips of gin and then sign up at a table outside the entrance.

The musical is an original called *Hippydrome: Hits of the Sixties and Seventies*. It's not so much a musical as a collection of hit songs strung together with a script written by the musical director, David Babbitt, and his drama students.

'Name?' asks a boy with fat fingers and big ears.

'Louise Connor,' I say.

'You're number eighteen,' he says. 'You can wait here if you want, or go somewhere else. It's gonna be about twenty minutes, at least.'

I sit and wait and I feel sick with nerves. Then I imagine singing on opening night with the Hardings in the audience and I am nauseated, even though one of the reasons I want to do this is to show off to them. I go to the toilet and drink some more gin.

My number is called and I go into the auditorium. A woman wearing a red poncho waves me over to the piano and I walk with my hand shielding my eyes from the floodlights. Only the front rows of the audience can be seen, but it's noisy out there. There must be a hundred people or more.

I don't care. The alcohol has settled in. I am edgeless,

tall, light, quick and powerful.

'What are you going to sing?' asks a man in the front row.

I have decided on a song from *Annie Get Your Gun*. A stupid idea, but I thought they might like it. I'm not even sure I know the right title. '"I Can Do Anything Better Than You Can",' I say.

'No you can't!' screams a joker in the back of the auditorium. I couldn't care less who it is. I even think this is a fairly funny remark.

A man cries out, 'Keep it down.'

The woman in the red poncho asks me what key I want her to play in and I don't have a clue. I want to say, *You could play the front door key for all I care* but instead I say, 'It doesn't matter. You choose.'

Somebody laughs with a short snort. It sounds like James. Perhaps it is James. I don't care. I'm indestructible. I'm not even blushing. I'm high as a kite.

I sing better than I ever have, as though some kind of spell has been cast. It's a voice I didn't know belonged to me and I don't want to stop singing. I don't have to stop. I get all the way to the end of the song without interruption. From what I know of what happens at auditions, at least in the movies, this must be a good sign.

I peer into the front row. The director introduces himself. His name is Paul, a skinny man with a skinny moustache. Beside him is David Babbitt, bald, without a moustache.

David calls out, 'Okay, we'll see you back here tomorrow. Six o'clock. Sharp.'

'Great,' I say. 'That's great.'

The morning after the audition I catch up with Bridget as she is heading out the door to go to the river to hang out with her friends. The top she's wearing under her jacket is small and tight, like a bandage worn to protect a pair of broken ribs. Bridget and I don't see each other at school, and she is hardly ever at home during the day on weekends. I want to talk to her; not just because I am convinced that she is the reason Margaret and Henry found out about my smoking, but because it's making me worry. Without her on my side, I don't think things will work out the way I need them to. Maybe I just want to be nice. Maybe I would enjoy being nice. Sometimes it's hard to tell what's making me do something.

'Thanks for passing on the tip about the audition,' I say. 'I really appreciate it.'

'What audition?'

She is still walking. As usual, her body tells me that she's in a great hurry and that she has somewhere better to be and somebody more interesting to see.

'James said you heard me singing and told him to tell me about the auditions.'

She scrunches her perfect nose at me. 'Nah.'

'Oh,' I say. 'Anyway, I went for an audition.'

'Awesome,' she says, without meaning it. 'I hope you get a part.'

I smile but she doesn't smile back. She is afraid I'm going to follow her.

'Do you know Tom McGahern?' I ask.

'Yeah,' she says, and keeps walking. 'James brought him over that night.'

In one way or another, she's always moving. I don't know what she looks like when her long legs aren't propelling her towards something: launching her onwards, towards something better. I decide not to take it personally, not to withdraw. But perhaps I have left it too late.

'What do you know about him?' I ask.

She walks a little slower, but doesn't stop. 'He's that millionaire freak who transferred from another school last year.'

'Why is he a freak?' I ask.

She stops out the front of a house, 'Just look at him,' she says, gazing anxiously down the street as though Tom might poke his pale head out of an attic window and spit on her. 'He *looks* like a freak.'

'Have you ever spoken to him?'

'I don't need to,' she says, pulling her bag close to her chest. 'Everybody knows he's a freak. Even his parents are freaks. And he doesn't have any friends.'

'Give me an *example* of this freakishness then.'

She flings her bag across her shoulder and juts her head forward in anger. 'Don't yell at me. It's not my fault he's retarded.'

'How can he be retarded if he's on the honours roll?'

'It's called the National Honours Society and why don't you ask him that? There's a simple and embarrassing explanation.'

'Like what?'

'Haven't you wondered why he's like at least *three* years older than everybody else? He was kept down. Practically brain dead from drug abuse.'

I cannot breathe and therefore cannot speak. I look at the ground.

'By the way,' she says, her chest rising and falling, hardly able to breathe with anger and the restraint of her tight white bandage, 'Mom can't drive you anywhere today. She's got lumbago again. Dad said if you go into town you could meet him at the office and he'll take you home.'

'I'll walk,' I say.

As I go up the stairs to my room, my nose begins to bleed. I go into the bathroom and let the blood drip into the sink.

I don't try to stop the bleeding. I watch the blood splatter on the white porcelain, 'as red as the nail polish Pushkin wore', as Mrs Walsh said once when my nose bled into one of her white handkerchiefs.

I watch my blood drip and pool in the sink like red milk. I like to see how much blood I can lose.

With blood trickling down my chin I say to the mirror: *May she have a terrible accident and lose the tip of her perfect nose and one long brown leg from the knee down.*

But when I get back to my room, I undo the curse and pray that Bridget doesn't hate me.

Then it suddenly occurs to me, like a thwack across the back of the head — it's so obvious. If things don't work out with the Hardings, and if I can't live with them, I can live with Tom, in his mansion. When school has finished and my scholarship ends, I'll move in with Tom's family and become a citizen.

I need to see him as soon as I can.

Margaret calls out to me from her bed. I go in and she removes her glasses, rubbing the lenses with her cardigan sleeve. She seems like a spectre; not a hostile one, but simply not palpable or present enough. There is something not quite real about her.

'You haven't told me how your audition went?' She sounds mildly affronted. I have left her out again. I'm not treating her like a proper host-mother.

'It was good,' I say, my head throbbing, 'I've been called back. I have to go later today.'

There's an odd musky smell in the room; a smell of satisfied human damp.

She puts her hand out for me. She wants to hold my hand. I can't. This is something I still can't let her do. My hand sweats at the mere thought of touching her, just as when my mum tries to touch me.

I say, 'I have to go now. I have to practise.'

She tries to sit up but her nostrils flare up with the pain.

I say, 'Don't sit up. You'll hurt yourself.'

She slides down again. 'Why don't you sing for me? I'd play the piano with you except that my back's not so good. Why don't you practise in here? I'd love to hear you.'

My bladder twinges sharply as though stuck with a pin. I stare at the box of tissues next to her bed to stop myself from crying.

'*Please* sing for me,' she says.

I stare at the perfect white tissue sticking out of the box in the shape of a big white molar. 'Oh no,' I say, going red as hell, 'I couldn't.'

'Why not?' she asks, offended again, or perhaps she wants to see me embarrassed.

'You'll be hugely disappointed. I'm not very good.'

She rubs her glasses again. 'That's silly and obviously not true,' she says. 'The standard of singing at that school is very high.'

Now she sounds like a school teacher and I wish she was a completely different kind of person: the kind of person who understands how another person is feeling just by looking at them; somebody who doesn't stare all the time or speak in a loud and confident voice. Somebody who knows when to look away.

'I better go,' I say and leave the room.

There's a supermarket around the corner but I decide to go to one further away. I ride Bridget's bike. The shop is crowded. I look all around to see if there is anybody I recognise or who might recognise me. I go to the counter and ask for a bottle of gin.

I ride home. I have one hour before the call-back audition. I go to my room, put a chair under the door handle, and drink as slowly as I can to give myself time to judge the gin effect. After twenty minutes I stand up and walk around my bed a few times to see how I'm going. I feel good, but I should have eaten something. *Gin-effect sounds like genuflect*, I think, and the phone rings in the hall. Margaret calls out, 'Lou, could you get that please?'

I pick up the phone. It's Tom.

'Hey,' he says. 'I was thinking about you all night.'

'That's great,' I say blankly, wishing that I could hang up and call him back on the phone downstairs.

'I think I'm either in love with you or I have rabies,' he says.

I know Margaret is listening.

'That's fine,' I say. 'How are you?'

'I'm good,' he says, confused. 'I didn't know if I should ring you at home. I don't know how cool your host-parents are about me?'

'Excellent,' I say.

I imagine him sitting up in his bed, nothing but underpants on, no longer smiling. 'Are you all right?'

'Yes. Great,' I say. 'Only Margaret has a sore back. Poor thing.'

'Oh,' he says. 'Anyway, I was wondering if you'd like to go for a picnic this afternoon. We could go to the park. I can't wait a whole day to see you and I need to know if I have rabies or not.'

'I'd love to,' I say, 'but I'm busy.'

'Whaddya doin'?' he asks.

I feel desperate. If I tell him about the call-back he'll get cross that I didn't tell him about the first audition and he might want to come along and watch me and this idea terrifies me. I'm far from ready to sing in front of somebody I know.

But if I don't include him in this and he finds out, I could blow everything.

I tap the receiver and say, 'Hello? Hello? Are you there?' I wait for what I think is a convincing length of time and then I hang up.

I call out in the direction of Margaret's bedroom, 'They must have been cut off.'

'Who was it?'

I stay in the hallway for fear of her seeing my crimson face.

'A friend from school.'

'Call her back,' says Margaret.

'I don't have her number,' I say.

Margaret must control every situation. 'I'll look it up for you,' she says. 'What's her name?'

'I don't know her last name.'

'Well, if she calls back I'll be sure and get her number for you. What's her first name?'

'Um, Judy,' I say. 'Her name's Judy.'

I go to the call-back audition and when I get home, still a bit tipsy, I find out that Margaret's back is so bad that she can't come down for dinner. Henry, James, Bridget and I sit at the dining table, eating dessert and swapping stories about our day.

'How was your audition?' asks Henry.

'Good,' I say. 'I might have a part.'

James has his mouth crammed full of spaghetti but he puts his hand over his face and says, 'You'll probably get the lead part.'

'How do *you* know?' asks Bridget.

James swallows as much as he can and speaks with his mouth half full. He suddenly seems about twelve years old. 'I was there yesterday.'

'Were you?' I say, 'I didn't know that.'

'You're different up on stage.' He smiles as though he's captured my secret and he's keeping it upstairs – like an insect in a jar – in his smelly room. 'It's weird. It's almost like you're a different person.'

'Aren't you nervous?' asks Bridget. 'Don't you, like, *blush like crazy?*'

I'm too exhausted to feel hurt by Bridget's cruelty and spite. 'Not really,' I say.

Henry holds up his glass of orange juice. 'I hope this isn't premature, but I think a toast might be in order.'

'That's really bad luck,' says Bridget. 'What if she doesn't get a part?'

The phone rings at half-past nine. I've got a part in the musical. The only thing that stops me from feeling pure terror is the knowledge that confidence, and a good night's sleep, are only a glass or two of gin away.

It's Sunday night. Margaret is out of bed and we are all in the living room watching a video Bridget has picked up from the video store.

'Pause it for a second,' says Margaret. 'I need an apple.'

'I'll get it,' I say.

I fetch her the biggest, roundest and reddest apple in the fridge.

'Thanks, sweetheart,' she says and pulls me towards her so that she can kiss me on the cheek. By the time I sit down again, tears of happiness are rolling down my face.

About halfway through the film there is an unexpected sex scene. The woman, who is wearing a summer dress, lies on a kitchen table, takes her pants off, and spreads her legs, and the man, still wearing his trousers, undoes his zip and climbs on top of her. The camera is stationed at the woman's head so that mostly what is seen is the man's body pumping her, his head going back, his face grimacing.

I think that the Hardings can see what is happening to my face and neck. I'm not blushing, I'm burning alive. My hair is singed. I cannot breathe. I am frozen with the shock of the impact of this thing I have seen. I can feel the pain between my legs and I can feel the table under my shoulder blades.

The scene seems to last forever. None of us moves a hair. The man and the woman are being watched from above, the man pummelling the woman.

The silence in the room can be felt, like pain. In the movie, another man comes into the kitchen. He is a friend of the first man and he begins to unzip his trousers.

'Stop it,' I say without intending to make any sound. 'Stop the video.'

Margaret has the remote control and she stops the movie. The room is silent, but only for a second. Margaret turns the TV back on and a gridiron game blares into the room.

Henry, with no sweat on his brow, no quiver in his voice, no blush, not even an invisible embarrassment that might show itself in the way that he swallows, says, 'I guess that was a pretty boring film.'

James is next. 'I hate when they put stupid sex scenes in films.'

Bridget is worst of all. 'As if anybody would have sex on the kitchen table!'

Not one of them is troubled. Not one of them disturbed. Not one of them ashamed or sick or bothered. My emotion is more than they can bear. They have shut down and they are in this together.

'I'm going to my room,' I say, pain and sadness shooting through me. 'I hate football.'

On Monday morning the results of the auditions are posted up at school. I see Tom in class but instead of sneaking glances at each other across the room and talking in code, using the hand signals we've developed, he bows his head and sulks.

'Why didn't you tell me?' he asks when we are leaving class. 'Why didn't you tell me you were going to audition?'

'I was too embarrassed,' I say.

'Crap,' he says.

We walk to our lockers together without speaking. Tom slams his locker shut and everything inside it falls. 'I was going to audition too, you know, but I thought you'd hate that kind of shit.'

'The Hardings really wanted me to audition,' I say. 'James put my name down. They were worried about me not being involved in anything at school.'

'Crap.'

'Ask them, then,' I say. 'Ask Margaret and Henry. They talked me into it and I just went along for the ride. I didn't think I'd even get a part.'

'Sure.'

'Sorry,' I say, thinking about living in his mansion house, 'I should have told you. I'm really sorry.'

'Yeah right,' he says.

'Maybe you should come to the first rehearsal and see if you can still get a part. Then we can be in it together.'

'No fucking way,' he says. 'I wouldn't be caught dead going to those stupid rehearsals every night for months.'

'Not every night,' I say.

Tom storms off with his bag dangling, straps trailing on the floor. I wish I could empty myself out like a trouser pocket. I feel filthy and nervous, standing here in the corridor, alone, surrounded by the noise and gay activity of happy students. I leave the building, my skin prickling with sweat, wondering what it is that happens between normal people, wondering what it is they laugh about.

I don't trust or even like Tom right now, but he's the only person I can even talk to without feeling surreal. I have run out of gin and I have run out of money and I have the first all-cast rehearsal tomorrow night. I wish that I hadn't let him go.

When I get home, Margaret is sitting at the dining-room table cutting an apple into small pieces. I see to my horror that she has the score of *Annie Get Your Gun* in front of her.

'I've been looking forward to you coming home,' she says, 'Look what Henry got at lunchtime.'

I look over her shoulder. 'Oh, that's terrific,' I say.

She holds my arm, 'My back's a lot better. I could play for you.'

'Oh,' I say. 'Maybe later. I had a really hard day at school. I need to go for a bike ride or something to clear my head.'

'Hell's bells!' she says. 'What's wrong with you?' She is holding my arm and I wonder if she can feel me shaking.

'Are you sick?' she asks. 'Your eyes are all glassy. Did something happen?'

'Not really. It's just that I ran into a friend who went for the part and didn't get it and as you can imagine she was upset and I wonder if she'll ever talk to me again.'

'I see,' says Margaret, letting go of my arm, 'You wonder if she's jealous of the interloper.'

'Exactly,' I say. 'I thought she'd never stop crying.'

'Is that Judy?'

'Yes,' I lie. 'It's Judy.'

I ride my bike to a nearby phone booth and ring Tom.

'Hello,' I say. A woman answers the phone. Tom's mum, I suppose.

'Is Tom there?'

'Is that you, lovely Lou?'

I nearly laugh. 'Yes,' I say.

'We're looking forward to meeting you,' says the cheerful, posh voice. 'I'm Tom's mom.'

'Hi,' I say.

'I'll get him for you.'

Tom and I meet in the park and sit on a bench and we kiss. I like him most when he doesn't speak and when I look at his eyes a flare goes up in my soul. I tell him I need a loan.

'Why don't you ask your host-parents for some money?' he asks.

'They won't give me any.'

'What do you need it for?'

'I need it for alcohol,' I say. 'I can't sing unless I'm a bit tipsy.'

He doesn't seem surprised, in fact, he seems pleased.

'Dutch courage,' he says.

'Something like that.'

'It's more than that, isn't it? It runs a lot deeper than that, doesn't it?'

'Maybe it is, maybe it isn't. I'd just like money to buy some gin.'

He puts his hand in his tight jeans' pocket.

'Shit,' he says.

'What?'

'I've only got five. I thought I had more.'

'Fuck,' I say. I don't believe him. 'I can only get a small bottle with that.'

He smiles. 'I've got a better idea.'

'What?'

'Ever taken speed? It's even better. Especially if your problem runs a little deeper.'

I don't care what I take but I wish he'd shut up about this running a bit deeper business, especially since it's obvious he's talking about his own problem, not mine.

'Give me some,' I say.

Tom has some in his pocket inside a plastic coin bag.

We sit inside a piece of playground equipment; a bright green ball that you sit inside while somebody outside spins you around. It smells of vomit. Tom shows me how to snort the speed but most of it seems to get stuck in my nose and a horrible acidic taste, like powdered headache tablets, crawls down the back of my throat. It's a dark and distasteful few minutes.

'That's revolting,' I say, climbing out of the round green ball. 'We should have got a few cans of beer to wash it down.'

'Then let's get some,' he says.

We go to the nearest store. I don't feel the effects of the speed until we are inside. Under the bright lights and with the music loud around me, the effect seems to kick in suddenly. When the shop attendant is giving me the change I start talking and can't stop. I'm practically dancing on the spot.

We go outside and I'm still talking.

'Good isn't it?' asks Tom.

'I think so,' I say and I keep talking and talking about nothing, and yet it feels as though I've worked everything out.

Tom and I walk down the main street. I see Bridget in a

parked car with her boyfriend, the rufous one. She is brushing her hair and looks as though she's been crying. There's a six-pack of Coors on the dashboard.

'Let's go and say hi to Bridget,' I say.

Tom takes my hand. 'You'd better not. She'll know you're out of it.'

'But I should get a lift home,' I say.

'Don't,' he says, grabbing my arm. 'You're too out of it.'

But I'm more awake than I've ever been and I can't stop moving. I head towards the parked car. It takes off just as I get close enough to see Bridget reapplying her pink lipstick. Rufus speeds off without indicating.

Tom and I keep walking and near the Town Hall there's a boy busker, playing the flute. There's a toy shop next to him and in the window – which the boy can't see – a mechanical toy unicorn is bobbing its head from side to side in perfect time with the boy's tune.

'Look,' I say, 'the toy's head is moving in time with the tune that boy is playing.'

'Huh?' says Tom.

'What a wonderful thing.'

'I guess,' he says. 'It's a pretty good coincidence.'

I sit on the kerb outside the toy shop. Tom sits down with me. I've got to tell him that it's much more than a coincidence. And so, I spend the next hour telling him that the unicorn's head swaying in time to the boy's tune sums up the whole of life. More than that, it tells us the very point of life itself.

It's after ten o'clock and Tom and I are lying on his bed. His parents are out. I'm thirsty but not hungry. I want to talk about the big things. I have all the answers.

I feel as though I could do anything, anything but sing,

that is. I might be full of amphetamine but I know that my mouth is loose and my words are fast and muffled. I know that the outside doesn't sound like the inside feels. What the world hears when I speak is probably something like a talking sock.

We lie on his bed until after midnight.

'I'd better go home,' I say.

'Sure,' he says sulkily. 'You better go home.'

We keep talking.

I know that either Margaret or Henry will be waiting up for me and I know they'll be angry, but I don't care. I am full of things I want to say to them. I have an enormous amount of insight and wisdom and confidence and I know it won't last. I am looking forward to talking to somebody other than Tom. I realise that I love Margaret and Henry and I can't wait to see them again.

Tom drives me home in his flash red car.

Henry is sitting in the kitchen with the radio on. He stands up when I walk through the door.

'Where the hell have you been?'

He searches my face so he can decide whether to keep his anger or shift to concern and sympathy. After all, something terrible might have happened to me.

All I want to do is get myself another cigarette, light it up, make a coffee and chat with him until the sun comes up.

My mouth starts to move of its own accord, as though it were stuffed full of mechanical, self-chewing gum.

I sit down. 'Do you think there's something different about the air between midnight and sunrise?' I ask.

Henry doesn't answer.

'I think the air is quite different and that's why people are different,' I say.

'Even you are different right now,' I say. 'Don't you think

184

that when the alarm goes off at five a.m. that there's something different about the air? Don't you think the air is airporty?'

Even though the face looking at me is hostile, I can't stop talking.

'At five a.m. the air is a packed suitcase or the phone about to ring for the first time in ten years,' I say. 'The air is full of calm emergencies.'

Henry is furious. He's also busy trying to work out what's wrong with me. I want to keep talking but I also wish this wasn't happening and that I could go and chain smoke with somebody really interesting. Somewhere where there is alcohol and music.

I think of home and of pubs with beer-sodden carpets and my sisters lying wasted and half dressed on the lounge-room floor; salt poured over red wine spilt from cheap casks onto the carpet. I change my mind and wish I were straight. I wish I were a completely different kind of person, straight and clean and tall and tidy, like Bridget, who drinks light beer with her friends but never gets drunk or foolish.

Henry's face is right up close to mine. 'It's two-thirty in the morning. Margaret's been driving around the neighbourhood all night. She's only just now got into bed!'

'Is she in bed now? Is the mini-bus in bed? Is the mini-van in bed?'

I love the sound of the words mini and van.

'Have I ever told you what I call the mini-van? It's called shitty shitty prang prang, or sometimes it's called . . .'

Henry smells my face. 'You've been smoking!'

'Not really.'

'Lou, look at me!'

I look at his nose.

'Have you been taking drugs?'

'Drugs?' I say. 'No. I haven't taken drugs. I'm just sleepy. I should go to sleep.'

'Lou-ise!' shouts Henry, nearly making me laugh. I hate the sound of that name. Loo-ease. Ill at ease. Loose eze.

'I only tried one cigarette but it was despicable.'

Henry grabs me by the elbows so that he doesn't get his hands dirty. 'How could you do this? Do you have any idea how worried we've been?'

I let myself go limp and his fingers lose their anger. He folds his arms across his chest. I realise for the first time that Henry isn't that old, he's probably only about forty or something, which isn't exactly old. He has a handsome face and if he wasn't an almost-albino I'd probably find it hard not to be attracted to him.

'After all the nights Margaret and I have sat up in bed arguing about you . . . this is what you do? And me wasting my breath defending you!'

'I better just go to bed,' I say. 'I better get out of your radio . . . I mean, out of your way.'

Henry has no choice but to let me sleep it off; whatever it is. He knows there's no point having it out with me while I'm under the influence.

He opens the door. 'Get to bed. Margaret and I will talk to you first thing in the morning.'

'Thank you,' I say.

I go to my room and smoke what's left of my cigarettes. When I try to sleep, I can't. All I can do is sit up and rock myself back and forth and rub my legs and arms, which ache as though they swam home and want to swim some more.

There's a knock on my door at nine o'clock. I'm under the blankets, fully clothed. I have fallen asleep just a few moments earlier.

'Come in,' I say, but Margaret and Henry are already inside.

Margaret looks awful. Her hair is lank and greasy and she looks much older.

She says, 'You'd better have a shower, then meet us downstairs in the kitchen. James and Bridget have already left for school.'

Henry opens the window. 'Keep this window open and your door shut until we say otherwise.'

'Sorry,' I say. I can still feel the speed in my blood, but I'm not high. I just want to sleep.

'Okay,' I say. 'I'm sorry.'

'So are we,' says Margaret, meaningful and serious as hell. I don't blame her.

I take the stairs on tiptoe and listen at the kitchen door. Margaret and Henry aren't talking. Margaret is blowing her nose. I go inside. The kitchen is the most cramped room in the Harding house and I have never liked being in it.

With its door at each end, a long table which takes up most of the space and forces you to stand close to whomever is doing the cooking, a small window which sees the branches of a tree and no sky, and the schedule on the fridge telling everybody what they must do, it is the most unnerving room in the Harding house.

'Aren't you guys going to work today?' I ask.

Henry stands up and pulls out a chair for me to sit in. Both doors are shut and there is no tea or coffee on the stove.

'No.'

I want him to say more.

'Lou, you don't really expect us to go to work after what's happened? What would your own mother do?'

I sit down and think to myself that it would be water off a duck's back for my mum. She'd keep brushing her hair in an earthquake and she doesn't believe in discipline. When Erin and Leona beat me to a pulp, she yells out from the kitchen, or over the din of the TV, 'Youse can fight your own battles, but break that table and I'll break your necks.' Afterwards, when I lie on my bed, she comes to me with a cup of tea. I take it and the tea on my swollen tongue makes me happy. 'Can you stay here a while?' I ask, and she does, and we talk until I fall asleep.

'I'm not taking drugs,' I say. 'I was just in a weird mood from lack of sleep. You know I have really bad insomnia.'

I'm not stoned, but I seem to have acquired a thicker skin, a layer of immunity. I feel as though I could say anything and not feel in the least bit skinless. How wonderful it would be to always feel immune; immune from things and people, what they think and what they say.

'Lou, please don't lie to us,' says Margaret. 'Lying is the worst thing you could do right now.'

Henry is less angry. 'We know how troubled you are, Lou, but that's no excuse for what you've done. There are two children in this house who we need to protect and we can't have you around them if you're taking drugs.'

They're using my name a lot. I decide the best thing to do is tell some of the truth; to cooperate. Make them feel as though they've cracked a hard nut. Let them get on with their lives. I'll deal with Tom later and make my move as soon as I can. I'll tell him that I want his family to adopt me.

'Okay,' I say, 'you're right. I did a really stupid thing last night and I can't believe I did it. I tried some drugs. But as you can see, I didn't enjoy the experience.'

Henry leans under the table and takes his diary out of his briefcase.

'We're going to have to call Flo Bapes. The Organisation has to know about this. Your parents will have to be contacted. The decision is not ours. It's out of our hands.'

The very sound of that name – Flo Bapes – makes me shudder. When I called her last week to ask her if I could see a doctor, she told me this was a matter for Henry, who I now believe is glad to have me out of his hands. He wants to wash his hands of me. In fact, he's at the kitchen sink doing just that. He feels cleaner already. He feels relieved. The manual has told him what to do and all he has to do is follow it. It hurts. I'm amazed at how much it hurts.

He reaches for the phone.

I start to sob; great gulps of air and heaving convulsions. I hadn't thought that it would be this serious. I would rather die than go home. Henry's hand hovers theatrically over the receiver, waiting for me to give him a reason not to dial the number.

Then I realise that it is only a threat. I feel like laughing.

I say, 'Is there any way I can stop you from telling them? It'd kill my mum if she knew. It'd kill my dad too. Can't you just ground me or something?'

Margaret is pale and small dark bags, filled with a foul blue liquid, sag under her eyes.

'Who gave you the drugs? We need to know who's behind this before we can agree to anything.'

I pluck a name out of the fluorescent kitchen sky. 'A girl called Simone,' I say.

My appetite is coming back. I feel like pancakes. I feel like being hugged and put to bed, but not my own bed, a new and different bed. Henry and Margaret's four-poster bed. I wish I was at the airport meeting Margaret and Henry for the first time.

I say, 'I've never met her before. I was walking home from school and she came up to me. She is really pretty and friendly. She said she'd seen me at the audition and wondered if I'd like to have pizza with her and her friends.'

As I tell this lie I can see Simone and her friends. They look like regular high school students. They are in the drama club and they have a 3.8 grade point average.

'And what happened?' asks Henry, wrapping his hands around an empty cup as though to warm them.

'We were having pizza and somehow I was telling them how lonely I'd been feeling and they asked if I'd like to try something that'd make me feel really happy. They told me it was one of those natural herb things, you know, like that guarana stuff you can buy in the shops.'

Margaret has been rubbing her eyes by sticking her fingers under the lenses of her glasses, as though she's too tired to take them off. She stops and slaps the table. 'And you believed this? You fool!'

'It sounded okay. They were so casual about it. They seemed like really nice people. Simone is bright. She's going to Yale and wants to do pre-law.'

I have no idea what I'm going to say before I say it. Margaret doesn't agree with Henry. She thinks I should be sent home. She wants me to be punished. 'Well, you're not as smart as you make out, are you?'

'I suppose not.'

She takes her glasses off, holds them in the air and peers through them at the calendar on the wall, affecting a strange toughness, as though she busts drug users for a living.

'And so you took this drug – this unknown substance – on the strength of a pretty face who claims she's going to Yale?'

'Yes, I was stupid,' I say. 'They just had a small brown packet and poured powder into my drink and then I drank it. I felt sick. Then I said I should go home and they offered to drive me. That was about eight-thirty. They drove around and around and I kept telling them to drop me off or let me out.'

As I tell this story, I can see Simone's car. It's a Saab with white sheepskin seat covers. She has two friends, one girl and one boy. The boy has blond hair. The girl has short red hair. They laugh a great deal and I laugh too. We are driving fast, listening to loud music.

'I was lost. I didn't know where they'd driven me. I wouldn't have known how to find my way home and I thought it would be more dangerous to get out of the car. By the time they dropped me out front it must have been late.'

'It was two-thirty a.m.,' says Henry, exhausted.

Margaret wants to know if she and Henry can search my room. I agree and stay downstairs with my head on the kitchen table. I have stashed an empty bottle of gin under my mattress and the rest of the speed is in my underpants.

They are taking a long time. I lie on the couch and watch some TV, hoping they'll leave me alone for the day. Then I remember that the first all-cast rehearsal is on tonight and that I still haven't solved my problem.

Henry comes in first. 'We didn't find anything.'

Margaret is still angry. 'We need to look in your wallet. Can I have it please?'

'Yes,' I say and hand it across the back of the couch.

'There's not a cent in here,' she says. 'Not a penny. Did these people make you pay for the drugs?'

I have no idea what the right answer is. 'Yes,' I say. 'After I'd already taken the drug and we were in the car, Simone and her boyfriend told me that I had to chip in or they might not be able to get me back home.'

This Simone girl and her boyfriend sound like lunatics. I hope I never see them again.

'Good God,' says Henry. 'How much?'

'Twenty dollars and all my change,' I say.

Margaret and Henry leave the lounge-room to confer for a minute.

'We want you to promise you'll never see these people again,' says Henry. 'They could have killed you and left you in a ditch on the side of the road.'

Margaret is still cross. 'Next time anything like this happens we'll be calling Flo Bapes. There'll be no more sympathy. We will not allow you to corrupt our children. If you ever consume alcohol or any kind of drug again, you'll be on the next plane home.'

'I'm so sorry,' I say. 'I'm really sorry. It won't happen again.'

I don't believe they'll send me home.

'You'd better stay home today,' says Henry. 'You look like death. But you won't be going anywhere tonight. We'll talk about your schedule later. And don't talk to James and Bridget about any of this. Just say that you were sick today.'

I feel like telling them that Bridget and her friends drink all the time and that she spends most Friday nights playing drinking games, like 'quarters' and 'spin the bottle'. I feel like pointing out that I haven't met a single American kid over the age of fourteen who doesn't drink.

'But I have the first all-cast rehearsal tonight at school. I have a big part in the musical.'

Margaret and Henry have forgotten all about this. They leave the room once again to confer and I listen to their hushed, angry voices. Henry must be sticking his neck out for me again.

He comes back in alone, his neck red, 'We've agreed you can continue to go to rehearsals. You'll need to give me a copy of the timetable and Margaret and I can show up at any time. You'll only be going to rehearsals and nowhere else. Besides rehearsals, you are grounded until we say you can go out again.'

'Thank you,' I say. 'You've saved my life.'

Henry and Margaret go to work. I sleep on the couch for a few hours and then wake up when the sun floods the room. I draw the curtains and lie down again, but the wave of sleep has washed up on the shore of my unhealthy skull and I am filled with dread again. I can't rehearse without alcohol and I have no money. In two hours Bridget and James will be home from school joyfully making cheese sandwiches with mayonnaise that squeezes straight out of the container, and then they'll lie on their bellies in front of the TV, talking and laughing before they do their homework. I have no choice but to try the booze cabinet.

The cabinet is locked and the key is nowhere to be found. I search the house for some loose change. I start with all the drawers on the ground floor and then the drawers in the basement. I leave the bedrooms till last. I find a grand total of one dollar and thirty-five cents. I imagine, for one startling paranoid moment, that my looting for coins has been filmed by a closed circuit TV and that they'll all watch it together when they get home.

I lie on my bed and pray for sleep. I say the Our Father about twenty times. This doesn't work. I go to my desk and write a letter of apology and put it under Margaret's pillow. I go back to bed. I panic. I take the note from under the pillow. She won't like the idea of my having been in the bedroom. I move the note under the piano lid and then take it out again. I move the note to seven different locations before tearing it up. I lie on the bed again and try to think of a plan.

Margaret knocks on my door as soon as she gets home. She hasn't taken her shoes off. She usually takes her shoes off right away and replaces them with slippers. Something must be wrong. She hates her corporate clothes.

'How are you feeling?' she asks.

I sit up. 'I feel rotten,' I say. 'I feel really bad about what I've done. I'm really sorry.'

'Apology accepted,' she says, 'but what I'm really interested in is a huge improvement in your behaviour. And no more lies.'

I'm confused about this reference to my behaviour. What else have I done wrong? I bet it's the outburst over James.

'We just want you to fit in. That's all we want.'

'Where's Henry?' I ask.

'He's staying back at the office late tonight.'

'That's my fault, isn't it?'

'Yes. It is.'

Margaret is using her special parent voice, stern and slow.

'Are Bridget and James home yet?'

'No, James has debating practice and Bridget has a science club meeting. They'll be home with Henry. He's picking them up at seven.'

She still feels some warmth towards me. I can tell by the way she isn't in a hurry to leave my room.

'I have rehearsal at six-thirty,' I say. 'I'd better get ready.'

'Well, just let me use the big bathroom for a while. I need a good bath. The cold is playing havoc with my back. Then it's all yours.'

'Okay,' I say. 'I hope it makes you feel better.'

I lie on my stomach for a while and then I realise what I must do. When Margaret is in the bath, I must borrow some money. I'll put it back next week when I get my allowance. It's medicine. That's all it is. It's just medicine. I only need it when I sing so there's really nothing sinister about it at all. That's all it is. The musical will be over in a few months and I'll be free. Anyway, I'm not just getting through rehearsals, I'm learning how not to be nervous. At the very worst, this is my way of finding out how ordinary people feel.

Margaret's handbag is on the swivel chair in her study. I open it and find that she only has two twenty-dollar notes and about two dollars in change. I take a twenty and go upstairs. I listen at the door of the big bathroom. She's still in the bath. I decide to get on Bridget's bike and leave even though it's only half-past five.

If I don't leave right away, Margaret will want to drive me. I have no choice. I write a note. I say I have to get to the auditorium early to warm up. I say that if she'd like to come along and watch, that'd be great. I sign off, *I love you* and as I'm writing it, I think I mean it, but I'm not really sure.

16

It's nearly midnight and I'm lying face down on my bed, reading a letter from my mum. In it she tells me about my dad's recent heart operation. I didn't know he was sick. I didn't know he needed an operation. Maybe there was something about it in one of the earlier letters I read quickly and threw out. Maybe there was something about him being ill in one of Erin's letters that I didn't read at all. I feel awful. Maybe I should write to them, or at least call.

Dear Loo-Loo,

It must be winter there by now as its summer here. You are probably ice skating to school and building snow men.

Your dear old dad is recovering well from his heart operation. He's sitting in his favourite chair peeling the sticker off his beer bottle and making faces at the telly. He says to say 'hello'.

There's nothing much to report except that Erins pregnant and hopefully Steve will find them a flat to live in. We were thinking she could use your room for the baby for a while when you get back if its okay with you.

Erin said that nursing was a bit too boring and too many exams. Shes got a good job at the hotel anyway which is good and she brought us our dinners when we went there the other night and looked fabulus in her black and white gear.

Your dad and me will get back to the meals on wheels when hes

fully recovered. Mr Smith died last week and left us his big
wardrobe. Its real mahogany wood and hardly fits in our room.
With all the old people dying by the time you get back there will be
some real good stuff for you. No need to buy you any birthday
presents next year eh?

Hope you are doing real well and that you are happy.

We love you heaps and miss you even more.

Your loving mum

xxxxxxx

p.s: When you get home I'll do my impersonation of Pam Ayres
for you.

As I read this letter, I want to feel sad for my dad and I want to
miss him but I can't help seeing them all sitting in the flat in
front of the TV chain-smoking and eating junk food and talking rubbish. My sisters are wearing heaps of make-up and tight
tops and long feather earrings. My mum is wearing a shower
cap and filing her nails with an emery board. My dad is wearing the tracksuit bottoms that haven't been washed for years
because he says, 'That's what I'm wearing on Saturday morning
when your mum does the washing.'

I remember the rancid smell of them when he used to
wrestle me when I was small. 'I'm the boogie man!' he'd yell as
he chased us around the house. 'Here comes the boogie man.'

I write something in my notebook that my science teacher
told us yesterday:

Human beings share over 98% of the DNA of chimpanzees. But he
didn't mention that human beings also share 50% of the DNA
of bananas.

Two weeks later, and my behaviour, as far as the Hardings are
concerned, has been impeccable. It's six-thirty a.m. and I'm

going downstairs early to make pancakes for breakfast as a surprise for Margaret and Henry. James and Bridget won't be down until seven-thirty so I have nearly an hour alone with them.

Our S.A.T. scores are out and Henry and Margaret have promised to take 'us kids' out for a celebratory dinner tonight. The atmosphere is right.

Margaret comes into the kitchen first.

'That smells great, Lou. What a treat.'

'Good,' I say.

Henry comes into the kitchen wearing his dressing gown. I can't take my eyes off his hairy white legs.

'Isn't this a nice way to start the day,' he says.

I am still grounded and have run out of money again. I have a dress rehearsal in five days and no alcohol to get me through it. Tom lent me some money so I could put twenty dollars back in Margaret's purse, which I've done. I gave her a little extra too, but it has been two days since I last had a drink and my whole body vibrates with unease. I'll need to borrow some more.

I have started drinking on days when there are no rehearsals because I can sleep better when I've had something to drink. Even though my sleeping problem seems to be solved, I find it hard to concentrate in class, find it hard to focus, and my face aches. My teeth feel too big in my mouth, and my mouth doesn't belong in my face; as though it has been roughly transplanted where there's not enough room for it. I can sense the relationship between my jaw and teeth and brain, which seem suddenly to be too close together. My nerves are camouflaged by drinking, but my body still suffers.

Margaret and Henry are more cheerful towards me now that my S.A.T. scores are out, and I am officially in the top one per cent of the country. This seems to prove that I can 'fit in'.

I put the pancakes on a plate and slice a banana, pour some honey, and cut a lemon in half.

I watch Henry pour maple syrup on his pancakes. 'We should have pancakes more often,' he says.

'I wondered if we could talk about something,' I say.

Margaret puts her knife and fork beside her plate.

'Of course. You can talk about anything at all, you know that.'

'Better out than in,' says Henry.

This is exactly what my mum says about pimples when she's trying to encourage Erin and Leona to burst them. *Better out than in.*

I look at the floor and then I say it.

'I don't want to go home. I want to know whether you can help me stay in America?'

Henry's reply is far too quick, as though he knows I was going to ask this question.

'Oh, Lou,' he says. 'I'm not sure about that. There'd be all sorts of difficulties with immigration laws and visas and as far as I can recall, there's a strict policy . . .'

I look at him.

'But there's *always* a way,' I say. 'What if you could sponsor an application for me to get permanent residency? I could go home for a week or something and then come right back. I wouldn't expect to stay *here* in this house. I'm not an idiot. I'm not asking to stay with *you*. All I wanted to know was whether you could help, that's all.'

Margaret wants to keep me happy, to shut me up. She gives Henry a conspicuously coded look.

'All being well,' she says, 'I wouldn't say that it was out of the question.'

I know she is uncomfortable. What she wanted from me was the short-term experience of a quaint and foreign visitor.

She does not want to be involved in changing somebody's life.

'Margaret and I have talked a great deal about your situation,' says Henry. 'We can see that it's not fair that somebody with your intelligence should have to study in a country with relatively few opportunities or resources compared to this country.'

Bloody hell, it's not the *country* that's the problem. I decide not to purge him of this narrow-minded untruth, especially since he seems to have spent some time working out how to say it. Still, I'd love to spit at one of them for so completely missing the point.

'Don't worry,' I say. 'Forget it.'

Margaret stands up.

'Oh, you'll be okay. How about if we forget about you being grounded?'

'Thanks,' I say and leave the kitchen so that they will not see my face.

The weather is cold now and every morning there is ice on the cars. It's Saturday. Tom and I are at his house, watching TV. His mom and the cook are making dinner for us. We've been together all day, playing Scrabble and watching videos. His mom has been home for an hour or so, and his dad, whom I've not met yet, is due home from a meeting in about half an hour.

'What's the meeting your dad is at?' I ask. Tom shakes his head and looks grave. 'You really don't want to know.'

I decide it must be a Ku Klux Klan meeting or something equally stupid, and that even if it is, I'm still going to ask if I can move in. I'll tell him what I think of bigots and racists after I've got a green card and I've got into a good college on a full scholarship.

Besides, I need to ask Tom for another loan and wonder if now is a good time.

'You can come sit over here on the couch with me,' says Tom, a terrible grin on his face. 'My mom won't mind. She's extremely liberal actually.'

'Oh,' I say. I'd rather stay where I am. If I move to sit with Tom, I'll be sitting directly beneath an enormous chandelier, which sways when somebody walks across the floorboards and sways even more noticeably when Tom's mom plonks herself down on the settee.

Tom calls out, 'Mom, you wouldn't mind if Lou and I sat close together on the couch, would you?'

'As long as I can see where one body starts and the other stops,' she calls out, laughing, as always, unduly amused by her own wit.

I move across and sit with Tom and he drapes his arm heavily over my shoulder. His shirt smells damp, as though he hasn't worn it for a long time. He smells like a box of broken crayons.

I don't like Tom a lot of the time and I don't like the person he is right now. I don't like his at home with Mom personality. It's infuriating and childish; always trying to sell his family to me, telling me that they worked hard for their millions, telling me that they struggled to make it here in the new country. But he's beautiful and I am more confident around him than I am with the Hardings, and around Tom, I do not blush. My body feels at home near him, even if I do spend a lot of time thinking he's an idiot.

'I bet she'd mind if I had a smoke,' I say.

Tom calls out, 'Mom, can Lou smoke in here?'

'I don't mind if she smokes herself to death, but I'd prefer if she did it in the old nursery.'

'Let's go,' says Tom.

The old nursery is behind the kitchen. I haven't seen, until now, any signs of the maid's four-dollar-an-hour industry, but this is where broken things are kept and where the maid stores her buckets and mops.

This room is also stuffed ceiling high with boxes and furniture. Tom takes two chairs. 'I'd like to sit on the floor,' I say.

'Wait,' he says, 'I'll get you a rug and a cushion.'

The smell of cooking meat fills the air. We sit against a wall, shoulder to shoulder, our breathing in unison, Tom talking about how happy he is to be with me.

He grabs my hands and says, 'I want to wake up every day with you and look into your eyes and say something good to you.'

'Me too,' I say, wondering if I could think of enough good things to say.

Even though there's risk involved, I'm too curious not to ask.

'Tom, did you move here from another state last year?'

He stares at his lap.

'I know you're repeating your senior year. I don't really give a shit, but I just want to know.'

Tom suddenly grabs my face and kisses me for a long time, desperately, pressing his lips too hard. The inside of my lip is cut by my teeth.

'Stop,' I say.

Tom stops.

'I'll be twenty in three weeks,' he says.

'You're such a liar,' I say.

Tom grins. 'As if you care about lies.'

'Yeah,' I say, wondering why he never looks embarrassed. 'You're right.'

Then he stares lovingly at me and I think I know what he's about to say.

'Lou, I want to marry me.'

'Typical,' I say, hoping to make a joke of his slip of the tongue.

'You know what I meant to say. I mean I want *us* to get married. I want you to marry me. Then you can stay.'

He adds this last sentence as though to suggest this is the only reason he's asking me to marry him. I look away and reach for another cigarette. He kisses my face and neck and the back of my hands, like an actor, and is so soppy all of a sudden that I don't like him at all. I feel repulsed.

'Maybe I should think about it,' I say, even though I know I should say yes.

'How long for?' He is angry in typical Tom fashion; too quick to joy, and too quick to anger if he doesn't get his way.

'I don't know,' I say. 'Just a while.'

But Tom wants to talk about us and marriage and how we could give it a few years and I could move with him to the East Coast.

He talks far too long in a persuasive and argumentative way as though I am an idiot and he needs to make me see things clearly. I don't think he's ever tried to twist somebody's arm without success before. If he only knew what I really think. I am tired of his monologues, which are really always about him even though he pretends he is talking about us. The whole thing with Tom is fast losing its deranged charm. Besides, his eyes are glassy, a mixture of self-pity and anger, and I want to kiss him again just to stop him from talking. So, I look at his beautiful face, which is by far the best thing about him, and I pretend he's a better, wiser person.

'I'd love to,' I say. 'I'd love to marry you.'

A few minutes later Tom's dad arrives home and we go out to meet him.

'Dad, this is my girlfriend, Lou,'

Tom's dad takes his jacket off and says, 'Nice to meet you. My name's Gerald.'

Tom takes his dad's jacket and we follow him, a few paces

behind, like little children, and sit down at the dining-room table, even though dinner isn't ready yet.

'Switch off the TV please, Tom.'

Tom returns and his dad uses a remote control to play some classical music on a machine behind him.

Tom's dad is tall and large. His arms and legs are thin but his neck and belly are fat. He has eyes so brown they are almost black.

Tom's mom, Betty, comes in and asks me if I'd like some wine. 'Yes, please,' I say.

She doesn't say hello to Tom's dad. I wonder where the cook will have dinner. Only four places are set.

'Do you have a preference? Red or white?'

I shrug as if to say I don't mind and Tom kicks me. 'Red, please.'

The cook serves dinner and we begin to eat. I drink my wine too fast and finish before the soup is gone. Tom's dad looks nothing like Tom and, unlike his son, eats his dinner slowly, with impeccable manners. Tom, like James, almost inhales his food. It's terrible to watch.

'What are the two of you going to get up to this evening?' asks Tom's dad, his knife and fork laid carefully beside a large plate piled with roast lamb and vegetables, his hands in his lap, ready to converse between thoughtfully arranged mouthfuls.

'We're going to a party,' says Tom. 'Around the corner.'

'Has Lou told her host-parents she'll be out late?'

'Yes,' I say. 'They know I won't be home until ten o'clock.'

Tom's mom takes the lid off a dish of carrots. 'That doesn't give you very long. Why don't you ask if you can stay the night here?'

I blush. 'I don't think they'd be into that idea.'

I notice that before Tom's dad takes food from his plate, he turns it round until the food he wants to pick up with his fork is at the bottom of the plate, at six o'clock.

'What a shame,' says Tom's dad. 'It'd be so nice to have you for breakfast.'

I laugh, but it seems I am the only one who finds this amusing.

'They're pretty strict,' I say, 'not like you.'

Tom's mom is pleased with this comment.

'Well, some people are just more old fashioned than other people.'

The cook goes home during dessert and nobody says goodbye to her. I'm fascinated and horrified.

After dinner I can hardly believe my ears when Tom's mom says that we should retire to the drawing room.

We talk about school and Betty's painting classes. I wonder if she and Margaret would get along, since they share painting in common. Gerald doesn't say much. He has a book on his lap, which he holds over his groin, turning it slowly, anticlockwise, in the same way he turned his plate during dinner.

After having not spoken for what seems like an age, Gerald clears his throat. 'It really would be fine for you to stay the night, Lou. If you like I could call your host-parents for you. With a bit of persuasion, I'm sure they'd agree.'

Margaret and Henry have been explicit on this point. Under no circumstances am I to stay out overnight. If I do, I'll be sent straight home. It's not that I believe them, but I'd rather not call their bluff (or have them call mine – I never have been sure how this works).

'I'm afraid they are very strict,' I say. 'You'd be amazed. They have an absolute rule against staying out after ten p.m.'

'What a shame,' says Gerald. 'We have so many rooms and so many of them are empty. It would be nice to see somebody emerge from one of those doors in the morning.'

When my sister Erin first stayed out all night, she was fourteen. She came home on a Sunday morning. I was vacuuming the lounge-room. My mum was in the kitchen doing the washing up. Erin looked awful: puffy and bruised under the eyes. She was wearing a long, grey jumper, stretched and thin. It looked as though it belonged to a very tall man and hung crookedly around her thighs, over her loose black stockings. 'I'm going to bed,' she said. 'Don't tell Mum.'

I was incredulous. 'But she waited up all night for you,' I said.

Erin grabbed me by the wrist and twisted my skin so that it burned. 'Well, it's not night now so what does it matter? If you say anything I'll rip your hair out.'

'I will tell her,' I said. 'You're too young to have sex and stay out all night.'

Erin put her hands around my neck.

'If you do I'll make you so scared you'll smell like shit.'

When Erin had been in her room for a few minutes I went to Mum in the kitchen. I said, 'I just checked Erin's room and she's sound asleep. She must have snuck in hours ago.'

My mum ignored me, acted as though she hadn't heard me, and used a tea towel to wipe breakfast scraps from the table. As I was leaving, she said to the table, 'I mustn't have heard her,' she said. 'I must be going deaf.'

By the time Tom and I get to the party, which is in a loft apartment, it's half-past eight. The loft is the home of a college student who I've never met before. She comes to the door and greets Tom by licking his face. She has a shaved head and the largest eyes I've ever seen.

Tom and I sit in a cushion-filled circle with a group of college students and drink beer for a while. I'm getting tipsy and feel quite nice, when somebody turns the music up loud and brings out a tray with small white piles of what I suppose is cocaine or speed.

I look at my watch. It's nine-thirty. I don't have time to get high but I desperately want to.

Tom leans over. 'Are you going to have any?'

'Okay,' I say.

He winks at me. 'Sure thing, Mrs McGahern.'

The tray gets passed around and I watch what people do. It only takes a minute to snort the powder and it doesn't appear to do anybody any harm except make them laugh a bit too loud. I could take a little bit and just go home and feel a little high.

The tray reaches me and Tom takes it for himself. I watch what he does, and do as he has done. He doesn't try to talk me out of it.

When I'm finished, Tom passes the tray to the next person. Then he stands up and tells everybody that we are getting married. People start singing 'Going to the Chapel'. I laugh, but I'm starting to worry about the time.

Once I get high, I want to dance. 'Just for five minutes,' I say. 'Then I better leave.'

I feel like a god. I feel perfect. I dance in front of people without fear, and after dancing for a while, I want to sing. There isn't much Tom can do to stop me and he doesn't try. He just keeps calling me Mrs McGahern and I am quite sure, all of a sudden, that I am madly in love. I have never felt this happy and all that matters to me is that I should continue to feel this way. I don't want to leave the party.

Tom walks me to the front door at ten past three. I know the exact time because I have spent ages staring at the green light on his digital watch.

'You should stay at my house,' he says, 'you're going to be murdered.'

'It'll be fine,' I say.

'I hope so,' he says, holding me tight as though I'm about to go on a long train journey. 'I don't want you to get in trouble. You're the love of my life.'

'How can that be?' I say. 'You've only had a bit of a life.'

'You know what I mean,' he says, pulling away to look into my eyes. 'I know I'll never be with anybody like you again.'

'How do you know?'

'I know for lots of reasons. I know because of your eyes, for one. They're so beautiful.'

'So?' I say. 'I didn't choose them.' ·

Tom lets go. 'All right, you're too high to talk. Go home. I'll see you at the dress rehearsal. Sleep well.'

'I feel so good,' I say.

'I know you do,' he says.

'Oh, I need twenty dollars.'

'You just love me for my money,' he says, taking a bunch of notes out of his wallet.

'I love you *and* I love your money,' I say, laughing like an idiot.

I clatter through the front door. Margaret and Henry are sitting at the dining room table with two empty bottles of gin between them.

'Hi,' I say, wondering if they've been having a party. 'I'm so sorry I'm late. I didn't want to get driven home by anybody who'd had too much to drink.'

Henry stands up. 'Florence Bapes is on her way over and your suitcases are packed. We're sorry, but you're leaving tonight. We don't know what else to do.'

I don't believe him. I think he's having a joke and I smile and consider giving him a hug.

Margaret picks up a bottle of gin. 'We searched your room

209

and found these under the mattress. Perhaps you wanted to get caught. Perhaps you were crying out for help. We hope you get that help, Lou. We really hope you do.'

As soon as I realise they mean business, I am filled with rage. Whenever I'm caught red-handed, it's the same. I get furious.

'I asked you for fucking help,' I say, 'and look where that got me!'

I collapse onto the divan in the entrance hall and cry.

'Will I get to say goodbye to Bridget and James?'

Henry comes over and kneels by the divan. He doesn't hold my hand or comfort me, he just kneels, with his hands awkwardly on his knees as though touching me now would breach some unwritten code of the exchange program. 'No, we think it'll be better if this is a clean break. Better for you, too.'

'But what about the musical? It's going on in a few months. I promise I won't go out or drink again. It was –'

Margaret rushes from the dining table across to the divan and slaps me hard across the face.

I do more than cry. I gyrate and convulse and speak deranged gibberish; a kind of disorganised, unconvincing speaking in tongues.

I'm not sure why I do this, since it can't possibly help my cause, but I feel intensely melodramatic and want to attract the maximum amount of attention and sympathy. Perhaps I want to create the impression that there is something beyond my control at work here; that it is not me that's bad, rather some demon I am possessed by.

Perhaps I want to suggest that what's really required is an exorcism. I flail around on the divan, fall to the floor and shudder about in a frenzy of upset, using language that's filthy and disturbed. Margaret and Henry leave the room and close the door emphatically behind them. Even then, I continue to rant and spit and fling my body against the furniture. The fact that I am covering myself in bruises comforts me. I will be injured tomorrow.

Flo Bapes comes in holding a wad of paperwork. Outside, the sky is becoming blue.

Two officers from the Organisation are with Flo – one tall, one a little shorter, both with beards. I stare at them, as though in a daze. They look so alike standing side by side, their beards and moustaches almost identical, and as they look at me, they lick their lips simultaneously, like twins, or as though they have decided to look the same because they are secretly in love.

I stare at the slightly shorter man who wears a brown track-suit and hasn't had time to brush his hair properly. I decide I will find him a brush when I go upstairs.

I am sent up to my room to gather my things. 'Effects' is the word Flo uses.

She says, with something close to relish, 'Lou. You'd better go upstairs and gather up your personal effects while we sort out the business side of things down here.'

I sit on the landing for a while then knock on James' door.

He is awake. 'Hi,' I say. 'I'm sorry about all this.' I sit on the edge of his bed. He moves his hand to turn the lamp on.

'Don't,' I say. 'I've been bawling my eyes out.' He sits up and moves across in the bed to make more room for me. 'I better not stay long,' I say. 'They'll be coming up to get me in a minute.'

James isn't sleepy.

'Are you leaving tonight?' he asks.

'Yes. Flo Bapes is here. They're doing all the paperwork now.'

'I was in the kitchen when Mom and Dad found the bottles. They called Flo from Dad's mobile but I could hear everything. They say you're an alcoholic.'

This pisses me off.

'I've just been drinking for rehearsals. There's a big difference. Alcoholics drink before breakfast and beat their dogs and wives.'

James laughs.

'The understudy will get your part now. She's pretty boring compared to you.'

'Thanks,' I say. 'Do you think Bridget will be awake? I want to say goodbye to her.'

'Probably. There was a lot of yelling going on earlier. It's the first time I've heard Mom and Dad yelling at each other. Mom thinks you've been using us all along and Dad totally disagrees. He says we didn't look after you enough. He says we didn't understand you enough. Mom was pissed about that and gave him a bit of a blasting.'

'Shit,' I say. 'I'm so sorry. Well, I better say goodbye to Bridget.'

'I don't think you'd better talk to her at the moment. She's totally on Mom's side. She told me earlier that she's furious with you. She also thinks you must have stolen money to buy the gin. But I'm not mad with you.'

'Thanks,' I say, and squeeze his hand.

James looks at the pattern on his quilt, 'Can you say goodbye to me properly. I feel like hell now. Couldn't you say goodbye to me properly?'

Little schmuck, I think.

He reaches out for my shoulder. He wants to hug me, and then more.

I'm wearing a blouse under a jumper. I lift my jumper and blouse up, under my chin, just enough so that James can see my breasts. His hand lifts, trembling, and reaches out. I move back a little so he can't quite touch me. He stares hard, his face flawless and clean in the half-light, just like the night we stared at one another in the back of the van.

212

I close my eyes and think of Tom while James silently jerks away under the blankets as though using a pump to fill a bicycle tyre. When he groans, I feel aroused and foolish and squalid. I stand up. James repulses me but I am not able to turn him down. I cannot abide him, but I cannot turn my back on him. The way I feel about him confuses the hell out of me.

Flo screeches from downstairs, with no regard for the fact that people might be sleeping.

'Lou, come down! We're all waiting for you!'

James stops and grabs hold of me. 'I don't want to be sick,' he says. 'I don't want to be dirty. I just want to be nice with you.'

I tell him I understand exactly what he means. I tell him that purity between people is what I always want and what I've always wanted between him and me. I tell him that my real family is foul; that my sisters and parents are foul and that the whole point of me coming here was to purify myself and that I never want to see them again.

I tell him that I wanted to be different, that I am different, and that's why I'm here. I tell him I wish we didn't have bodies at all. I tell him that I don't know how to live.

'I don't know how to live properly either,' he says, pushing tears out of his eyes so that they are easier to see.

I lean over and kiss him softly on the forehead.

I tell him to make a wish about our futures; something pure, something to do with love. Nothing to do with sex.

He reaches out to touch my breast and I sit again to let him do it. He puts his hand under my shirt, feels my breast, and closes his eyes. I pretend that I like it because I wish I did.

'Goodbye,' he says.

Flo is coming up the stairs.

I lean with my back against James' bedroom door so she won't be able to open it.

'Did you make a wish?' I ask.

'Yes,' he says. 'Can I tell you what it was?'

'Yes.'

'I wished we could meet again when I'm eighteen and you're nineteen.'

'I wished we could meet again too,' I say, lying.

'Oh my God,' says James. 'I'll go mad waiting.'

'I hope you do,' I say.

'Me too,' he says. 'Goodbye.'

I open the door and Flo takes me by the elbow.

'Just let me see my room one last time,' I say.

'Well hurry up then,' she says.

I begin to sob when I see how little remains in my room. There's nought but a pile of letters tied up with string; they are all the letters and stories and short plays that I have sent to Margaret and Henry and James and Bridget. The rubbish bin is full of sweet wrappers and shop receipts. The bed has been stripped and the cupboard is bare. There is an oil burner on the desk, its small white candle purifying the room. I slam the door and go back downstairs.

Flo Bapes hands me two copies of a document and gets my signature. Margaret is clearing cups from the table. Flo has already called my mum and dad.

I am angry now. 'Do I get to know what's happening next?'

She tells me that my mum and dad have given their consent to have me placed with a new, temporary host-family. What happens to me next is up to her, she tells me, not Margaret or Henry, and certainly not me.

'All right,' says Flo, 'we better get going.'

Henry puts his hand on his throat, and speaks softly, 'You're being taken to the home of an intermediate host-family a few miles from here and then you'll be sent . . .'

'Sorry, Henry, I'll have to interrupt you there,' says Flo, in her best officious voice, concerned not to let too many cats out of the bag at once.

'We don't know what will happen from here. What happens next partly depends on Louise and partly on the rules which, as you will understand, I didn't have enough warning to read, considering the very grave circumstances.'

Henry is angry now too, for having been put in his place by an ignoramus. He walks towards me, winks, and picks up one of my suitcases. 'I'll help you out to the car with these if that's all right with the rules.'

'Thanks,' I say.

Margaret doesn't come out to the car. She stands in the doorway, crying, holding a piece of paper to her chest. She doesn't look at me as I leave. Henry waves at me from the kerb. I wave back, like the Queen waves, and wonder if he'll get this terrible joke.

Part Three

17

I sit in the back seat of a black car with one of the bearded men. Flo is driving and the other bearded man is in the front passenger's seat. When we have driven a few blocks, Flo tells me that I'm going to Chicago to stay in a 'hostel for wayward exchange students', until a decision is made about my 'long term future'. She tells me again that my parents have given her permission to take custody of me and that I am now in her 'charge and care'.

'I thought I was going to stay with a new family or something?'

'No,' says Flo, 'you're going to stay in secure accommodation.'

She loves this.

'You mean a prison,' I say.

'No, young lady. It's secure accommodation.'

'Then you lied to Margaret and Henry,' I say.

'They've suffered enough,' says the bearded man sitting next to me.

We stop only once so that Flo and the bearded men can get some coffee and food. I don't eat and don't speak until we arrive, even though when it starts to snow I would love to tell somebody I've never seen snow before and how beautiful it looks.

We pull up outside a four-storey building in a busy city street in the heart of Chicago.

The entrance to the accommodation is next door to a pizza parlour. Flo gets my suitcases out of the boot and says goodbye to me on the kerb.

'I'll be keeping in touch with Margaret and Henry,' she says, as though the three of them are life-long friends, 'and if you have anything you'd like to say to them I suggest you put it in writing.'

'Whatever,' I say and hear Bridget's voice in my head.

The two bearded men let themselves in and take me up the three flights of stairs to my dormitory. On the way up we pass through a big room with barred windows and about ten teenagers sitting on couches.

'This is where we leave you,' says the man with the smaller beard who sat next to me in the car.

'Good luck,' says the other.

I sit up on the bottom bunk in my small dormitory, which has two bunk beds, a small cupboard, a barred window and a single chair. It's a dark, cold room.

One of the accommodation staff comes in.

'Hi, my name's Gertie Skipper,' she says. She's short and thin and looks about eighty.

'Hi,' I say.

She gives me a cheese sandwich on a small white plate, tells me why I am here and some of the rules.

The essential rules for wayward exchange students are as follows: I am not permitted to leave the accommodation unless accompanied by a chaperone. She will keep my allowance. There are weekly excursions to tourist attractions and, depending on one's religion, there are chaperoned trips to nearby churches, synagogues and mosques. Other than that, I will leave the building only to attend various rehabilitation appointments with doctors, psychiatrists, counsellors, and, if I am lucky, for interviews with prospective new host-families.

Bedtime is ten o'clock and the kitchen roster is on the notice-board in the common-room downstairs.

Gertie sits on my bed and pats my leg.

'You'll be staying here until you are either sent home to Sydney or another suitable family is found for you. What happens will depend on your progress.'

'What do you mean by progress?' I ask.

'Your rehabilitation, I suppose you could call it. Your counsellor will tell you more about this when you meet him tomorrow.'

One by one the other inmates – there are eleven of them – are brought to my door and introduced to me.

They stand in the doorway and say 'Hello' then leave. I sit up with my back against the wall with the uneaten cheese sandwich on a plate resting on my legs.

I'll be sharing with three girls: Miranda, Rachel and Veronique. I'll find out why they've been sent here later.

Gertie tells me that she and the other staff are here to help me and that I should take a few quiet moments to eat my snack and unpack my bags.

'When you're ready, why don't you come downstairs and mingle with the others.'

She makes it sound like a holiday camp.

'Thanks,' I say.

Gertie leaves and shuts the door behind her.

I begin to unpack, but when I feel like I might start crying, I stop for a moment to look out the barred window at the busy street below. I realise how much I've missed being in a big and noisy city. Perhaps if I could live here, things would be completely different.

I lie down to sleep, but can't sleep, so I stare up and count the springs under the bunk bed above me. I let myself get colder and colder. I lie like this for what seems like hours, thinking about how nothing feels real, then feeling sorry for myself for being in such a cold, dark room.

I am about to go downstairs when there's a knock on the door. A tall, skinny boy with shoulder-length black hair comes into the room.

'Hi,' he says, 'my name's Lishny. I'm from Russia.'

He has a very big nose.

'I'm Lou,' I say. 'I'm from Sydney. Australia.'

He sits on my bunk bed.

'I just arrive two days ago,' he says. 'Can I help you to unstuff?'

'You mean unpack.'

'Yes.'

'That's okay,' I say. 'I can do it myself.'

I begin to unpack. He stares at my pile of books.

'Can I check at your reading materials?'

There's something fishy about Lishny's struggle with English. I wonder if he's been sent to spy on me: to find out if I'm remorseful.

'Yeah, all right,' I say.

He scatters all my books on the floor and rummages through them like he's starving and the books are loaves of bread.

'What do you read?' I ask, standing with my back against the window, my arms folded.

He is flicking through the pages of one of my books and doesn't answer.

'What kind of books do you like?' I ask.

He screws up his face. 'What a banal question.'

I agree.

'I agree,' I say. 'You're right.'

He smiles. What a charming smile. I smile back.

He points to the cover of my collection of short stories by Gogol.

'This is one of the worsted translutions of Gogol I have ever witnesses,' he says.

'Is it?'

I have copped on to his fake bad English routine and I think he knows I have, but I don't want to stop him speaking in his silly pidgin. It's cheering me up, which is, perhaps, what he intends.

'Sure. It's really dreedfoul.'

'I see,' I say with a grin on my face that tells him I've definitely copped on to him.

He flicks the pages and rants in Russian.

I nudge his back with my foot.

'Yes?' he says. 'Can't you see I'm busy?'

I smile at him. He smiles back.

'So, doctor translution,' I say. 'What exactly is wrong with this book, then?'

'If you would like to sit down, I will explete.'

'Explain.'

'Sure. If you are so creezy about this creezy Russian odour.'

'Crazy, not creezy,' I say. 'Author, not odour.'

'But why? You can say this creezy odour stinks.'

We start laughing and it is hard to stop.

'Your English is perfect, isn't it?' I say. 'This pidgin rubbish is just some kind of quaint gimmick.' My voice sounds formal and forced. I wish, sometimes, that I could remain silent but silence is an art I know nothing about. I must add silence to my list of things to get better at.

'You might be right.'

I take a pillow off the bunk and hit him on the head.

'Don't hit me! I'm quaint,' he says. He takes a pillow from the other bunk and hits me back. 'I've never been quaint before.'

When we stop playing with pillows, we each sit on a bunk, under the blankets, and Lishny tells me why the translation of Gogol is no good. He says it captures none of Gogol's irony.

'I'll go to my dorm and get my copy and show you,' he says.

Lishny takes ages to come back and when he does, he not only has his Russian copy of Gogol but two enormous pieces of chocolate cake. He holds a piece in each hand. He has a smear of chocolate on the end of his nose.

'Thanks,' I say. 'I was getting really hungry.'

'There's a party downstairs for Gertie's sixtieth birthday. Do you want to go down and join in?'

I can hear tinny music, the way music sounds when an old tape is playing. There's some talking too and a bit of laughter, but it sounds flat and boring. I hate people in groups.

'No,' I say. 'I'd rather stay here.'

'Me too.'

We eat our cake with our fingers and talk about books. It is such a relief to be talking to someone who isn't an idiot.

Gertie comes to check on me. She stands in the doorway, holding a clipboard, and tells me that I'll need to come downstairs soon, for dinner and to sign some papers and to have my induction session.

I thank her and she leaves.

When she's gone, Lishny tells me that this so-called hostel is really a prison and that the chaperones are really guards. He tells me that it's partly run by the Organisation and mostly run by the immigration department and the police.

'They say the bars on the windows and the locks on the doors are to stop us from doing ourselves harm, but it's really about making sure we don't escape and make ourselves at home in this allegedly wonderful and free country.'

When it gets dark we don't turn the light on.

Lishny comes over and sits on my bunk and we talk until it's too cold to stay still.

'I feel like going downstairs,' I say. 'It's freezing in here.'

'It's freezing all over this building. A polar bear would think it was too cold.'

We laugh.

'Why are you here?' I ask.

'I can't talk about it,' he says. 'I'm being questioned by the police and forbidden to discuss it.'

'Oh.'

'And what about you? What is your crime?'

'I drank too much,' I say.

'You should get the hiccups from drinking too much. Not a prison sentence.'

Lishny and I go down to the common-room where the others are watching TV and playing board games. There are two couches, four armchairs and a small square table.

A Christmas tree sheds its needles in the corner by the barred window and snow adheres like breadcrumbs to the frozen glass.

Lishny and I sit on the end of one of the couches. One of the other inmates sits on the floor by the wall next to the only heater in the room. He has one trouser leg rolled up to the knee and holds his bare leg close to the heat. He scratches at his shin, which is covered in scabs and fresh welts; blood trickles into his socks.

'Why can't they give him something for that?' I say. 'He's covered in sores.'

'Maybe he has something to help him but he doesn't want to use it.'

We sit and talk until a bell rings for dinnertime, then we gather around the kitchen table to eat stew. Gertie and one other guard, Phillip Tanzey — a medical student who works here part time — sit with us through dinner. The other inmates talk about the snow and pop stars and film stars, and excursions they've been on, and other places in Chicago they'd like to visit. Nobody talks about incarceration or wanting to be freed.

'What percentage of inmates end up being sent home?' I ask.

Phillip puts his knife and fork down and wipes his hands on a napkin.

'You're not an inmate and I don't know what the percentage is,' he says, 'but probably more than half. But lots want to go home. There are lots of complicated reasons.'

Gertie smiles at me.

'Don't you worry,' she says, 'it's early days for you yet. You just settle in and we'll cross that bridge . . .'

'When we come to it,' I say. 'God, I hate clichés.'

'Me too,' says Lishny. 'I hate and avoid them like the plague.'

Lishny and I smile at each other. Nobody else has got the joke.

One of the other inmates, Mike, from England, speaks with his mouth full.

'Do you know about the points system yet?' he asks.

'No.'

'You start with sixty points and you lose two points every time you give cheek or swear or miss a meal or don't make your bed or talk after lights out.'

Phillip wipes his hands on a napkin again.

'Mike, you know it's not that simple. Lou, we'll talk about this more after dinner.'

I wonder how many points I've already lost.

After dinner, I stay in the kitchen with Gertie and Phillip. They close the door and take me – point by point – through the induction program. At the end of this long lecture, Gertie asks me to sign a form. I'm agreeing to be sent home unless a new host-family is found. As I sign it, I wonder whether I might be able to escape.

Lishny and I sit together on the floor behind the couch huddled under blankets he has pulled from his bunk.

Tonight, there are three guards on duty, and one of them, Lily Beesman, who arrived after dinner, is on her way over to talk to me.

'Hello, I'm Lily.'

'Hi,' I say.

We shake hands.

'You're not supposed to be on the floor,' she says, crouching down. 'You'll get a kidney infection. You should be sitting up on the couch.'

Lishny has told me that Lily was once a kindergarten teacher. She says she has enlarged kneecaps from years of bending to talk to children. Her tall, waistless body is roughly made of three segments, with a strange bulge in the middle. She looks like an enormous finger.

'Why does it matter,' I say, 'if we sit on the floor?'

'Well, I suppose it's all right,' she says, standing up and dusting her swollen knees.

Lishny and I spend the rest of the night talking and laughing. I find out that he's only just turned sixteen and that two months ago he won a chess tournament in Seattle. He wants to be a GM.

'What's a GM?' I ask.

'A grand master. I made it to the semi-finals when I was fourteen at Sudak in the Crimea. I lost because my end game sucks. When I go home I will work on it.'

I wonder what it's like where he lives and whether I could go and stay with him.

It's my second day. I didn't sleep at all last night and couldn't turn on the light to read. The door to the common-room was bolted shut so I couldn't go in there to watch TV.

All the other inmates have been taken on an excursion to see a movie, with Phillip and Lily as chaperones. I have to stay because at three o'clock I have an appointment with Rennie Parmenter, the counsellor.

I have a pain in my stomach. I go downstairs to look for Gertie.

She's in the kitchen, standing on a crate at the sink, and she wears her watch on the outside of her cardigan sleeve.

'Are there any pain-killers?' I ask.

'Do you have a headache?'

'No, it's a cramp.' She leads me into her bedroom, which is on the same floor as the common-room and kitchen.

'Sit down,' she says and I sit on her single bed.

Gertie shuts her bedroom door and I am overcome with a sad tiredness, a craving to lie down on top of the floral eiderdown, to cover myself in her crocheted blanket and her smell of lavender, and be read to sleep.

She puts her small warm hand – so warm it's like a hotwater bottle made of flesh – on my shoulder. It's remarkable how much heat is coming out of her old body.

'What kind of cramp is it?'

I look at her eyes and realise I haven't looked properly at them before. I never pay enough attention to people's eyes. It's time I learnt to pay closer attention to the details of people's faces. I can't remember what colour Margaret's eyes are. This is something I should know. Maybe if I paid more attention to this kind of thing, I'd feel better and none of this would have happened.

So I look into Gertie's eyes, and she looks into mine, and a shudder rips through me like a root being pulled from the soil. Suddenly what I feel has nothing to do with what I'm thinking. I'm thinking she's old and senile and I don't like her, but I feel like I want her to hug me.

'I don't know,' I say, 'just a cramp.'

She holds my hand. 'Is it your undercarriage?'

I want to say something sarcastic about the word under-carriage but I decide not to. I want to be kind. I want to see what it will feel like to act in a different way. I will practise on Gertie.

'No,' I say, 'it's just a stitch I get sometimes. Like someone's sticking a knife in my side. I get it when I haven't slept properly, which is nearly all the time.'

'Okay,' she says, 'but don't be afraid to tell me anything at all. I know teenage girls sometimes have things go wrong downstairs.'

I smile at her instead of saying something mean, and she squeezes my hand and then she hugs me and I feel as though I've been drugged. Maybe it's because it's warmer in her room.

'Could I lie on your bed for a while?' I ask.

I'm sure it's against the rules for me to be in her room or to sleep in her bed.

'Well,' she says, 'just this once.'

Gertie wakes me from my nap with a hot cup of tea, and I feel completely resuscitated. This is the best I've slept for months.

'Better get up now. Rennie's here to see you.'

I feel as though the sleep I've just had is my reward for being good to her, for something marvellous I have done. Maybe this is how life works.

'Thanks for letting me sleep here,' I say. 'I'm really grateful.'

She nods and sits by my feet.

'I know you've already made friends with Lishny,' she says, 'but it might pay to make friends with the others too. Lishny will be leaving soon.'

'Why?' I ask. 'What's he done?'

'That's for him to tell you. I just think it would be a good idea for you two not to get too attached.'

'Does he know he's leaving soon?'

'Yes, of course. This isn't the terrible place he likes to pretend it is.'

'Then why can't he tell me why he's here?'

Gertie sighs.

'He *can* tell you. There's absolutely nothing stopping him. Maybe he just doesn't want to.'

Rennie Parmenter is waiting for me in the counselling room. It's a small room upstairs where the dormitories are. It has no window, a round table in the centre, two chairs, a small heater, and a box of tissues on the floor. Rennie is short, has greasy red hair and is wearing a loose woollen v-neck jumper without a t-shirt underneath.

When I sit down, Rennie gets up and slams the door shut.

'Oopsie,' he says. 'Sorry. There must be a blizzard outside.'

I wonder if it's still snowing and whether I'll get to go out and walk around in it. I've never walked in snow before. This will be my first white Christmas.

Rennie talks to me for what feels like hours. His vocabulary is pretentious and annoying.

When I say, 'You use a lot of very big words,' he doesn't realise I'm being sarcastic and says, 'Well, you see, I like to think of myself as a member of the wording class. That's my little joke. Perhaps you might see yourself in the same way one day, but you'll need to value yourself a lot more than you do right now.'

'I see,' I say.

He tells me his entire life story and a heap of information I don't need to know. He tells me that he visits every Tuesday and Thursday, without ever breaking for lunch. This business of not eating lunch might explain his bad breath; the bad breath a person gets from not eating.

'Gosh,' I say.

Rennie is bursting with gormless good intentions, proclaiming – when his life story is done – that it's time for a 'nice two-way chat'.

I am being 'briefed' for my 'new journey' he tells me, as he leans forward.

'So,' he says, 'I wonder to myself . . . how did pretty young Louise with the big IQ get herself into this mess? How did a capable sixteen-year-old girl manage to turn herself into an alcoholic?'

How could such an idiot be a counsellor? What kind of moron thinks that there's a rational explanation for all human behaviour? What kind of fool thinks that perversity can be explained? It's obvious. I felt like garbage for one reason or another and drank to make myself feel better even though it could ruin my chances of escape. What's so hard to understand about that?

I would like to kick him in the shins, but instead I turn what has happened into a story with a tidy beginning and middle and end, throwing in all kinds of motivations for my behaviour. He seems happy with this version of events, especially when I talk about my behaviour being motivated by a deep need for approval and acceptance.

I tell the story without blaming anybody but myself, except that towards the end I make the mistake of saying that Margaret is a smothering kind of individual and that the house was riddled with rules and that maybe this made some of my behaviour worse.

He pounces on this comment as an excuse to launch into what Lishny has warned me is Rennie's famous *How many people are at this table?* routine.

'Okay, Louise,' he says. 'So you're in a terrible mess. Let's logically analyse the real cause, shall we?'

This is so ludicrous I'm even more amazed that I don't kick him.

'Sure,' I say.

He gets up from his chair and opens the door.

'I can hear Gertie downstairs in the kitchen,' he says, waving in that general direction. 'Is it *her* fault that you're in this mess?

'No,' I say. 'It's not her fault.'

He shuts the door and sits down. 'Okay. Well then, is it *my* fault?' (he puts both hands on his chest, one hand crossed over the other as though he's Jesus Christ lecturing an apostle).

'No, it's not your fault,' I say.

'All right, then. How many other people are sitting at this table, Louise?'

'There's one other person sitting at this table.'

'Correct,' he says, his buttocks flying off the seat with all the excitement. 'And is that person Louise Connor?'

'Yes it is.'

'And is *she* a person who points the finger at other people for her own faults?'

'No, she isn't.'

He nods his head and swallows something that isn't food. 'Then you are ready to accept that you have nobody to blame but yourself.'

Rennie leans even further across the table. His face is too close to mine; a breathy claustrophobia. I have to move back in my chair to escape him. Oblivious to the effect of his breathing on my face, he remains in this thrusting forward position and wipes the table down with the sleeve of his sloppy jumper.

The impression this gesture creates is that he intends to have me lie down on my back across the table for some dubious, and possibly naked, examination.

'Well, are you ready to accept this? Are you willing to accept this adult responsibility for your own actions?'

'I am,' I say, remembering Lishny's warning that this is the only way to make the interview stop.

Rennie stands up. 'On that basis I think we can make real progress.'

He comes around to my side of the table, and rests his hand on the top of my head like an amateur priest at a dry christening.

'Perhaps you'd like me to leave you alone for a moment to think through what we've talked about, all right?'

'Okay,' I say. 'Thank you very, very much.'

18

It is the afternoon of my third day. The others have gone on their second excursion this week, which, Gertie tells me, is unusual. It's just because it's so close to Christmas and people need 'extra cheering up'. I couldn't go, because I had my first appointment with a psychiatrist this morning.

Her name is Dr Trevor. She gave me a prescription for some sleeping pills and I talked her into giving me two right away from the sample packet on her desk. I took both of them straight after the session, which is probably why I've slept most of the day. I feel drowsy.

I write a letter to Henry and Margaret. I write like an automaton, hardly thinking about what I'm saying at all. I say that I am sorry, countless times, and say that I miss them and I ask them to forgive me. I can't say whether I mean any of it. All I know for sure is that I wish I had been a different person and that they had been different people. I ask them to take me back. I tell them that I don't want to go home. I tell them there's no way on this earth I can face my sisters.

When I've finished this letter, I think about calling my mum but I can't face the prospect of Erin or Leona answering the phone and gloating about my downfall.

Perhaps I'll ask Gertie if I can go outside so I can buy my mum a card. She likes cards, especially Hallmark ones with printed messages inside. She reacts to them as though they have been composed especially for her, even if all I've added is *Dear Mum, from Lou*. Still, I'd like to send her something.

It is nearly four o'clock. I go to the bathroom to have a shower. I am desperate for some hot water but it has run out.

We are permitted one shower every two days and I may not get another turn tomorrow. I pick up my towel. Even with two days to dry on the rail, it is still damp.

I go down to the kitchen. Gertie is doing some knitting and I sit at the table and talk to her. I ask her why one of the bunks upstairs has been stripped of bedding and she tells me that Greta left this morning while I was with Dr Trevor. I met Greta last night. She had a very loud laugh.

'Why was she here?'

'She wasn't well.'

'She seemed well to me. She was laughing her head off all night.'

'Did she tell you that she changed her name from Greta Le Paige to Lumpy Green Cheese?'

Gertie starts to laugh even though she knows she shouldn't, and I laugh too.

'Maybe she was just eccentric,' I say.

'Maybe. That would explain why she rode her bike to school naked.'

'Wow,' I say, impressed. I might have liked Greta.

Gertie and I talk for an hour or more until she says, 'I need to start cooking. You better scat.'

'I can help,' I say.

'No, you go and rest. You look very tired.'

I hate when people tell me I look tired. Especially when I'm tired.

'Okay,' I say, 'thanks.'

I go to the common-room and turn on the TV but there's

nothing decent on, unless you like mawkish crap about angels, pointless violence or evangelical brainwashers. This common-room isn't very comfortable, but if I spend any more time lying on my bunk, I'm sure I'll get bedsores. My limbs are starting to suffer from a squashed feeling.

One of the things I dislike about this place, besides the cold, is the bright and cheerful mural that covers two walls of the common-room. Over the years, inmates have painted sickening and happy pictures of mountains and meadows full of daisies and horses. It looks like the picture of Mormon heaven Yvonne showed me. Maybe I should find out where Yvonne is. Perhaps her family could take me in? It's an option worth exploring, even if it means living with Mormons. At least I'd be with Yvonne.

The sleeping pills have really helped me out. I feel more resourceful, more relaxed, and I know, in one way or another, I'm going to find a way to stay.

I sit at the table and flick through a stupid fashion magazine (the kind that girls are meant to like). I turn the radio on, but it's a country and western song followed by a commercial for cars. After a few bored minutes of sitting at the table, my fingers are so cold it's hard to believe that the heater in this barren room works at all.

Just when I'm about to go back to my dorm, the others come back from their excursion. Lishny walks over to me, lifts me out of my seat, gives me a big hug and asks me how I am. Nobody seems surprised by this. Probably because almost all of the others have paired off in one way or another. Even though it's against the rules for boys to go into the girls' dormitories and *vice versa*, Lily is the only guard who seems bothered by us doing it.

Lishny tells me what he thinks of Chicago.

'I would love to live here,' he says. 'It may be possible.'

I don't take this comment particularly seriously.

'So why did your host-family throw you out?' I ask, again. 'Gertie says you can tell me if you want.'

'She's not lying. I can tell you, but I don't want to yet. Can you wait a few more days?'

'Okay,' I say.

At seven o'clock the bell rings for dinner. Gertie tells us we can eat dinner on our laps tonight. She brings each of us a bowl of soup and puts a plate with about a hundred slices of buttered bread on the table. Lishny and I take four slices each and sit behind the couch, huddled under our blankets. Unlike Lily, Gertie doesn't ask us to move.

'It's pumpkin,' she says. 'Nice and warm.'

Lishny and I wrap our hands around the hot bowls and thank her.

'You're very welcome,' she says and winks at me.

I wink back and feel happy.

Gertie puts her hand over her mouth. 'Oh, I forgot. There's a message for you.'

'Who from?'

'Tom. He said to call back tomorrow.'

'Thanks, Gertie.'

I have no desire to talk to Tom. But I probably should if I want to keep my options open.

After dinner, Lishny and I play a game of chess. He slaughters me and says, 'I bet nobody has ever beaten you so easily before.'

'That's a bit vain,' I say.

'You're a bit vain if you think you should have been able to beat me.'

'Fuck off,' I say.

'No. You fuck off.'

We carry on like this for a while. It's a real fight, but a nice fight. I've never had a nice fight with anybody before. When we finish, we laugh and he grabs both of my hands.

'It was a compliment,' he says. 'You play a really beautiful game.'

'Thanks,' I say.

Gertie is in the kitchen washing up with the two inmates on cleaning duty and Lily comes around to the back of the couch to inspect us.

'You should teach me to play one day,' she says. 'I like checkers and games like that.'

I smile weakly but don't insult her. I say, 'I'll teach you. Maybe tomorrow.'

Lishny and I go up to my dorm. I go first and he follows about twenty minutes later.

We sit in separate bunks in case Lily bursts in. We read and talk. Lishny goes to his dorm and comes back with a pair of mittens.

'I want you to try to tie your shoelaces with the mittens on,' he says.

'How come?'

'Because it makes it easy to remember what it was like to be a child.'

'Okay.' I put my shoes on, then try to tie the laces with the mittens on. 'You're right,' I say. 'I feel completely helpless.'

'Interesting isn't it?'

What I feel like saying is that he is the most fascinating human being I've ever met.

'Yeah. I thought you were going to try and push me over or something.'

'Do you want me to?'

'Yes please.'

239

He pushes me over and we fall onto the bunk and laugh. We start undressing. I take Lishny's t-shirt off and he lifts my shirt.

Lily barges in without knocking.

'You know you're not allowed in here,' she says.

'Sorry,' I say.

I feel bad that we have made her blush. I stand up.

'Sorry. We were just playing.'

'You two are just like little children,' she says.

Lishny nods solemnly.

'That's exactly what we are,' I say.

'That's the whole point,' says Lishny. 'We are just children.'

'Anyway,' she says, confused, 'it's time for bed and lights out.'

Gertie comes to my dorm after breakfast and asks me if I will come with her to visit a girl in hospital.

'She has anorexia. She was staying here until last week. She'll die if she doesn't eat soon.'

I wonder if this is part of a secret test; part of my rehabilitation.

'Of course,' I say. I wonder about Miranda, one of my roommates, who is also anorexic.

'What about Miranda? Will she go into hospital if she doesn't eat soon?'

'Maybe. But this girl is much worse.'

Gertie and I get a taxi all the way to the other side of the city but because she has written down the wrong visiting hours, we are three hours early and have time to kill. I wonder if this is also part of a secret test.

'Is there anywhere you'd like to go?' she asks.

I'd like to go to a pub or a café where I could drink strong coffee and smoke.

'The museum,' I say.

We spend the afternoon at an exhibition of Mexican art from the Day of the Dead. There are giant papier-mâché coffins and miniature skeletons frolicking in the afterlife: skeletons engaged in everyday things, like reading in bed, eating a packed lunch and walking the dog. And there's a girl skeleton on a bicycle, wearing a small red top with sleeves too short, and long black plaits tied with velvet ribbon.

'This is great,' I say, and Gertie squeezes my arm.

We go to the hospital and into the ward where the anorexic girl is. She has a tube with cream-coloured fluid feeding into her arm. We sit at her bedside and although neither of us says a word, we are stunned to see that the Anorexic is wearing a red top with sleeves too short and that her long dark hair is in two plaits, tied with red ribbon.

Gertie clutches my hand and speaks in a soft voice about the weather (last night there was a blizzard) and then offers to read quietly from a book.

'If you want,' says the Anorexic. 'I don't really care.'

Gertie reads in a whisper, as though the Anorexic has grown large ears and loud voices would hurt her.

'That's really boring,' says the Anorexic. 'Don't read any more.' I ask her what it feels like to be ravenously hungry all the time.

'I'm not hungry,' she says, and closes her eyes.

Even though Gertie tries to talk to her, the Anorexic refuses to open her eyes again, and so we leave.

In the taxi Gertie starts to cry. I don't know what to do.

'Do you think she's going to die?' I ask.

Gertie sighs. 'I don't know. If she wants to, I suppose.'

'Where are her parents?'

'They flew out from Germany last week, but they've hardly left their hotel room. Strange family.'

'All families are strange,' I say. 'They all have people in them. People who probably wouldn't talk to each other if they met at a party.'

Gertie laughs.

'Can we get out of the taxi a few blocks away from the hostel and walk in the snow?' I ask. 'I want to buy a card to send to my mum and dad.'

'Sure,' she says. 'Have you seen snow before?'

'Only in a snow dome.'

'It will be a great joy to show you the snow then,' she says and I realise I don't think she's senile and old, like I did at first. Or maybe I just hope she'll take me into a café and let me smoke a cigarette.

I spend the next morning in the common-room hanging out with the others. Lishny has been taken away by the police for an interview. I ring Tom and we have a long and boring conversation. He sounds like he's reading from a script, playing the part of the boyfriend. 'I miss you,' he says. What does that feel like? I wonder. When I tell him I have to get off the phone, I sense his relief. Perhaps we are not so different.

I write another letter to Henry and Margaret and I give each of them a list of the twenty things I like most about them. As I write these lists, a strange thing happens. I begin to feel nostalgic – it's like a wave of nausea and sadness, a heat in my stomach and a stinging in my eyes. And I think that while I was with them, I was truly happy. I tell them that my time with them is the only time in my life I've ever been happy and that they are my true kin. 'I love my own mum and dad,' I write, 'but they aren't my true kin. I can talk to you in ways I could never talk to them.'

This, of course, is rubbish. In theory it should be true. In theory I should be able to talk to Henry and Margaret in ways

I would never be able to talk to my parents, about all manner of things, but this never did happen. It was meant to, but it didn't. I was no more at home with them than I am with my real family. The only real difference is that here I have a chance of becoming somebody else, of transforming myself. At home, they know me too well and I can only be my old self.

So, I tell Margaret and Henry that my sisters are heroin addicts and that my mum and dad don't know this. If they did – I write – it would kill them. The truth is this: I don't want to go back to that stinking council flat where every dollar spent gives rise to panic, and I don't want to reverse my original decision never to go home again.

I decide to spend a few hours getting to know the other inmates. There are five girls including me. Other than Miranda, I share with Rachel and Veronique. Rachel was sent here because she drove her host-father's car into a wall. She has the bunk above mine. She tells me she has persistent nightmares about bricks being in her bed and is haunted by the sensation of tiny shards of brick in her ears.

Veronique smothered her host-family's dog, allegedly because she believed that her host-parents weren't paying her enough attention. She says it was an accident.

The fifth girl, Kris, has a dorm to herself. I don't know why she is here. She never comes downstairs to the common-room.

The six boys are here for drinking, drug-taking, drug-selling, stealing, attempting or conspiring to escape from their host-families in order to avoid returning home, and for driving cars under the influence.

All but Lishny. He is accused of drowning his four-year-old host-sister in a bath.

During the day the inmates wander in and out of each other's dormitories, while Lily moves from room to room wearing her sack-like dresses, checking the dormitory bunks in pursuit of inmates in the act of sexual wrongdoing. This morning I went into Lishny's room and saw Lily with her arm under his bedclothes.

Unlike in a real prison, there are no locks on the bedroom doors. Sometimes it's as though we are all sedated passengers on the same long train journey, desperate to be the first one off; wishing in the meantime that we had a carriage of our own.

I wish I had a private silent carriage with a door that slides shut. A carriage in which I could draw the small curtains then lie down, swathed in soft blankets that I have found in the cupboard in my first-class compartment (along with two small white pillows), and gaze out at the passing landscape until I fall into a deep sleep.

The days are long and cold. So much snow has fallen, and the sky is so dark, that during the day, when you look out the barred kitchen window, it's not possible to see the cathedral spire, which usually juts into the pale sky as blunt as a shape cut from a sheet of black cardboard. Our coats, scarves and hats, along with our suitcases, are locked in the attic behind a thick wooden door, bolted and chained. But who would seriously consider escaping in these conditions?

It's morning and the heater has been fixed. I haven't heard from the Hardings. I take my bowl of cereal to the window of the common-room and stare down at the mannequin lighting up in the dress shop window across the road. It's an untidy haberdashery; a few bolts of sombre, sensible material leaning against the dusty window. Only elderly women go inside, where they rub against each other's fur coats for warmth, and talk at the counter.

The window dressing is always the same: four dark woollen dresses dangling from stiff wire, like dead trapeze artists, and a female torso on a stick wearing a white, thermal top. The torso is made of a glassy translucent material and has no arms or legs. At night, its bulb lights up in the darkness at four-second intervals, glows as white as larvae, then blinks off again, casting a ghostly wash across the pavement.

19

It's the evening of my tenth day. Gertie comes to my room. I have only my bra and underpants on.

'I have good news for you,' she says.

'What?' I say.

'Mr and Mrs Harding are coming to Chicago tomorrow. They'd like to meet with you.'

'Oh,' I say, happy for a moment.

But then I imagine sitting with Margaret and Henry in some bare room on hard-backed chairs, embarrassed, giving them my tearful apologies, hands cold, wishing I could simply start again and that I could change my personality – and theirs – completely.

'We have an apartment for host-family reunions and farewells, just out of town. The Hardings would like to rent it this weekend so you can all get together again.'

'To see if things can be patched up?' I say.

'To see if there's any way forward.'

She tells me I'll be leaving tomorrow afternoon.

'But I hope this won't be a farewell for you and the Hardings,' she says, watching as I pull my jeans on. 'I hope you'll all make the most of it.'

'That's great,' I say, this time picturing a fancy apartment with good heating, a full fridge, big TV and a soft warm bed.

'Will Bridget and James be there?' I ask.

Gertie smiles. 'Would you like to see them again?'

'Of course,' I say, hoping this is the right answer. 'I'd love to see them all again.'

'Well, I'll see what can be arranged.'

I want to touch her. I rub my arms.

'A hug?' she says.

'Yup,' I say.

Lishny isn't back yet so I spend the night sitting on the couch with the others watching a boring movie set in Spain and I realise that I'm not as excited about seeing the Hardings as I should be. I'm sure I want to go back to their house and back to school. But I'm fantasising about how great it would be if I could be in the house with just Henry and Lishny. We could sit in Henry's study and he would smoke his pipe and we'd read books and I'd learn to play the piano. These are the things I think while I wish the movie could distract me more than it does.

It's Friday afternoon and I'm leaving for my reunion with the Hardings. Flo Bapes comes to get me in the Organisation's black car. She's driving again and the bearded men are with her.

'We're not coming with you all the way,' says the longer beard. 'We're getting dropped off at head office.'

We drive slowly though heavy traffic and they have a good time drilling me about my rehabilitation.

'Are you craving alcohol?' asks the beard in the back seat.

'Not one bit,' I say.

I wish the back seat were much bigger so that when I turn to look at him I didn't have to see up his nostrils.

'What about the insomnia? Are you still not sleeping?'

'I'm sleeping like a baby,' I say. 'Like a baby.'

I don't mention the sleeping pills or the fact that my eyes sting and my jaw feels swollen.

'That's wonderful,' says Flo. 'That's terrific.' As though she suddenly cares about me.

The bearded men get out of the car. I stay in the back seat.

Flo turns to me. 'That's very rude, Louise. I'm not your chauffeur.'

And so I get out and into the front passenger seat.

'Sorry,' I say.

We drive for another hour through the snow, in silence.

We arrive at the apartment.

Henry and Margaret wait for me outside the smoked double glass doors to the foyer. They are standing side by side, Henry's arm is over Margaret's shoulder, her hand resting tenderly around his waist.

I say goodbye to Flo without looking at her and she drives away with a brutal honk of the horn.

Neither of them hugs me. Margaret leads me up the narrow, uncarpeted stairs to show me to my tiny room.

There are two pink towels folded into a neat square bundle, and a small bar of gift soap at the end of the bed. The bedframe is black cast iron and groans like a sore animal when I sit on it.

'You'll have a nice view tomorrow,' Margaret says nervously, as she opens the stiff window about half an inch. The air is bitterly cold. Why is she opening the window?

'That's great,' I say.

I look at the window but all I see is the black of the glass and my tired white face.

'This is nice,' I say, as I pick up the bar of soap.

It's a small round bar, wrapped in lavender paper with a lavender scent, like Gertie's bedroom. I stare at the squiggly patterns on the bedspread as Margaret starts to put my clothes in the cupboard. The sound of clothes hangers, a tinny, erratic sound, makes me panicky. We are doing it all over again. I feel no different from the first time she showed me my room. I'm nervous and edgy.

'You shouldn't do that,' I say, too sharply.

She stops. 'I don't mind.'

'I meant that I'd do it,' I say.

'I know what you meant,' she says, and I sit there and watch as she cries without sound and continues to put my clothes on clothes hangers. The mood between us is tense and I don't know why she wants this reunion. She seems to be regretting the idea. I want to tell her a good lie, something like that I love gift soap wrapped in paper and that it's so nice of her to put it on my bed and to make me feel like I'm in a nice hotel. Instead I say, 'Did you nick this soap from a motel room?'

Margaret doesn't realise that I am trying to be funny. She walks over and takes the soap from me, turns it over in her hand and says, 'No, it was a gift from Henry's mother. She died last week. It was his idea to come here. He wants you to have a second chance. I don't know if I agree.'

She puts the soap in the pocket of her blazer as though it's contraband.

'I'm really sorry,' I say.

'Are you?'

'Yes, I am. I'm really sorry about everything.'

She sits on the bed, exhausted.

'I really like you, you know. I don't understand why you betrayed us the way you did. It doesn't make any sense.'

I stop myself from crying by taking a deep breath.

'I don't understand either,' I say. 'But I know I'd never behave that badly again.'

She stands up and looks down at me. I've never seen Margaret look so real, so human, and I realise one of the things

I could never understand about her was her almost robotic ease in the world; as though nothing ever got in.

'Perhaps not,' she says, almost smiling. 'We'll see.'

I wonder if this means I'm coming back.

'Where's Henry?'

'He's downstairs. He has a few calls to make.'

'Where're Bridget and James?'

'Downstairs. Watching TV.'

I didn't know they were here.

She takes me to the shower and points to the taps and to the cupboard where the extra towels are kept. 'Do you think I could have a shower now?' I ask. 'It might help me relax a bit.'

'Of course,' she says.

I want to sleep. I want to get into bed while Margaret is still with me.

'Could I just go to bed after my shower? I'm really tired.'

'It's still early. But if you want,' she says.

She leaves the bathroom and I undress quickly.

I close the window and wrap myself in a towel while I wait for the water to reach the right temperature. The shower water smells like rotten eggs.

I block my nose and breathe through my mouth, but the smell is gluey and solid and makes itself at home in my stomach.

I get under the shower. The water pressure is weak and I am so cold when I get out that the bones in my back and legs feel broken. I go back to my room, smelling of sulphur, and get under the cold covers. A few minutes later, I begin to sweat. The inside of my elbows sweat, the back of my knees sweat, and my head sweats.

I can't sleep. My legs won't stay still. I have to run them back and forth across the sheets to stop them from aching.

It's the morning and I'm sitting up in bed, not sure what time it is, waiting until I hear the sounds of breakfast being made. I don't like breakfast, but I like the smells it makes and the sounds of people making it. Henry comes to my door. He looks at the bed and wonders whether it would be wrong to sit down on it, next to me. He stands, a little stooped, and talks to me from the doorway.

He is skinnier.

'How are you feeling?' he asks.

'Fine,' I say. 'How are you?'

'I'm good,' he says.

Silence.

'I'm sorry about your mum,' I say.

He nods.

'I'd have woken you for breakfast,' he says, 'but Margaret thought you'd probably prefer to sleep in.'

'God. What time is it?'

'Twelve-thirty.'

'Oh no,' I say. 'I must have been very tired.'

I know I should get out of bed right away so we can start to talk things over. What I really want to do is go back home with the Hardings – see a movie, read a book, watch some TV, play a board game and go back to school. I'll be much happier this time.

'Well, then,' says Henry, 'I'd better leave you alone. I'll be down in the kitchen if you need anything.'

'Wait,' I say. ' I just want to say I'm really sorry.'

He looks out the window and clears his throat.

'Okay,' he says. 'Thanks for your letters. But why don't we see if you can do more than just say the right things, eh?'

He leaves before I get a chance to answer, ducking under the door frame, putting both hands on his head, to make me laugh, wishing he could have said more; leaving me to wish precisely the same thing.

My eyes are hot suddenly and full of tears. It is always sad when two people have been thinking the same thing at the same moment and neither can find a way to say it out loud. Henry is like me. He wishes that people could be better than they are, that they could behave more like the way they sound in their letters; that they could say kinder things out loud – the kinds of things I say in my letters. We both wish for more truth, more emotion, less strain, less pretence, but we are both too shy, too self-conscious to even approach behaving like the better selves we carry around in our minds.

When Henry has shut the door I say 'I love you', knowing nobody will hear it. Perhaps simply to test if it is true.

I get dressed without showering and go downstairs. It's snowing and a fire has been lit in the apartment's fireplace. I go into the kitchen.

'Can I have some coffee, please?'

'Sure,' says Margaret. 'Where do you want to sit? I'll bring it to you.'

'I'll sit in here with you.'

'Do Australians always drink a lot of coffee?' asks Henry, keen to get some conversation going.

'All the time,' I say. 'It's much more popular than tea or soft drinks.'

I have no idea whether this is true or not.

'More popular than Coke or Pepsi?' asks Henry.

'Definitely,' I say.

'How interesting. In such a hot place.'

'It's not always hot,' I say. 'We have cold winters and the nights are often cold, even in summer.'

It occurs to both of us that we should have had more con-versations like this a long time ago and we look at each other, pleased, happy to be getting along.

I drink my coffee and when Margaret and Henry start

talking about work I go into the lounge room and slouch on the couch in front of the TV. I know I shouldn't lie about, but I'm so tired, there's not much else I can manage. I should have taken two sleeping pills last night instead of one.

Margaret makes my bed and washes my clothes.

'Where are Bridget and James?' I ask Margaret as she passes through the lounge room.

'They've gone to see a film. When you didn't get up they decided to go.'

'When will they be back?' I ask.

'They'll be back by three, then we can sit and talk.'

I'm not nervous. I just want this to be over so I can get back to the Harding house. I sit on the couch with a book, which I pretend to read.

'Can I do anything?' I ask. I feel like a cigarette. 'Do you need anything at the shops?'

'No, you just rest,' she says.

Neither of them has said what this reunion is for. Perhaps they don't know. Perhaps they are waiting for me to say something but I don't know what to say other than sorry.

The sounds of Margaret's domestic industry – her whistling, the smell of soap powder and the opening and closing of doors – causes another wave of nostalgia; causes me to think that I was completely happy with the Hardings from the moment I set foot in their big house.

I often remember in this false, distorted way, and the memories are often cloaked in the colour of sun. Sometimes I feel nostalgia for things I know I hated when they were happening; for days spent at the beach or the swimming pool with my sisters.

When I pick my memories apart, I realise that my mind has merely played back the objective ingredients, the clichéd apparatus of happiness; the sun, the sound of splashing water, ice-cream on parched lips and cold fizzy drink on a hot tongue, and laughter too. My memory often peddles in the falsehood of past happiness. I should know this.

The early months I spent with the Hardings – our summer road trip, our dinners, our nights in the garden under moonlight, our long conversations in the kitchen – flood back to me now as happy times in which I laughed, as other people laugh, at ease in the world, in real and spontaneous enjoyment of life's great, simple moments. And yet I know that I did not register any part of it as happiness – not any part – and that I was never at peace. But not this time. This time it will be different.

I drift in and out of sleep, a stale-mouthed, heavy stupor, and my memory lies to me again. It tells me that I was always happy when I lay on my clean white bed, in my clean bright room, at the top of the landing in the Harding house, listening to the sound effects of family.

My memory tells me that I was happy when I heard the sounds of Margaret and Henry moving about the rooms after dinner, talking and laughing, and the sounds of Bridget and James going in and out of each other's bedrooms, between bouts of dedicated homework, sitting at neat wooden desks; the sound of pages turning in books I promised myself I would read one day.

It tells me I was happy then, and a fool not to notice it. *It's too late now*, my memory tells me, *they were happy times and now that they are gone they will never return. There will never be happiness like that again.* I wonder if there is such a thing as happiness.

James and Bridget come home in a taxi and James sits down on the couch next to me.

'Hi,' he says.

'Hi.'

Bridget looks at us and frowns, narrowing her eyes, like Henry does.

Bridget is wearing a long white coat, high black boots and pink lipstick. I smile at her. I want to tell her she looks good. But I don't. I'm worried about blushing again. I haven't blushed since I left their house.

'Hi,' she says. 'What time did you get up? We thought you were dead or something.'

She is smiling at me.

'I was really tired. I can't sleep very well in a dormitory with three other people and it's really cold there.'

James reaches for the remote control, even though the sound is turned down and he won't be watching the TV. He changes from a black and white movie to a sports channel. His arm brushes my leg.

'I hate those corny movies,' he says. 'All that love crap makes me puke.'

Henry and Margaret come into the room and sit in arm-chairs opposite the couch. Margaret is holding an envelope, which she smooths with her hand.

Bridget stays standing. 'What's it like in that place?' she asks.

There is nowhere for her to sit.

'It's awful,' I say. 'Do you want to sit here?'

She strokes her coat, which she doesn't want to remove, in spite of the heat from the fire.

'Okay. Scoot over,' she says. Before I can move to the other end of the couch, so that she can sit in the middle, James moves closer to me.

Bridget sits on the other side of James and now that we are squashed together, he wastes no time making sure his knee knocks mine. He swings his legs open and closed, open and closed, in pretence of coldness or nerves. I look at Henry and Margaret to see if, this time, they will choose to notice what their son is doing.

Henry stands.

'I'll make some coffee. James, turn that off.'

'I'll have root beer,' says James.

'I'll have Diet Coke,' says Bridget.

When Henry is in the kitchen, Margaret asks Bridget and James about their day in the city. They tell her that she should have come. It was awesome. The movie was great. The shops were awesome and the cab ride was awesome. They wish they could live here. I wish the word awesome didn't exist.

'I felt like a quiet day,' says Margaret, 'and I wanted to do some reading this morning.'

Bridget sighs. 'God, Mom. You never take a break!'

Margaret chews her lip.

'Where did you eat lunch?'

They ate lunch at an Italian restaurant. It cost more than James' shoes. James pulls his new hi-tops out of a plastic bag.

'Cool, huh?'

He seems to have regressed about six years since I last saw him but when his leg rubs up against mine, I still like the feeling it conjures, as though his body has nothing to do with the rest of him.

I want a cigarette and hope that we'll go out somewhere for dinner.

When Henry returns, the talking – the meeting – begins.

'Well, Lou,' says Margaret, 'you must already know how disappointed we are in you. You betrayed us and all the trust and faith we put in you.'

She is staring hard at me and so is Henry; two sets of sad eyes and two pairs of knees and two armchairs aimed straight at me. I feel like laughing.

'I know,' I say.

257

Henry has a runny nose. He uses a handkerchief to wipe it and nobody speaks; we all stare at him until he finishes.

'We just want to know why you did it. If it had anything to do with anything we did, we would like to know.'

The truth is too complicated.

'It had nothing to do with you or anything you did. You were all perfect. Like I said in my letters. It was just me. Mainly it was my insomnia. That's why I drank. But that's fixed now. It wasn't anything you did wrong. You were perfect. I've been having counselling and it's really helping.'

Henry looks at Margaret and she hands me the envelope.

'We want you to read this and if you think you can agree to what's there, you can come back and live with us on a trial basis. But it's a two-way street and you've got to keep your end of the bargain this time.'

Bridget stands and storms out of the room.

I turn red and feel very hot.

'And you might be able to finish your senior year and go home with your head held high,' says Henry. 'We've told your mum and she's happy for you to come back with us.'

'On a trial basis,' says Margaret, her lips pulled into a tight, anti-smile.

'Thank you,' I say, 'thank you so much.'

Henry wipes his nose. 'You'd better read that first. There are a few new rules.'

A door slams upstairs.

'Is Bridget mad with me?' I ask.

'She wants a personal apology,' says James, 'because you stole money. She says she can understand why you drank because you felt depressed and all that, but she hates that you stole after all the things Mom and Dad bought you.'

I agree that this is the worst thing I did and I cannot speak. I've never stolen before and it makes me sick to remember that

I did. I don't want to sob, not with James beside me. I look at the floor.

'I'm sorry,' is all I can get out. Sorry is short, less likely to make me cry. It's a good thing sorry is such a short word and so easy to say. If it was a long word, like recalcitrance, I think I'd be in a lot more trouble.

Nobody speaks. Henry wipes his nose. Margaret crosses and uncrosses her legs. James stays sitting close even though there's plenty of room. I think of Gertie. I look at Margaret and see her sad face, and I look at her eyes the way I looked at Gertie's eyes, and suddenly she is real. I look at Henry's eyes and he seems more real too.

'I'm really, really sorry,' I say.

They stand. James stays seated. I hug them both; it's awkward, but it's right.

'I'll go upstairs and read this letter now,' I say.

James stands.

'Let's have dinner out,' he says. 'I'm starving.'

I remember Bridget.

'I'll go and talk to Bridget,' I say.

'Okay,' says Margaret. 'Then we'll go get something to eat. You can read the letter later if you like.'

Now she seems happy.

Bridget is lying face down on her bed.

'Hi,' I say. 'I just wanted to talk to you for a second.'

'Sure,' she says.

I sit on the floor, to avoid being too close.

'I wanted to apologise to you in person about borrowing money from Margaret.'

'Stealing more like it!'

I feel more embarrassed each time I think about the theft, as

259

though it is suddenly real and before it was part of a peculiar dream. I am stunned at what I have done and what I have been.

Bridget sits up and takes a clip out of her hair.

'What about James?' she asks. 'Are you still going to fool around with him?'

This knocks me out.

'What?' I can barely breathe. I need to hold something, reach for something: a glass, a cigarette, the light switch.

'I know all about it,' she says. 'He told some of his friends and, you know, that kind of news travels pretty fast.'

'What news?' I am hoping she doesn't know a thing.

'You know what! It's pretty obvious. Anyway, I could hear you doing it.'

There was never any noise. She's lying.

'That's crap,' I say. 'That's total crap.'

'No it's not,' she says.

I stand up. I fold my arms. I look down at her.

'James knows the truth,' I say. 'Talk to him. This is stupid.'

She shrugs.

'Whatever.'

'I wanted to say I'm sorry,' I say, 'but now you hate me again and this time for something I haven't done.'

I sit on the bed. She's playing with her hairclip.

'Look,' I say, 'I'm really, really sorry.'

I reach out for her hand and hope she takes it. Instead she hugs me.

'I don't blame you,' she says, 'I just wanted you to like us. I didn't think you liked us.'

Is this true?

'I liked you heaps,' I say, 'I liked you all so much. Right from the start.'

She pulls away, tears on her face.

We make eye contact.

'I knew James was lying,' she says. 'I knew he'd lied to his friends.'

She wants to talk about him too much. Bridget has always wanted to talk about James too much. He gets under everybody's skin.

I look at her.

'Forget James,' I say. 'Are you okay?'

'Yep,' she says.

'I think we're going out for dinner.'

'Oh, cool,' she says. 'Hey, where's my hairclip?'

We find the clip, we smile a bit, I borrow one of her coats, and we walk downstairs laughing at something she has said about the coat being too big for me.

It's Sunday. Henry has set the table with bowls, plates, coffee, cold toast — which has been cooked only on one side under the grill — and four kinds of cereal. I want to try a little cereal from each box, like a sampler of cereal and I decide to do it, because it's the kind of mildly eccentric thing that makes Henry happy.

James and Bridget are in good moods; they joke and make fun of Margaret. She's been out this morning getting a haircut. Her hair's short now and an unfortunate bowl-shape. Still, it makes her look younger.

'Like a Lego-man,' says James, and Margaret clips him across the ear and laughs.

Henry offers me some more toast and Margaret starts to clear away the bowls.

When we have finished eating, Henry stands by the kitchen sink and pretends to look out the window.

'This cereal reminds me of travel,' I say. 'My dad used to always buy tiny boxes of cereal in travel packs of six or twelve.

I've always liked them. They make me think of cars on open roads and caravan parks with table-tennis tables.'

We all spend the next hour or so talking about our memories of childhood holidays.

I didn't sleep well last night, so I take another sleeping pill and fall asleep on the couch. I want to be relaxed. James wakes me by putting a can of soft drink on my forehead.

'Fuck off,' I say.

'I love you too,' he says.

After lunch, Margaret tells Bridget and James to go upstairs so she and I can be alone.

I drink my coffee and she asks me what I think of what's in the letter.

'It's all fine,' I say. 'I completely agree to everything you say.'

'That's great,' says Margaret.

I don't mention how ridiculous the no-boyfriend rule is, or the rule about keeping my room spotless. But fair's fair, and it occurs to me that I haven't said one properly affectionate thing to any of them; that I haven't lifted a finger to help Margaret and Henry around the apartment and that without realising it, I have spent most of the weekend asleep, or watching TV.

I don't even know their middle names. I don't know what makes them feel happy or what they do, exactly, at work. I hadn't even thought of asking.

'What are we doing today?' I ask, disgusted with myself but keen to make this day my first real day of being kinder, more interested in their lives, more helpful.

'Oh,' says Margaret, 'Flo Bapes is coming to collect you at three o'clock and we're leaving at five.'

'Oh,' I say. 'I didn't realise.'

We talk about what will happen next. Margaret tells me

she wants me to come home after Christmas. She wants me to get some more counselling and to see my doctor a few more times. I agree with this and she seems happy.

I get up as soon as we've settled on the plan, go into the kitchen, and start washing the dishes. Then I ask if there's anything else I can do to help around the apartment and when Margaret says no, I go to my room.

While I wait for Flo, I look out the bedroom window, my hands warm in the pair of mittens Margaret gave me to wear last night.

I put the mittens next to my cheeks. I want to cry but nothing happens. I feel like I've been kicked in the gut. Waiting for Flo feels like rejection. It might be the prospect of spending Christmas in the accommodation. I wonder if Lishny will be there. But even this doesn't seem like much consolation. I feel a premonition of something much darker than I've known before; of something very bad about to happen and soon.

I go back downstairs. Margaret and Henry are sitting in silence at the kitchen table, which has been cleared and scrubbed. I notice a small vase of flowers in the centre of the table. Without the fire going in the next room, this apartment is cold and sad.

Bridget and James come in and sit at the table. We make small talk and James puts his foot on top of mine. I kick him on the shin. He sulks.

We sit and wait, listening to the snow creak on a nearby roof. I want to get into Bridget's silk pyjamas (she told me last night I could borrow them), and lie on the couch in front of the open fire and pretend to be unwell. But the day has been packed away. Now is the time for me to say it.

'I just want you to know that I really like you all and I'm really happy that you're going to take me back. I just want you to know that.'

Margaret looks like she wants to cry. She stands up, grabs my head and squashes it against her belly.

'We all love you, you know,' she says and before I know what to do it feels like I'm sobbing and the whole room is flooded with sunlight and happiness.

A car horn blares and I know it is Flo. I dread the goodbye at the front door, the fidgeting and the grasping for words.

I stand on the doorstep and wonder if I could find something funny to say about the smell of sulphur in the shower (which everybody has noticed), something about me being a bad egg. But when it's time to get into Flo's black car, I change my mind.

Besides, Flo digs her claws into my arm and introduces me to another man from the Organisation, who stares blankly at me through the passenger-side window.

'Hello, Louise. My name's Roger Franson.'

'Hi. It's awesome to meet you.'

Now my voice is sarcastic like James' but Roger doesn't seem to have noticed.

I want to say goodbye to Margaret and Henry, and tell them how much I am looking forward to coming home.

'Can you wait for just one second?' I ask.

I take a piece of paper out of my notebook and write a note. I hand it to Henry and then we hug, a short and clumsy hug, but it feels good. Then I hug Margaret and she kisses my eyebrows. Nobody has ever done this before.

Flo starts the engine and I climb into the back seat.

Mr Franson tells me he's a surgeon and that he's taken a whole day out of his work at the hospital to take me back to the hostel.

He strokes the lapel of his expensive coat as he tells me how sorry he is that 'things haven't been going so well'.

I am struggling with my seatbelt when he turns to me, 'We'd better stop and help you with that.'

'I can do it myself,' I say.

'I'm sure you could do just about anything but that doesn't mean that people can't help you sometimes.'

I stare at the road. 'You should write that down. It's very inspirational.'

Nobody, not even Flo, could fail to detect the sarcasm in my voice. But Roger turns in his seat, looks at me, then looks away, his mealy mouth clamping shut over the second pair of imperfect teeth I've seen in almost six months and says, 'Thank you.'

20

Gertie tells me that although the Hardings have agreed to take me back, they want me to spend some more time in counselling. I don't tell her I already know this.

'You'll be going back after Christmas. In the New Year. It'll be a new beginning.'

Beginnings are always new, I want to say.

'That's fine,' I say.

'And you'll be spending Christmas with a host-family who already have a host-daughter from Sydney.'

'But why?'

'Don't you think it'll be nice to spend Christmas with a family?'

'Maybe, but why would anybody want to take in a stranger just for a few days? It seems like a lot of trouble for nothing. I don't mind staying here with you and Phillip and . . .'

'Well, that's just it. We'll be with our own families.'

'Oh yeah,' I say. 'Of course.'

Three long and boring days have passed. I've only been on one excursion and am never left alone. I've been visited by students of sociology, criminology, penology, ethics, anthropology, biology, ethology, psychology, psychiatry and statistics.

I know by the way they look at me that they would like

to measure the size of my cranium but are too polite to ask. The question they want to ask is an inane one: how could somebody with a good brain have been so relentlessly stupid? The only other inmate who gets as much attention from the students is Lishny.

Because it is so close to Christmas, we have eaten a special treat of pizza for dinner and we've each been given twenty dollars so that when we next go on an excursion we can buy ourselves a present.

At seven o'clock the police will be here to interrogate Lishny again, perhaps for the final time. I sit with him in the common-room on the straw-mat floor behind the couch, under blankets. The other inmates sit on couches and stare numbly at the flickering television screen. They have copied us and are also cloaked in grey blankets pulled from their dormitory beds.

I pull the blanket up to cover my neck, but the wool is so cold it feels wet.

Lishny looks at his watch again. It is half-past six. He smiles at me, ducks under the blanket and rests his head on my lap.

Lily comes over and sits down. She wants to distract Lishny with endless prattle about the cold.

'Lishny,' she says, 'take that blanket off so I can see you.'

Lishny takes his hand from my thigh and lifts the heavy grey blanket from our bodies.

'Why don't you two go and sit with the others?'

Lishny's eyes are black.

'Do you have any oranges or sardines?' he asks.

Lily doesn't think this is as funny as I do, and she goes away to watch the television.

'I'm in love with you,' he says.

I put my hand on Lishny's back, rest it lightly over his thin white shirt. 'I saw you today,' I say, 'you were standing alone in the dark upstairs hallway, sliding the backs of your fingers across your face. I've been watching you a lot.'

'That's good.'

'Then I saw you looking at yourself in the boys' bathroom mirror examining your nose and I . . .'

Lishny lifts his head from my lap and comes out from under the blanket.

'I'm lonely,' he says. 'I'm so lonely I wore your socks as gloves to bed last night.'

For the first time I am worried about what will happen to him. Until now I have only worried about what will happen to me when I don't have him to be with. I've never worried about what will happen to somebody else before. Not that I can remember.

'And,' he says, 'I licked your eyebrows in my dream.'

Lily is on her way over to us again. She stands over us with a nasty face like my mum's when she's wringing out wet towels and telling me how hard it is to raise three ungrateful daughters.

'Terrible cold night, isn't it?' says Lily, her back stooped so that she looks less tall.

'Sure it's cold,' says Lishny. 'It's worse than Norilsk.'

That's where Lishny is from.

Lishny pulls the blanket over our heads and Lily walks away again.

'I have left you a note,' he says. 'It's under your pillow. It explains everything.'

I know the note will say something about his plans to escape. Lishny has an uncle who lives somewhere in Illinois and he plans to find him. He wants me to escape and come and live with him and his uncle. He's told me that he loves big libraries and that I will probably find him there if I can't find him anywhere else.

'I don't want you to go,' I say.

He puts his head on my shoulder. I put my hand on the back of his neck and he moves it to his thigh. We stop here, suspended, our breathing in unison, my hand on the inside of his thigh, his head on my shoulder.

'I don't want to talk to the police again,' he says.

I put my lips on his face and neck. Lishny is always warm in spite of the iciness in the air and he wears fewer clothes than the rest of us, as though he were living elsewhere. His cheeks are always pink, and I don't think he's guilty of the crime they say he has committed.

At seven o'clock there is a loud knock at the door and Lishny comes out from under the blanket, sweat on his nose, his neck blotchy with a rash.

He kisses me and says, 'This is not the end. Do you know it?'

I nod and we kiss some more.

Three police officers come into the common-room, snow clinging to their coats and boots. They put their black hats on the table. One of the male inmates, Ari, turns off the TV and runs upstairs.

Ari ran away from his host-family so that he wouldn't have to return home to compulsory military service in Israel. He is nervous of the police. A few months ago, he was captured as he stepped off a train to buy a cup of coffee. He is so afraid of the police that at dinner, before they were due to arrive, his cutlery clinked his plate uncontrollably like nervous marionettes and he asked if he could use a plastic knife and fork from the pizzeria downstairs.

The other inmates are in a voyeuristic mood, glad of the distraction, perhaps glad to be seeing the back of Lishny. They turn around in their seats or stand along the wall next to the mural of counterfeit cows and meadows.

The police officers wear black turtle-neck skivvies under bulging, black leather jackets. They carry their walkie-talkies in black bags strapped tightly across their chests.

One of the police officers has been here once before. He has an olive face and neck and white hands, as though he is a different person from the neck down. He takes his notebook out of his top left pocket and flips it open. I wonder if he has one olive parent and one white parent; so marked is the difference in skin colour on his face and hands: a half-and-half cookie in the human world.

Lily, Phillip and Gertie huddle with the police in the kitchen doorway and speak in urgent whispers. It is impossible to know whether they are encouraging the police to take Lishny away or beseeching them to let him stay.

The half-olive, half-white officer says, 'Okay, everybody clear the room except for Lishny's chaperone.' Lily puts her hand in the air like a girl in a classroom who is busting to answer a question, 'That's me,' she says.

Phillip goes to the front door and slides both bolts across and fastens the chain. When he comes back into the room he seems to find his hands too large. He picks up a police officer's cap and moves it across the table.

The room is quiet with the television turned off and we can hear, more acutely, the taxi horns and police sirens, wailing in the busy street below. An ambulance passes, followed by the sound of more police cars. These are the noises I listen to at night when I cannot sleep and they are noises I have grown fond of and find comforting.

The second policeman, short and square, clears his throat, 'Everybody upstairs. We need to have this room cleared pronto.'

When I don't move he comes to drag me away. He smells clean and sharp from the night air, and the blizzard. Tiny gusts of cold air come from his glistening uniform buttons. I smile at him. 'Hello, ossifer,' I say.

'You'll have to go upstairs,' he says.

I have no plan and stupidly turn away from him, hoping stubbornness alone will permit me to stay downstairs. His hand is on my elbow and I shrug it off.

'Miss? You'll have to come away from that window now. We need to be alone with Mr Bezukhov.'

'I'm going,' I say.

I pass by the kitchen door and look in at Lishny.

He looks back at me, and smiles a horrible, defeated smile with his small white teeth and thin, crimson-red lips. The face that only minutes ago looked perfect to me now seems the ugliest I have ever seen.

Phillip takes me upstairs and stands with me by the door to my dormitory. He wipes the sweat from his lip and keeps his finger resting lightly on the side of his mouth when he speaks.

'How are you feeling?' he asks, hoping my answer will be short and non-violent.

'Fine,' I say.

'Good. The police will probably be a while. You might as well get some sleep.'

I sit at my dormitory window and look across the street at the large digital neon clock in the shape of a spinning blue globe, advertising a telecom company. Further down I can see a lit-up bus-stop advertisement, 'Welcome to First Class.'

Rachel gets out of bed and stands next to me in her slippers. I say, 'Don't you think the sirens make a comforting sound?'

'Sort of,' she says and smiles.

We rest our elbows on the windowsill for a while. She says, 'Do you think they'll arrest Lishny?'

'I hope not,' I say.

'They will,' says Miranda from her bed. 'There are usually

only two cops. They must have brought an extra one to sit with him in the back seat of the cop car so there'd be two of them to restrain him and one to drive.'

Miranda's in a bitter mood, probably because she hasn't eaten for a month. A cold shiver travels from my coccyx up my spine. It waits there for a moment then travels, burning, into my groin.

'Go cannibalise yourself,' I say, and Rachel grabs hold of my hand and kisses it. People are strange sometimes.

'I'm getting into bed,' I say.

I lie in my top bunk and stare at the ceiling, which appears to be made of porridge. I have remembered Lishny's promise of a letter, reach under my pillow and find it.

Darling Lou,
   You know how to find me and I know that you will. Please read to me at night.
   All my love,
   Lishny

I imagine Lishny getting into a car, alone. There is no steering wheel, but the car drives smoothly out into an empty road and disappears.

He is going to stay in a posh hotel like the one he told me about, the one where he stayed after winning a chess tournament in some hot country.

Lishny told me that the hotel's restaurant had wall-to-wall fish tanks so that he was surrounded by fish while he ate a meal. There were sharks and giant fish close to his dinner plate, with colours the likes of which he had never seen before. His hotel room had a spa, unlimited videos to watch, chocolates and a big bowl of fruit by the bed and a fridge full of alcohol.

There was no chess playing for an entire week. He had been

happy then. He told me that we'd go back there together one day.

I hug my pillow and imagine Lishny and me lying together, face-to-face, asleep with our lips together, breathing into each other's lungs, in that hotel-room bed.

The police took Lishny away three nights ago and the chaperones still refuse to discuss what has happened to him. It's boring here without him.

When I ask Lily about him, she smiles weakly at me, puts her hands in the apron pocket of her starchy pinafore and says, 'It's out of my hands.'

When I press her, she moves her hands in the baggy pocket in an obscene and excited fidgeting, as though her bulging pinafore is about to give birth to something with too many knuckles.

'But is he still in the country?' I ask.

Her fingers twitch inside her pinafore with increased agitation as she thinks of what Lishny and I might have done. 'I can't say,' she says. 'Anyway, maybe it's time for you to let go.'

I have slept little these past few nights and tonight is no different. The sleeping pills don't work at all any more. I leave my bunk bed to visit Phillip in his room at the end of the hall. He is awake and sitting up, a book open on his lap.

'Lost the knack of sleep too?' he says, with no apparent surprise at seeing me at the end of his bed.

'Yes,' I say. 'Can I sit and talk with you a while?'

'Sit down,' he says.

He's wearing a t-shirt with an iron-on transfer of a naked male body, laid out on a stainless steel mortuary slab. Heavy black stitching, crude like tacking, rips through his torso and seals the pathologist's incision.

Phillip pulls the orange blanket up to his neck. 'Sorry about the t-shirt,' he says. 'The others are in the wash.'

We talk for a long while about insomnia. I tell him I think that I have lost my mind when I close my eyes to sleep only to find that this causes me to become more awake.

'It's like sitting down to a plate of food, only to find that you have no mouth to eat it with. Even worse than that, it happens when you are hungriest, when the food is of most use to you, and when you are quite sure you have a mouth,' I say.

'In fact, only yesterday you were sure that your mouth worked very well indeed. You even saw it there on your face when you looked in the mirror, and you confirmed then that you were quite normal and had a mouth.'

Phillip smiles with recognition and a hint of something else; as though he likes what I've said but wishes it were somebody else that had said it. Perhaps this is the way I looked at James. He looks down at his book. 'It's a desperate and lonely feeling.'

'Yes it is,' I say and wish that we could lie in his bed together and talk ourselves to slumber.

'You look as though you'd like to climb in,' he says.

'Could I?' I ask, a surge of blood travelling to my face, warming me, filling me with a sudden desire to feel his skin; not for the sake of skin, but for the proof it would bring that he might care for me.

He doesn't move at all. 'I don't think that would be prudent.'

'But you're gay. Why does it matter? It would be like two girls, that's all.'

Phillip yawns with his mouth closed. 'We'd both be in a lot of trouble, and you have a lot to lose.'

I can see that Phillip is sleepy, that he is about to ride the wave without me. How is it possible for him to drift now when I am so sore with rejection, so far from sleep?

'I'm sorry, Lou,' he says, suppressing another yawn, his eyes leaking sleepy water. 'You're a nice person.'

I look through the dim light at the milk-bottle-shaped birthmark on Phillip's chin and wish he would bring at least one hand out from under the blankets.

'Do you want me to go back to bed now?'

'You better,' he says. 'Just try not to think too much.'

'Sure,' I say. 'I'll see you tomorrow.'

I leave Phillip in his bed and watch from the door as he drops his book to the floor and turns onto his side, his hand going deep under his pillow. I wait until he is still and imagine what it might have been like to sleep with another person, just to lie with him; head on the same pillow, my stomach up against his back, and to wake face to face, to share some of the same breath.

I've been through another dreadful session with Rennie Parmenter, and all of the inmates who eat have just finished dinner and now sit around the TV in the common-room, huddled beneath grey blankets on the threadbare couches.

The room is filled with the noxious odour of fresh paint. The cows and rabbits and daffodil-filled valleys painted on the hideous floor-to-ceiling mural have a fresh and lopsided new friend.

Two new arrivals, both girls, have last night painted a unicorn onto the mural. The unicorn is twice as big as any of the cows, with a disproportionately large horn which impales a bloated pink cloud. I wish Lishny was here.

I am lying on my bunk, holding the twenty dollars the Organisation has given me to buy a Christmas present. The room is dark and smells, as it always does, of a strange suffocating dampness, like a chicken coop; the coarse matting underfoot like a mixture of straw and poultry feed and dead feathers.

It has been snowing heavily for weeks and it is so cold inside the damp-walled rooms that tomorrow we are all to be issued with thermal underwear and extra blankets. It is also promised that a new electric heater will be installed in the common-room.

The kitchen will continue to be heated only by the oven, which we light whenever we sit in there, the door left ajar, a small trickle of gas heat warming only the surface of our numbed skin. My fingers, especially my knuckles, are so cold it feels as though they have been burned.

I go down to the common-room and sit at the barred window and watch Christmas shoppers in the busy neon and lamp-lit street below. They wear long dark coats, scarves and hats, and carry several bulging plastic bags in each arm. I am full of craving.

I think until I ache about their warm lives. I pick one of them and imagine him arriving home, laden with gifts and food. He slides a key into a familiar front door and feels on his hands and face, and on the hair on the top of his head, the instant warmth of porch light. He smells burning butter or baking bread, hears his wife calling 'hello' from a bedroom, half-dressed and drowsy, or sees into the bathroom, the door ajar, her happy face in a mirror looking out or calling 'hello' from the seat of a toilet; there is nothing he is not allowed to see, nothing he can't have. He is welcome to everything. His children are coming down the stairs in nightclothes, fresh from their showers or baths. I wish I could go home with him; with one of these shoppers in the street below.

It is my turn to do the dishes. I am alone with Gertie in the kitchen. She asks me to sit for a while because there's something important she has to tell me, but first she says she is angry because another health inspector has paid a visit.

'That's three times this year,' she says. 'I don't know why they keep coming.'

I tell her that I think the accommodation is clean and that I also don't see why they should keep coming. I tell her that my mum delivers meals on wheels for elderly people and that she has to wear gloves when she handles the trays, even though the food is covered in foil. I rang my mum last night, but nobody was home. Erin's horrible voice was on the answering machine, so I hung up.

I tell Gertie that wearing slimy plastic gloves sometimes causes the trays to slip out of my mum's hands and then old, sick people miss out on their food altogether.

Gertie smiles at this story and arrives finally at the subject that most interests me.

'Well, I have some good news for you,' she says, her small eyes wet with a kind of glee I had not expected to see.

'Really?' I say.

'You're leaving tomorrow to stay with the family you're going to spend Christmas with.'

'Fantastic!'

I want to thank her and say all the things I have been rehearsing to say, but she hands me a pair of pink dishwashing gloves, as if to tell me that I must keep my feet on the ground.

She says, 'This is your final chance. If you make a good impression on this family and it all goes well, the Hardings will certainly be taking you back.'

'That's great,' I say.

I didn't know that my return to the Hardings was conditional and I want to ask whose idea this was. I'm angry about this, and want to say so. I should have written to the Hardings again, or sent them a Christmas card. What if they change their minds?

Instead I smile.

'I want to see your high school graduation photo.'

'Thank you,' I say. 'I appreciate the opportunity. I want you to know that I really appreciate your faith in me.'

She takes a dirty cereal bowl from the table and puts it on the sink. 'Almost everybody deserves a second chance,' she says.

In the morning, Gertie helps me pack, but my throat is too constricted and fat with pain to talk to her. I am surprised by my fear.

It's the kind of fear I used to feel when my sisters and I wagged school and pushed each other around in shopping trolleys. In those underground shopping-centre car parks I was afraid like this, but more afraid to admit it and so succumbed to the awful joy-riding, being pushed down those steep ramps by sisters I have never trusted. And I was right not to trust them. They'd take me to the top of a steep ramp in a trolley and then let it go. I broke my arm once because I trusted them.

I stopped tears then, the way I do now, by convincing myself that excitement and danger are better than boredom. But even when I breathe deeply, there is a strange burning in my nose, like the tingling you get when you are about to fall.

Gertie sits on the bunk bed with me and puts her small clammy hand on my lower arm and holds it there, holding onto me as though to keep me for herself. Even through the thick wool of my jumper I can feel the intense heat of her skinny old body, and I wonder if the body stores up its heat as it grows older, if it stews away like something left for a long time on a stove.

She looks into my eyes and says, 'You must conjure up

Louise Connor in ten years and wonder what will happen to her if *this* Louise Connor takes another wrong turn. You must make the most important decision now, about your future, even though you have no concept of a future and no concept of a continuous life.'

I can tell by the look on Gertie's face that she thinks this is the best speech she has ever made. It's probably giving her goose bumps.

'Lou, you have to pretend to be somebody else for long enough to get yourself out of this mess.'

Gertie suddenly seems embarrassed, even confused, as though at some point along the way she didn't get something right.

'I've seen signs of change already. I've seen you being patient and even listening to people you don't like. We think it's because you have become less self-centred.'

The idea of me being self-centred comes as a bit of a blow, but I smile at Gertie and her hand falls from my arm, the heat and dampness lingering. Nobody has ever said so much to me before.

When Gertie has left my room, abruptly, full of drama and silence, I sniff at my arm. The wet patch of wool reeks and I smile at Gertie's strange smell.

The other inmates are being taken out to do some Christmas shopping, perhaps to distract them from the fact that one of us is being set free.

As I sit and wait, I remember when I shared a room with Erin and we spoke of our fantasies. It was not so long ago. I was fourteen and had just started taking elocution lessons. Erin had been out drinking with her then boyfriend, Shane, an air force pilot, who was more than ten years older than her.

I told her that my favourite fantasy had a number of parts to it but always involved waking up in the morning to discover that miraculously I had become equipped with an extraordinary talent for the piano or the violin or an exceptional facility for new languages.

'I don't want to just wake up and find I can instantly play the piano or speak several languages, but to find myself with the will and drive and capacity to learn them.'

Erin laughed at me. 'Why wouldn't you just fantasise about being able to speak like a hundred languages straight away. Just because you wake up with a sudden thingo . . . what's the big deal about that?'

I told her that she had completely missed the point but she wasn't interested in the reason why she had missed the point. She didn't care what she had missed. She said, 'Anyway, that's a stupid fantasy.'

I thought I should ask her what her fantasy was, to be nice, or to try to 'keep the peace' as my mum is so fond of saying. 'What's your fantasy then?' I asked.

'Well,' she said, 'ever since I've been going out with Shane I can't get this fantasy out of my head that what I do is get on a crowded jumbo jet full of hundreds of passengers and Shane is in the cockpit steering the plane and we leave the door open and start having sex and then . . .'

At this point I was quite sure I knew what Erin's fantasy involved, but unfortunately I was quite wrong. It was much worse, far more explicit and violent than any of her previous grubby tales.

My sister's sordid cockpit fantasy made me cry. She stopped talking, not to make me feel better, but so that she could listen to me sniffling for a while.

In quite a sinister way, I fascinate my sisters, and they love to watch my reaction to the horrible things they say. If my parents weren't complicit in all of this, perhaps I could love them.

'God,' said Erin, 'what's so fucking sad about wanting a root in a cockpit? When the time comes, you're gonna have really big issues, kiddo. Really big issues.'

I sobbed more than I usually did, maybe because of the 'when the time comes' part. I said exactly what was in my head even though I knew it would mean nothing to her.

'It's all violent,' I said. 'Everything about you is so violent. In your head it's like an abattoir where all the people are horny all the time and it makes me afraid. I mean, how do I know how many other people are living with horny abattoirs in their heads?'

'Go to sleep,' she said. 'Just go to sleep.'

But, of course, I couldn't.

21

Gertie is driving me and as she drives she tells me all about the new family, as though I am going to be spending the rest of my life with them.

'They already have an exchange student. She's also from Sydney. Her name's Mandy. Do you remember her from the orientation camp?'

'No,' I say.

'Oh well. Maybe you'll remember her when you see her again.'

'Maybe.'

'The mother is a clerical worker and the father is unemployed at the moment.'

'That's great,' I say, stupidly.

'They're not very well off.'

'Right.'

'They're being very generous offering to take you in like this, at such short notice.'

'I know.'

'Mandy may feel a bit threatened by your presence.'

'Fair enough,' I say.

'Well, Lou, I'm sure you can figure out for yourself that you'll have to be extra careful not to step on any toes.'

My new host-family lives on the barren, industrial outskirts of the city. Gertie keeps her gaze fixed on the road, her arms held out straight and rigid at the steering wheel.

She says, with a smirk I have never seen on her face before, 'I don't know what's going to happen to you, but I hope I never see you again.'

'Yes,' I say. 'I hope I never see you again either.'

We laugh and before I know what I'm doing, I reach out and hold Gertie's hand. She keeps my fingers squeezed tightly in hers and my chest swells. When I can speak again, I ask, 'Do you happen to know what desquamation is?'

Her hand returns to the steering wheel, as though she needs both hands steadied in order to think.

'I do,' she says. 'It's a scaling of the skin. It can be caused by too much vitamin A. My nursing days come in handy sometimes. Why do you ask?'

I can hardly believe Gertie is the first person to know.

'I've seen it in books about Edwardian explorers and they always seemed to be getting it when they died in the snow. Do you know why they got it?' I ask.

'Too many polar bear and dog livers.'

'Wow!' I say. 'How horrible.'

It's lunchtime and we stop for a sandwich in a roadside café. I feel comfortable with Gertie and eat two sandwiches. Gertie is the closest any person has come to answering my question and I wish that I was going to be living with her and not this poor new family who live in the sticks and already have an Australian exchange student. Gertie tells me that she often wonders how Lishny is doing. I haven't thought about him all day.

We cross a narrow, derelict bridge and arrive at the house.

The day is unnaturally dark and yet I feel lighter than I have for a long time, and calm, as though I can see the future and the future is calm too.

When I get out of the car, I spin around on the gravel path. My boots crunching the ground makes a great noise and a big flock of starlings stir and whoosh in the brooding sky. They look like leaves in a cup of black tea. Gertie looks up at the sky and smiles and I smile too.

'I feel good,' I say.

'I can tell,' she says.

'I love it when the weather is serious. When it makes you take notice.'

She holds my hand and I don't mind. My hand is dry.

The house is small and grey, rectangular and wet looking, like a rain-soaked concrete bunker, a single scrawny tree in the front yard like the last hair on a dying animal.

A small man greets us at the door.

'Hello,' he says and makes a most unusual gesture with his hands, clapping them together as though about to pray and leaving them together, his fingers pressed against his double chin. Unlike every other person I have met in this country, he does not offer to shake our hands.

'Come inside,' he says. 'We'll take care of your belongings later.'

He leads us into the kitchen, a small dark room directly inside the front door. His wife and her two children get up from the kitchen table where they have been sitting in front of bowls of soup, and the sound of chair legs scraping the concrete floor, all at once, is like sudden, heavy rain. The soup is an intense green and they eat it with slices of brown bread.

Without any hand shaking, the introductions begin.

My new host family are: Mr and Mrs Bell, and their two small boys, George and Paul. The boys look remarkably like their mother, and like her, their hair is loose, curly and ashen, oddly dull and dirty. Their faces are long, with serene stares of boredom and fatigue. They look like sheep but bear no resemblance to their father; it is as though Mrs Bell gave birth to them without his involvement.

'Sit down,' says Mrs Bell, whose long white neck is dotted with a vivid red rash.

'Thank you,' I say, and Gertie and I sit at the small wooden kitchen table. 'Would you like some soup?' asks Mrs Bell.

There's a small old dog under our feet, who snorts and snuffles, his bared teeth grubbing and shovelling for fleas, digging into his raw, hairless groin.

The soup looks like spinach soup and smells like hot weeds rotting beneath a summer sun. The boys continue to eat it after they have said hello, the spoons scraping against their teeth.

I know this is going to be the kind of silent house in which every nerve-jangling noise is amplified; it's something about the lack of furniture, the bare floors, the thin curtains and the cold. I've been in a house like this before, in the countryside, and I rode a motorbike around a paddock until it ran out of petrol just to make some noise.

'No thank you,' I say, 'we've just had something to eat.'

The boys haven't spoken since saying hello, but as they finish their bright green soup, they find a moment to smile at me. They have the strangest of smiles for children, full of welcome, void of suspicion or competition. Mr Bell is unloading my luggage and taking it to a room at the back of the house.

'Let's go into the family room,' says Mr Bell when he returns, running his fingers through two small squares of neat grey hair on either side of his otherwise bald head.

We cross the narrow hall and enter another small room, only slightly larger than the kitchen and equally dark. There are six hard-backed wooden chairs scattered about as though a game of musical chairs has recently been played. There is no couch. No bookshelves.

There are only the chairs, a pile of cushions in the corner, with names stitched in them, and a wooden table, which is identical to the kitchen table, piled high with board games. I see myself and the sheep-boys, sitting around on the floor playing games, with bowls of grass soup on our laps.

Mrs Bell brings a pillow in from one of the bedrooms and I am given the biggest of the hard-back chairs to sit in. I put the pillow on my lap. Mr Bell comes up behind me.

'Move forward a bit,' he says, and puts the pillow nicely behind my back.

Mrs Bell says, 'Why don't you take off your mittens? Is it cold in here? We could bring a heater in.'

It is numbingly cold. Paul offers to fetch me a blanket. 'I'm fine,' I say, even though I should take it.

This house is even colder and damper than the accommodation and I am sure I can feel a frigid gust of wet wind shooting up through the floorboards. It is as though the whole house is a series of refrigerated boxes sitting on a frozen lake.

But the Bell family all wear summer clothing. How can this be?

This is such an odd, cold home. I wonder if there is a hidden camera somewhere; a team of psychologists hidden behind a one-way mirror waiting to see how I react.

I look at Gertie. She has her hands inside her cardigan sleeves and her knees are jumping up and down.

'So,' says Mrs Bell when we are all seated, 'what do you like to do, Louise?'

The boys look at their mother as though she has accomplished something fine.

'I like reading,' I say.

George stands up before he speaks, 'We get our books from a mobile library that comes around every second Sunday.'

'Do you like reading?' I ask him.

'Yes. I've nearly read all the books for my age group.'

Mrs Bell makes a tiny gesture with her right hand and George sits down.

'Well, Louise, you'll be sure and let us know if there's anything you need for your hobbies and interests.'

I look at an Alice in Wonderland chess set, which is on the floor under the table, 'Perhaps somebody could teach me to play chess.'

'I will,' says Paul.

'That'd be great,' I say.

Paul stands again, just long enough to say, 'I tried to teach Mandy but she couldn't remember how to move the knights or how to castle.'

I am about to pretend I don't know what castling is, to keep the conversation going, when Mr Bell appears in the doorway. 'Paul, you shouldn't criticise a person when they're not in the room.'

Paul faces his mother. 'But it's true!'

'It may be, but how is Mandy to defend herself?'

Gertie stands up.

'Could we take care of some business before I go?' she says.

Gertie leaves the room with Mr and Mrs Bell and the kitchen door closes firmly behind them. I know that Gertie is telling them about the AA meetings which the Organisation has decided I must attend.

The boys take a game I don't recognise out of a big box stashed inside a cupboard and start to set up the pieces.

'Do you want to play?'

'No thanks,' I say. 'I'll just watch.'

I sit for as long as I can just watching. 'Could I look around the rest of the house?' I ask.

'I'll show you,' says Paul.

He shows me the bedrooms. There are no drapes on the

windows, only thin, white net curtains; no rugs on the floors, and no sign of a radio or CD player. And then I realise what it is that makes this house what it is: there is no TV.

It is dark now, and although I am calm and relieved to have been given this opportunity, I cannot remember ever having felt so bored; so bereft.

It is well past dinnertime but there has been no dinner. We are sitting at the kitchen table, tea in the pot, and the boys are sharing what looks to be a left-over Easter egg, smashed up into small pieces, which they pass to one another.

It has been decided that I will stay with the Bells for one week, to see how I get on. If it all goes well, the Hardings will pick me up in a week.

So now it will all work out. I'll finish my senior year and marry Tom immediately so I can stay in the country without needing to bother asking the Hardings if I can live with them. I'll go to a good college, get a job tutoring, or whatever it is medical students do to pay their bills, and then when I'm a doctor, or just about, I'll leave Tom and get on with my real life.

Maybe I'll find Lishny or somebody as good and funny as Lishny. Perhaps I'll have fallen in love with Tom. Either way, I'll never have to go home.

Mrs Bell reaches her hand across the kitchen table. 'I already know it's going to be a pleasure having you here,' she says.

I take my mittens off, smile, and hold her hand as though I've done this a thousand times before. I'm getting good at this. A few moments ago I was bored and now I am peculiarly peaceful.

The boys wipe their mouths with napkins and take it in turns to come over to hug me. I hug them back.

Gertie offers to stay until I am settled in.

I am shown to my room, which has been evacuated by George. I can't imagine where he will sleep, perhaps in the pantry.

It is a small, tidy room, with a window looking out onto a field. Paul shows me the cupboards, which have been cleared out, and tells me I can read any of his books.

'Where does Mandy sleep?' I ask.

'She sleeps in the bungalow out the back,' says Mrs Bell.

A shudder travels up my spine. I might have been asked to share with her, one room, two girls, changing clothes in front of a stranger, having to talk in bed, frightened of being seen.

Gertie and I say goodbye at the car.

'So this is it,' I say. 'I'll never lay eyes on you again.'

'That's right,' she says.

'Thanks for everything,' I say, wondering if I should hug her.

'You don't have to hug me if you don't want to. I guess I'm a bit bony.'

I laugh.

She opens her handbag. 'Oh, I almost forgot to give this to you. It's a letter from your parents. It came yesterday. Sorry.'

I wave Gertie all the way down to the end of the street and long after she can see me. I think, *Perhaps I am being watched. Maybe I should always behave as though there were somebody watching me.*

I lie on my new bed and open the letter. It's from my mum – sent before the news that the Hardings have agreed to take me back – scrawled on the inside of a musical Christmas card, with a fifty-dollar note sticky-taped inside. I wonder where this kind of money is coming from.

Dear Lou,

I have very exciting news for you! Your not going to believe your ears with this news, but both your sisters are pregnant at the same time!!!!

Leona just bowled up last night with her news that she's missed her period and took a pregnancy test. Can you believe it? I'm going to be a double grandma twice and they didnt even plan it that way.

Erin and Steve had a big fight only just a week ago and he's taken off somewhere but we know for sure he'll be back soon. You can imagine Erin is very keen to see him specially as its x-mas time. Happy x-mas to you!

Anyway this means that when you come home your going to be an Aunty (!!) and there might even be a few wedding bells as well when you get back too.

We heard from the Organisation that you were in a different place now because that family you had didnt approve of you having a few drinks. Sounds like they were a bit snobby like I thought they might be. As I've said a thousand times, sometimes rich people are like that. They don't understand certain things as you know now I suppose. I'm sure your better off where you are and anyway you always have coming home to look forward too.

Lots of love

Your mum

p.s: Remember Bill Fanucane who runs that new restraunt down near the new shopping centre? Well, he says hes going to need somebody to help with managing the bar part of the restraunt and he said you might have the right brains to be an assistant manager!!!

Anyway, he said he wants somebody to start pretty much exactly when you come home! So hows that for good luck! You even have a good job to come back to and its a lot more than youd make in an office or something. So make sure when you write next time you thank your dad for organising everything. With all the little ones on

the way its going to help having some more money coming into
the flat.

p.s again: Everybody misses you and loves you!!!!!!!

So many exclamation marks, I feel unwell. The one and only
test Leona ever passed.

22

Mr Bell brings a dusty portable radio with him when he returns from the backyard shed where he makes the chairs we are sitting on. He sits with us in the lounge room and puts the radio on the floor by his boots.

Tinny music catches in the air between our shy words: a box of broken instruments shaken by a violent wind somewhere far away. The boys squint when they look at the radio, as though to hear better.

The small Christmas tree with its single strip of fairy lights flashes in the corner; dozens of small presents, wrapped, lie underneath.

One of Erin's ex-boyfriends, who was a bikie, rode his bike on Christmas Day wearing antlers attached to his helmet. He also had a small plastic Christmas tree strapped to the passenger seat and a dozen gift-wrapped copies of his favourite novel in the panniers.

It drove me mad when I asked Erin what the book was and she said she didn't have the foggiest idea. I was not surprised when the bikie threw her over for a woman who worked in a museum and liked books and history.

I stare at the Bells' shabby Christmas tree and have a brief and irrelevant fantasy about a magic Christmas decoration which is a beautiful hand-painted sled affixed to the end of a mechanical arm, run by electricity, of course, which orbits the tree for a few minutes every hour. The sled is pulled by a troop of reindeer, of course, with Santa crying 'Ho, ho, ho' and gaily throwing tiny gold-wrapped presents from his sack onto the floor, and these presents are, in fact, tiny chocolates which can be picked up and eaten whenever you feel like one.

'Brian makes all the furniture in the house,' says Mrs Bell.

'Wow,' I say and wish, once again, that the word hadn't been invented.

Mr Bell raises his hands to flatten the tufts of grey hair on either side of his head. His hands are large and his fingers fat and calloused.

'You'll meet Mandy soon,' says Mr Bell, looking at his watch. 'What time you got?' he asks Mrs Bell.

'It's after eight,' she says.

'She'll be home from her fencing class soon,' says Mr Bell.

'I can't wait to meet her,' I say and as I say it a strange shudder travels from my coccyx to the middle of my back, then stops, panic over, as suddenly as it came.

It is cold tonight and the emptiness of this room surely makes the air colder still. The emptiness also causes everyone who speaks to sound too loud, as though there are tiny microphones hidden under the chairs.

I cannot sit still.

I look around. The boys seem comfortable in the hard-backed chairs and talk happily about school.

Mr Bell says, 'You'll come with us to visit the children's grandparents on Christmas Day?'

'Yes,' I say. 'I'd love to do that.'

Mrs Bell, whose eyes are large in her long and narrow face, lowers her voice and leans towards me, but the sound still clatters around the walls, 'We have a special surprise for you for Christmas Day.'

'You shouldn't get me anything,' I say.

Mrs Bell looks across the room at her boys and I look across too. I make an effort to record the details: the colour of the children's eyes, the shape of their mouths and the size of their ears. I would rather listen. I don't want to think about what to say next. I don't care whether I ever say anything witty again. This must be a better way to be. I want to listen and so I do. I sit and listen until it is nearly nine o'clock and I wonder why the children aren't going to bed.

George has blobs of jam around his mouth and nobody does anything about wiping them away.

My hands are so cold they feel skinned alive and my toes feel as though they have joined together in a stiffened, woody block and can no longer be moved as individual toes. The Bells are still wearing light summery clothes. Mrs Bell is wearing a t-shirt and underneath I can see her big bra.

It is half past ten when Mandy arrives home, carrying foils, and head armour – which looks like the head of a giant white fly.

'Hello everybody,' she says, dropping a long black bag heavily on the floor.

I stand up to greet her but she does not look at me; instead she hugs the boys and kisses them on the cheek.

'How are my favourite family?' she says.

'Hi, I'm Lou,' I say. 'It's nice to meet you.'

'Yeah,' she says, smiling weakly, 'it's nice to meet you too.'

I shake her hand and when we are finished, she folds her arms across her chest. I notice that the irises are too high up in her eyes; there is too much white showing.

Suddenly, I realise that I do remember Mandy from the orientation camp.

She is much fatter now. What was once a small, perfect face, framed by a neat blonde bob, is now mumpy and wan and folds of skin engulf her blue eyes. Her hair has grown and it hangs limply around her chin, perhaps to hide some of the flesh around her jowls.

During those hot orientation days in Los Angeles, I remember I was bored and wanted to play table tennis in the recreation room. Mandy and her mob of pretty friends sat around talking and eating lunch at a table.

I stood in the doorway.

'My mother told me never to cross my legs. She never crossed her legs and she never had one varicose vein,' said one of Mandy's friends.

'Yeah, my mother says the same thing. Don't cross your legs if you don't want to have any bad veins,' said another.

A girl with a sandwich uncrossed her legs and pushed her long fat tongue out to greet the bread, as though she intended to lick it. I was revolted by that tongue and by the conversation and the sound of the chirpy voices of these pretty girls.

I walked into the room, took hold of one end of the table tennis table and began to drag it across the floor. They looked at me and Mandy put her fingers in her ears, but I didn't stop. The broken wheel screeched against the floor. I continued to drag the table.

One of them said, 'Do *you* mind? We're trying to have a conversation in here!'

I continued to drag the table across the floor. I dragged it all the way to the double gymnasium doors and then left it there, blocking the exit. It was Mandy who said, 'Are you nuts or something?'

I didn't look at any of them. I left the room by climbing out of a window near where they sat and fell hard on my arm.

Mandy and her friends wore scrunchies around their wrists so that they could make efficient ponytails with their thick blonde hair during meals and sporting activities. They had all been water and snow skiing. They wore make-up, dieted and drank lots of water. Eight glasses a day. Their socks were white and stayed white; I examined them in the dormitory. Even the heels of their white socks were white. Like Bridget's.

Mandy lifts George out of his seat and puts him on her knee. There is something strange about the way her hands run through his hair.

'Hello, gorgeous,' she says. 'How was your day?'

George wraps his arms around her neck and giggles. 'I didn't have a day.'

Mandy's voice is so full of spark, and so loud, it is almost violent. 'Oh, but, Georgie, you *must* have had a day. You *must* have done something?'

George looks out from under Mandy's mane of hair, at me.

'I like Lou,' he says.

Mandy looks at my face for the first time. 'That's great,' she says.

'Thanks, George,' I say.

Mr and Mrs Bell are watching us, but their benign and curious faces show no concern at all. My throat is tight and my face is starting to go red.

'Are you learning to fence?' I ask Mandy, whose wobbly face is rubbing against George's face with a kind of unabashed affection that doesn't seem quite true.

'I've been competing for seven years,' she says, her nose pressed against George's nose, acting as though she likes the way she looks while she does just about anything.

There is a faint smell of urine in the air. I wonder if it is coming from George's pants.

'That's impressive,' I say. 'You must be good.'

Mandy squeezes George around the chest, and rocks him sideways, the way I've seen people do with children before.

I've never laid hands on a child.

'I used to be better. I've put on a bit of weight in case you didn't notice. It's the fatty food.'

'It's the food in the school cafeteria,' says Mrs Bell.

'You don't look like you've put on weight,' I say, smiling hard at Mandy. She will not make eye contact so I have an idea. I will look carefully at her face, with a smile playing on my lips, and send her a message. I play the message in my head, send it over to her with my eyes: *You look good, Mandy. You'll always look good. Don't be angry at me for being here.*

'Nearly eight kilos,' she says. 'You *must* have noticed.'

Mr Bell stands.

'How about a cocoa for everybody, as a special treat to welcome Lou?'

The boys leap out of their seats. George says, 'I'll help' and Paul says, 'Me too.' Mandy and Mrs Bell follow them into the kitchen and I am left alone.

Tomorrow, somehow, I will get some cigarettes. After Christmas, I'll give up.

It's morning. George and Paul run down the hall to see me.

'I'll show you Mom and Dad's big room,' says Paul and he takes me in there.

The walls are covered in dozens of photographs of the boys, taken at yearly intervals, sitting in the chairs that Mr Bell makes. In every photograph they wear the same thing: a pair of overalls over a yellow t-shirt.

'My dad sells chairs,' says Paul, 'and this is how he remembers them all.'

'They're beautiful photographs,' I say. 'You look beautiful.'

Paul jumps up and kisses me on the cheek. 'You're nice,' he says. 'You're nicer than Mandy.'

George holds my hand and leads me into the kitchen.

Everybody is sitting around the table. There are flapjacks for breakfast. I should eat enough for the whole day, maybe even a few days, camel style, just in case there's more green soup on the horizon. I am beginning to feel life's atmosphere, or to feel that life has an atmosphere: a good mood that cannot be named, that goes missing when you are anxious.

I am ready for a good breakfast, followed by some games with the children.

Mandy has washed her hair and wears it in pigtails. She is also wearing splodgy red lipstick, the size of her mouth exaggerated, like a clown's. Her teeth look orange.

'Up at last,' she says without looking at me. 'Did you sleep well?'

'Yes,' I say. 'It's a very comfortable bed.'

'Good,' she says as she uses a small spoon to scoop out a small amount of cereal from the bowl and guiding the spoon between her lips, the way women do in order not to ruin their lipstick.

'I won't eat pancakes,' she says. 'So you can have mine.'

She wants this to sound like a sacrifice, like a favour, but I know it has nothing to do with kindness and everything to do with her diet.

'That's very kind,' I say. 'Are you sure?'

She does not answer. I try to find her eyes so that I can look at them. I need to send her a message.

She will not look at me.

I decide to speak to the whole family. 'I just want to say thanks to everybody for letting me stay and I want to say a special thank you to George for letting me have his room.'

No matter what I say, or how I say it, it never sounds quite real.

After washing the dishes I tell Mrs Bell that I'd like to go for a walk.

'Would you like one of the children to show you where the store is? It's about a mile down the road.'

'No,' I say, 'I'm sure I'll find it. Anyway, I feel like a nice long walk.'

'Don't get lost now.'

I buy my cigarettes from a café next to a twenty-four-hour petrol station. It is one of the dirtiest cafés I have ever seen, with plastic furniture coated in greasy bacon and petrol fumes and darkened plastic fruit hanging off the walls. But I am glad of its warmth. I order a coffee and take a copy of the local newspaper from the counter.

'Have a seat,' says the waitress.

I sit. She brings my coffee, offers me cream and then cleans some tables. She is petite and light-footed. She glides from the tables to the kitchen as though she is filled with helium. Her singing is tuneless.

'Where are you from?' she asks when she brings me a refill of coffee.

'I'm living with the Bells, just up the road. Near the little bridge.'

'I know the Bells,' she says, excited. She sits down. 'I used to baby-sit for them. But that was before I got this job. I hate it pretty much but it's more money than sittin' for babies.'

She speaks quickly. I mostly listen. I notice the colour of her eyes, the shape of her mouth and the size of her ears. But after a long time of listening to her, I am disappointed. My mouth aches with the effort to smile.

I want to talk to somebody I really know, to talk about something bigger. I want to talk to Lishny. I wish somebody

I loved and hadn't seen for years would walk through the door, so that we could have a heartbreaking reunion. But when I try to name somebody that I would like to meet, I realise that I am somebody who could never feel that way about anybody and when I think about those TV reunions I wonder if there might be a distinct sub-species within the human race that is capable of this kind of joy. Or is it merely that cameras make people cry, and even I would do the same?

I get back to the house in time to be taken to an AA meeting in a nearby school hall. I say goodbye to Mr and Mrs Bell, who are both reading in the kitchen. 'You're a brave girl,' says Mrs Bell and I flinch at the word girl.

My chaperone comes to collect me in his car. He's a local high-school teacher. He's about fifty and wears tinted spectacles.

At the AA meeting, the walls are decked with plastic holly and faded decorations. The meeting's chairman wears a red Santa hat. The room is packed and full of smoke. There is an ashtray at both ends of each row of seats, but not everybody uses them to ash their cigarettes.

I ask for a cigarette and a man gives me five. My chaperone doesn't tell me not to smoke. In fact, he says nothing, as though stunned. I join with most of the people smoking and use a polystyrene cup with some cold water in the bottom to ash my cigarettes.

I amuse myself by closing my eyes and trying to guess what somebody looks like from the sound of their voice. When I open my eyes there are usually four old men staring at me. I try to look unhappy so that this is what the men will see.

I bet they don't believe I'm a *bona fide* alcoholic and they're right. If I speak, it will at once prove them right and probably both enrage and sadden them. I don't blame them for wishing

I didn't exist, for wishing I had suffered more.

Is there an old alcoholic man who could feel happy for the likes of me? Nobody could expect the old men to feel glad for me when my very appearance will remind them that their own point of salvation was crossed perhaps forty years too late. The fact that I will probably suffer one-tenth of their pain should make these old men want to hurt me.

My dad would say that these ugly, snotty-eyed old men have made their beds and should lie in them. My dad would say they had a choice and have nobody to blame but themselves. But nobody chooses pain. A lifetime of pain – the kind that makes these old men so revolting – is what follows as punishment for choosing to do something to avoid pain in the first place.

I lower my head and send a message to each old man in the room: *I don't blame you for hating me.*

The meeting ends with cups of tea and instant coffee. I can tell the room is a happier one because of my messages. I watch two old men exchange an embrace and two others laugh. One of them stomps his foot to stop himself from choking on laughter. 'Cut it out,' he says to his friend. 'Are you kidding me?'

I am whisked from the room before I reach the urn. My chaperone says, 'I've been told to get you home straight away.'

'That's fine,' I say and as we drive home our silence fills the car until there is so much silence, my ears pop.

The school teacher does not walk me to the door. 'Next week,' he says, 'my wife will pick you up.'

'I won't be here next week,' I say.

I close the car door as gently as I can but this causes it to stick halfway.

'Leave it,' says the school teacher. 'I'll fix it.'

I don't like him. Who will I ever like?

When Mr Bell opens the door, and as he reaches for my long black coat, I almost ask him if I can call Lishny.

Last night I said I was a vegetarian, so that I could change something about myself, and the Bells have saved me a plate of leftover mashed potatoes. I pick out the hard green bits.

George and Paul are nowhere to be seen and the silence is causing my eardrums to slide back into my skull.

'Why don't you have a TV?' I ask Mrs Bell, stunned to find myself craving a few loud hours in front of something pointless; to be anaesthetised by advertisements.

'Rots the brain,' says Mrs Bell.

'Yeah,' I say, 'that's probably true.'

Mr Bell has a sudden coughing fit and leaves the room, embarrassed. He manages to say, 'I beg your pardon' as he goes spluttering along the hallway.

Mrs Bell is sewing a name onto a handkerchief and I watch her for a while.

Then I clear the plates.

Then I run the water and soak the plates.

Then I put the kettle on.

Mr Bell comes back with watery eyes.

'Are you all right?' I ask.

He looks happy. 'Yes, thank you. Just a bit of that chicken,' he says.

I wish I hadn't lied about being a vegetarian. I wish I'd just said I was allergic to liver, and fish with heads still on and green soup.

'Where are the boys?' I ask.

'At their Aunt Sarah's place,' says Mrs Bell. 'She's just around the corner.'

'What do they do around there?'

'Watch TV,' says Mrs Bell, laughing. Mr Bell laughs too. They both laugh loudly. Their heads go back and they cover their mouths with their hands. This involuntary trait is so similar, it is as though they are siblings.

Mandy comes in and stares at me. She's been listening out-side. 'They might not be watching TV,' she says. 'They're good kids. They might be helping Uncle Stipe remove the wallpaper.'

I wonder how the hell Mandy has heard the conversation.

Mr and Mrs Bell laugh even more. I don't laugh. I think – for Mandy's sake – I probably shouldn't.

We sit at the kitchen table and drink tea and eat biscuits and there's more talk of Christmas Day. It's so cold my hands feel bruised. Mrs Bell peels some potatoes and puts them in a saucepan of water when they are done. I wonder why she's cooking more potatoes.

Mandy's legs are crossed and one leg is swinging violently, kicking the underneath of the table.

'I can't wait,' she says in a loud and spoilt little girl's voice. 'I love Christmas. It's my favourite day of the whole year and I bet you it snows, like in the song.'

'That reminds me,' says Mrs Bell, 'Lou can sing, can't you, Lou? We heard you have a big part in the school musical.'

It occurs to me that I haven't thought about the musical for ages, or the Hardings. They might as well not exist.

'Yes,' I say, 'but I'm shy about it, really.'

Mandy stops kicking. 'How can you be shy about it if you were going to be on stage and everything? You would have had to sing in front of the whole school.'

I don't think she got my mental message. 'I just am. Take my word for it.'

Mandy grabs my arm, just below the elbow so that my funny bone squeals at me. 'I know!' she cries. 'You can sing on Christmas Day. Grandma Bell has a piano and I could sing with you. I'm probably not as good, but I could sing along.'

My face burns. I need to get outside. I want to get drunk.

'Maybe,' I say. 'If you'd really like me to.'

'We'd love to hear you sing,' says Mr Bell.

I stand up. 'I might go for a walk,' I say.

'Really?' says Mandy. 'But it's freezing out there.'

'I like exercising after dinner,' I say.

Mr Bell stands quickly, as though the phone has rung, his small body vibrating with enthusiasm 'Perhaps we could all come for a brisk walk.'

'Okay,' I say, dreading the idea.

Mandy has put even more lipstick on and in the darkness the red looks blue. She tells me about school and all her new friends, her arms linked through the arms of Mr and Mrs Bell. I fondle my half-empty pack of cigarettes and want to be alone.

We have been walking for nearly an hour when Mrs Bell says, 'By the way, Lou, we've moved all of your belongings into Mandy's bungalow . . .'

Mandy cannot wait for Mrs Bell to finish her sentence because she'd been hoping to say all of this herself. 'Yeah, I thought it would be cool fun for us to share after all. George can have his room back.'

'It's warmer in there,' says Mr Bell. 'Mandy bought a big heater with some of the money her parents sent for her birthday.'

Not able to bring myself to feign joy, I say 'Happy birthday' instead, and wonder why the hell she doesn't drag the stupid heater into the house once in a while.

'But that was ages ago,' says Mandy, lamely.

I let Mandy go to bed first and spend some time at the kitchen table with my frozen hands resting on top of a hot-water bottle. When she has been gone for an hour or so, I walk out the back door.

She is still awake and the bright overhead lights and big noisy heater are still on.

'Hi,' I say. 'I thought I'd let you have some peace and quiet before barging in on you.'

Mandy sits up with a magazine on her lap. The cover shows a bony model in a ball gown and I catch a glimpse of the headline, *Star's Nightmare Diet*. The very skinny model on this magazine cover makes me imagine her skeleton, which is not far from her sheath of skin, and this makes me imagine death and coffins and the skull without eyes.

Mandy puts the magazine down with a sigh. 'I couldn't really go to sleep knowing you'd be coming in and waking me anyway. The door always slams in the wind.'

'I'm sorry,' I say. 'I'll turn off the light now, then.'

I turn the light and the heater off and the moon fills the room with a faint and milky fog. Mandy lies on her side with her eyes wide open and watches me undress for bed.

'I can see your ribs,' she says. 'They really stick out.'

I pull a buttoned-up cardigan over my head. 'Do they?' I say. 'That's funny, I was just thinking about death.'

'What?'

'Nothing.'

'Are you going to sleep in that?' she asks, sizing up my cardigan.

I move away from the window. 'Yes,' I say. 'I get cold.'

She watches me get under the blankets.

'What's AA like?' she asks.

'It's okay,' I say. 'I've only been to one meeting.'

'What did you do?'

'We talked and we told stories about why we used to drink and why we've decided to stop drinking.'

She's incredulous. 'But you were forced to stop!'

'Yes, but I'm glad,' I say. 'I was sick of myself.'

'Why?'

'Because I wasn't real any more.'

'Oh,' she says. 'What else did you do there? How come you were gone for two and a half hours?'

I put my hands between my thighs.

'We held hands, and sang songs and walked in straight lines with our arms outstretched to make sure none of us were drunk and we . . .'

'Shut up,' she says, without the slightest trace of humour. 'What did you *really* do?'

'We said the Serenity Prayer and then drank cups of tea and talked a bit more.'

'What's the Serenity Prayer?'

'Do you really want to know?'

I'm only talking to her because I feel like talking and it passes the time and it's reassuring to hear my voice, especially when it sounds confident.

'Sure I do.'

'It goes: *God grant me the serenity to accept the things I cannot change, courage to change the things I can, and the wisdom to know the difference.*'

'Do you believe in God?' she asks.

'Not particularly.'

'Then how can you pray?'

'I pray to myself.'

She suddenly props her head up with her fist, ready to argue. 'What's the point of that?'

'It's hard to explain.'

'Explain it anyway,' she says.

'Well, to me God is just a word for what I do when I talk to the best possible version of things: perfection. Or maybe God is the best possible version of myself. Maybe when I say this prayer, I'm appealing to a future, possible and perfect chair.'

I throw the word chair in there to check her listening skills. But she hasn't heard the last bit of my sentence. She clicks her tongue on the roof of her mouth. 'It's not God if it's just all about you.'

'It's not God if it isn't me. It can't be God without me thinking of God,' I say.

'You're not God!'

'I'm not saying that. I'm saying that God is the thought of God. The very thought of God is what God is. There are no words for that thought and the thought is different for every person and by necessity, beyond language.'

I sit up and start using my hands. I'm starting to feel as though I understand what I'm saying. I don't care for her, but I want to say this.

'The whole point of God,' I continue, 'is that God can't be explained. God is the very thing that causes the thought of God and the thought itself. I have God thoughts and that's what God is: the fact that my brain has the thought is . . .'

I have no real idea what I'm saying after all.

Mandy rolls over noisily to face the wall. 'That doesn't make sense! How can God be just the thought of God? You're just going around in circles! I'm going to sleep.'

Mandy falls asleep quickly (as I thought she would) and she snores; a kind of vacant rattle.

I lie on my back for hours and think of life and whether I believe in anything at all. I open my mouth and exhale my final answer into the silence. *God is like all those bits of wood in Mr Bell's shed waiting to be made into a chair and God is what happens when Mr Bell talks himself into making the chair even when his hands are cold and his stomach is full of bright green soup.*

'G'night,' I say to myself. 'Sleep well.'

23

It's Christmas Eve morning. The boys are wearing red and green. Mr and Mrs Bell are in their Sunday best. They are out of bed long before I am. I offer to make some scrambled eggs, knowing that we have run out of eggs and that I'll have to go to the shop.

'We have no eggs,' says Paul. 'We ran out yesterday when I made a cake.'

'When *we* made a cake,' says George.

Both boys look extraordinarily happy, as though there really is something in the air at Christmas time. They are sitting up straight in their chairs eating watery porridge as though it tasted like chocolate.

'I'd be happy to go down to the shop and buy some eggs,' I say. 'I really feel like some eggs.'

'I know,' says Mandy. 'I'll get some from Aunt Sarah's place. She's got chickens.'

Mr Bell stands up, abandoning a piece of toast and a half cup of tea. 'I'll go,' he says. 'I've got to pop over and deliver a chair today, anyways.'

'No,' I say. 'Why don't I go? You stay here and finish eating your breakfast. Just tell me the way.'

'Well,' says Mrs Bell. 'I suppose it's not so hard to find.'

Mandy makes eye contact, sudden and serious. 'I'll go too,' she says.

When we get outside I realise I have no choice but to tell Mandy I want to smoke a cigarette.

'Mandy,' I say. 'I have to tell you something, but you have to promise not to say anything to Mr and Mrs Bell.'

'You want some cigarettes,' she says, pleased with herself. 'And guess what?'

My skin is suddenly cold in spite of thick layers of hot thermal clothes. 'What?'

'I've got some. I smoke too. I could smell it on your clothes in your suitcase.'

I would like to kick her in the shins for sniffing my clothes.

'Thank God,' I say. 'I didn't think you'd be a smoker. You look far too healthy.'

'It's good for weight loss,' she says. 'I've lost about three kilos since I started.'

Mandy is further proof that you'd have to be a moron to smoke. I should introduce her to my sisters one day. I imagine us both as skeletons. 'And in the end it's the best weight-loss program of them all,' I say.

She frowns. 'What do you mean?'

'It doesn't matter,' I say. 'Where shall we go?'

'There's a park, around the corner. Then we'll go to Aunt Sarah's.'

'Thanks for this,' I say.

She puts her arm over my shoulder, heavy and abrupt. 'What are friends for?'

'For cigarettes,' I say, forgetting to put my arm over her shoulder.

When I do not touch her, she withdraws her friendly arm and walks a little way ahead of me until we reach the park. This new aloofness is my punishment, I suppose, for not putting my arm over her shoulder; for not knowing what to do with her body.

'I usually sit on the merry-go-round to smoke,' she says, 'and keep an eye out for the children.'

We smoke three each of her menthol cigarettes and I feel gravely ill; as though the merry-go-round, which hasn't budged, has been spinning at great speed with me tied to its centre.

'Thanks,' I say. 'You saved me.'

On the way home Mandy asks me, 'Why haven't you put on any weight?'

'I don't know,' I say. 'I haven't really thought about it.'

'You look great,' she says. 'You look really fit and everything.'

'Thanks,' I say. 'I really haven't thought about it.'

'Well you do,' she says, her mouth bulging with words she won't speak. 'Does alcohol help you stay skinny?' she asks.

'I don't know,' I say, wishing I had some.

When we reach the front gate she stops. 'Didn't you have a boyfriend when you were living with the Hardings?'

'Yes,' I say. 'Kind of.'

'I guess you miss him a lot.'

'Not really.'

'You must,' she says. 'How could you not miss him?'

'I forgot about him when I met somebody else.'

'That's obscene!' she says, her face scrunched with anger and disappointment. It's as though she wanted me to be a different kind of girl and that because I'm not, I have wrecked the world.

She's not the person I want her to be either. The difference is, she seems to hate me for it. While I, on the other hand, am just sad that I can't like more people and that I am forced to add Mandy to the list of people I don't like.

'That's really sick that you can just go from one guy to the next,' she says.

'Is it? I don't know,' I say. 'I haven't really thought about it that much.'

'God,' she says as she lifts the lock. 'I'd think about the guy a lot if he was *my* boyfriend.'

It is Christmas morning and after breakfast we open our presents under the tree in the lounge room.

I am about to tell the boys about my fantasy Christmas tree decorations (I have thought of some others) when the phone rings in the kitchen.

It's Gertie Skipper. 'You can talk on the phone in our bed-room, if you like,' says Mrs Bell.

I go into Mr and Mrs Bell's strange bedroom with the photos of boys in chairs all over the walls and pick up the phone. Gertie must have bad news. I have a terrible dead feeling in my chest. It feels like everything has closed down.

'Hi,' says Gertie.

'Hi,' I say. 'Merry Christmas.'

'So, how are you enjoying your stay with the Bells?' she asks.

'It's great,' I say.

I feel like I can stop whatever bad thing is about to happen by telling Gertie how I feel about everything.

'I mean,' I say, 'there's nothing particularly great about it but it's great to be here and to have another chance at staying on and not being sent home. I'm really looking forward to going back to the Hardings and it's great that I'll be able to finish high school. It's great that I am better and that I'm not ruining my life any more.'

'Well, then you'll enjoy hearing this. I've been told you've been a model citizen. The Hardings are very pleased and you're leaving on the third of January.'

'That's the best news I've ever heard,' I say. 'I thought you must have had bad news. I had a really sick feeling in my stomach, like you get before bad news.'

'Well, it's all good news, so not to worry. How's the other girl. Mandy?'

'She's okay, I suppose,' I whisper. I'm surprised how pleased I am to be talking to Gertie. I want to stay on the phone for as long as possible.

'But,' I say, 'she's obsessed with how fat she is and with being fat in general and she hardly talks about anything else and she reads stupid teenage magazines full of models and make-up.'

Gertie is smiling, I can tell.

'That's all understandable,' she says, 'don't you think? Maybe you could help her talk about other things. Use your brains on her.'

'Maybe you're right,' I say.

When I go back into the lounge room I realise that the Bells have been waiting for me. Paul and George have presents half unwrapped.

'Come on,' says Mr Bell, 'it's time to open your present.'

Mandy walks in, from the kitchen, with an angry face, and my bloodstream feels the heat of its own poison. I know by the look on her face, by the feeling in the air about her, that she has been listening to my conversation with Gertie, on the other phone, in the kitchen.

I open my present: a hand-carved box containing dozens of miniature elephants, the whole lot covering no more space than the tip of my baby finger. My hands are shaking.

'They're hand-carved in India,' says George. 'They use a magnifying glass to make them. We knew you'd love it.'

I kiss George on the forehead and withdraw just in time to vomit on the rug.

But it takes a few more hours for things to really go wrong, and I am forced to go on behaving as though nothing is about to happen.

After dinner, Aunt Sarah arrives, and we are going to Grandma Bell's house. Mandy is the last to emerge from the house.

'Has anybody seen my purse?' she says.

I am in the back seat of the Bells' car with Paul and George.

'That's the strangest coincidence,' says Mrs Bell, who is sitting in the front seat. 'I was about to ask the same question.'

Mr and Mrs Bell get out of the car. 'Why don't I help you look for it?' says Mr Bell and I know these will be the last ordinary words I hear spoken for a long time.

I stay in the car and wait for it.

A few minutes later Mrs Bell emerges from the house with a handkerchief to her face, partly for somewhere to hide, partly for comfort.

'Lou, could you get out of the car please?' Her voice is choked, as I expected it would be.

'Walk with me for a minute,' she says.

We walk to the bridge.

'We found my purse and Mandy's purse hidden in the bottom of your suitcase. Not that it really matters now, but we also found a packet of cigarettes.'

It is remarkable to me how such a sudden, shocking moment can also feel inevitable. I look over the bridge and feel like laughing. I lean my head against the wood and wrap my arms around my head to deaden the sound of Mrs Bell's voice.

'Surely you knew you'd get caught? We know about the money you stole from the poor Hardings.'

I bash my head against the rail of the bridge. I have never been as angry or as ashamed.

314

'Stop that!' she says. 'Haven't you got anything to say for yourself?'

I am a deaf mute with snot running from my nose. I bang my head again.

'You knew you'd be caught. You had to be caught. I don't understand. And on Christmas Day.'

I am letting the tears roll off my face and onto my coat. Mrs Bell hands me her handkerchief.

I use the handkerchief and start to walk back to the car. Mr Bell is coming towards me. He's shaking his head.

'Somebody is coming to pick you up in a moment,' he says. 'You'll be taken back to the hostel. Then we'll all get on with our Christmas.'

He seems like a different person.

But the person who is coming to pick me up is late, and I must wait in the kitchen. Mrs Bell sends the boys to their rooms and they protest.

'But, Mom, it's Christmas!'

'What's the matter with Lou, Mom?'

Mr Bell eats half a Christmas pudding, which was probably intended to last a week or more. He does not look at me.

Mandy looks at me and shakes her head and says *tsk*. I want to kill her.

I look at the ground and I do not look back up again until I leave the house. When the driver asks me whether I want to say anything about what I've done, I recognise the voice. It's Rennie. I smash my head against the window and scream until he shuts up. I look down and don't look back up until I reach the door of the hostel and look to see who is letting me in. It's Gertie and I want to break my silence and I want to hug her, but she takes a deep breath before I reach her and I know she thinks I'm guilty.

'Fuck everything,' I say.

24

Every morning at the hostel, the chaperones and inmates say and do the same morning things, but now I find this a comfort.

This morning I have an appointment with my psychiatrist, Dr Trevor. I have seen her six times since I got back and I cannot tell her the truth. She is short and chubby and has long blonde curly hair, which she ties in two annoying plaits.

'Please sit,' she says when I am already getting into my chair.

My chair faces her desk, and the window, with its view, through slanted peach-coloured blinds, of a car park.

'How are you feeling?'

I am stony silent with Dr Trevor and her motherly gentleness, in spite of the fact that I am desperate to tell somebody everything about myself; to answer this question and countless questions like it; to have somebody say some things that might help me know what is wrong. She has asked me the question I want to answer, but I am cold.

I look carefully at her eyebrows, which I know will pass for real eye contact. 'I'm okay,' I say.

'Are you sleeping well?'

'Yes,' I say, my resistance extravagant and pointless. I am making her bad at her job when what I need most is to encourage her to do her job well.

'You look tired,' she says.

'Do I?'

'Yes, and your leg is shaking.'

I realise that one of my legs is jumping up and down and I put my hand on my knee to stop it.

'I didn't notice,' I say.

She is silent now, trying to force me to spill the beans on myself. I can see that she is running a professional pep-talk with herself; reminding herself that it is important to maintain some patience, to win this game of verbal chicken.

She occupies herself in subtle ways while she waits. I watch her tongue as it licks the corner of her mouth and I notice that she has developed a rash there, at the corner, a pink wound, with creases in raw flaky skin. She moves a box of tissues on her desk to get a better view of the picture of whoever it is she has on her desk.

I smile at her with genuine warmth and for a moment I believe that I might be able to tell her – telepathically – that I would love to talk, but that I simply cannot.

What I really want, is for Dr Trevor to do something about my silence without me having to do anything. I want her, not me, to know, miraculously, what to do about it. It isn't good enough that she is an ordinary human being; that she isn't the sharpest knife that was ever pulled out of a drawer. It isn't good enough for me that she tells me things I think I already know.

She asks me questions about vegetables. She wants to know if I like them. I go so far as to tell her that I don't like them, or fruit, especially not apples.

She asks me about maths and whether I enjoy doing it.

'I know you are very gifted at math,' she says, 'but do you enjoy it?'

I tell her that doing maths for very long makes me feel dizzy and that I don't, therefore, particularly enjoy it.

She says, 'It's not uncommon for delinquents to hate both

318

vegetables and math. Almost without exception a delinquent teenager will perform poorly at math and possess an almost pathological distaste for vegetables, and in your case, also fruit.'

I swear at her without meaning to and then apologise.

'It's okay to be angry with me,' she says. 'This is an appropriate place for your anger.'

'Thank you,' I say. 'I appreciate that.'

Gertie comes into my dormitory, which I now share with Kris and Ivanka. Both were thrown out of their host-family homes for taking drugs.

'I want to talk to you about Lishny Bezukhov,' Gertie says. 'He's gone missing from the juvenile centre where he was being held.'

'So?' I say.

'We were wondering whether you might be able to help us. Maybe you might have some idea where he could have gone?'

'Fuck off.'

I spend the next day on my bed trying to remember everything about Lishny; testing the memory of him, testing myself for real feeling. I still care about him. In fact, I miss him and would do anything to see him again.

I ask Gertie if they have found him yet.

'No, and we're all getting really worried,' she says. 'Aren't you worried?'

'Not really. He's better off on the run than being locked up for something he didn't do. Especially in a country that executes people when it can't even be sure they're guilty.'

I regret how immature I sound, but I mean what I say.

She smiles at me. 'Do you have any idea where he might be?'

'Is he going to be sent to prison?'

'The evidence against him is very convincing.'

'As convincing as the evidence against me?'

'I'm afraid so.'

'Then he's probably innocent.'

I burst into tears and can't stop. Gertie holds me. I don't feel sad exactly, mostly embarrassed and angry. I tell her what happened at the Bells. I tell her everything.

'I didn't take the money,' I say. 'I swear I didn't take it.'

'I believe you,' she says.

When I've sobbed enough, I tell her I want to lie down. I'm so desperate for sleep it feels like it could make up for everything.

'Can I sleep in your bed again?'

'Of course, dear. Come with me.'

When I wake up, Gertie is sitting on the end of the bed. She has a cup of tea for me and some chocolate biscuits and wants to talk about Lishny. She tells me that maybe things will work out for him. The police are thinking of just sending him home. She says there's new evidence in the case and it looks like somebody else might have drowned the girl. A psychotic and childless next-door neighbour, for instance.

I don't believe her.

'I shouldn't even be telling you this,' she says and reminds me that if Lishny stays on the run he'll have a miserable life; that he'll be an illegal immigrant forever or permanently unemployed, or in slave migrant labour along with all the poor Mexicans, or he'll be deported. Whatever happens, as long as he stays on the lam, he won't be able to finish school.

On the lam. *On the lamb.* Lishny would love this expression.

I drink my tea and eat my chocolate biscuits and Gertie talks for a long time. She paints a convincingly dim picture of Lishny's life on the run.

'There'll be no more chess tournaments,' she says. 'He'll never get to be a GM.'

'Poor lamb,' I say. 'Poor running lamb.'

Gertie's hand lifts, her fingers rigid, and I wonder if she's thinking of slapping me.

'Come on, Lou. You've got to help us. *Please* don't make light of this.'

Gertie gets up, as though to leave, and I worry she may never speak to me again.

'Wait,' I say. 'I'll tell you where I think he might be, on two conditions.'

I tell her that the first condition is that the police must say they figured out where he was without any help. The second condition is that I get to see him again before either one of us is sent home. I'm not exactly sure why I tell her. I even suspect I might have fallen into a trap. I don't believe anything any more. I just want to see him.

The phone rings early on Monday morning. It's Phillip who brings me the news.

'Lishny's been found. He was at his uncle's. He was going to come back to the hostel tomorrow. He wants to go home to his family. There's a female officer who'd like you to call her back. Have your breakfast first.'

I have been afraid to swallow before, but now I am afraid to chew. I sit in the common-room with morning television droning on in the background.

There are two black dogs at the gate of the juvenile detention centre. Gertie comes with me to the reception desk, then leaves, so that Lishny and I can be alone.

Lishny is wearing a long-sleeved jumper and his hair is longer. He is sitting in an armchair near an open fire. I am led to a chair opposite his by a guard who tells me we have half an hour and then leaves.

We say nothing for a while. His eyes look too blue – as though they have given him nothing but food colouring to drink. We stare at each other and then laugh, but since we don't talk about why we have laughed, it seems to be the perfect response. It's a surprisingly beautiful room, lined with book-shelves and lots of dark wood furniture. Lishny looks so comfortable, almost as though he were pretending that this is his home and I am his visitor. This gives me an idea.

'We live in a nice house, Lishny,' I say. 'We're doing well for ourselves these days.'

'We live in an excellent house,' he says. 'Even better when the dogs are on holidays.'

'I'm so glad we didn't have those children.'

'More love for me.'

'More for me too.'

Lishny stands up and I hope he is going to kiss me. He prods at the fire with a poker.

I hold out my hand for him.

'Do you know that the worst feeling in the world is to be wrongly accused,' he says.

'I know,' I say.

'Do you? It's not the consequences of the accusation. Not even because of the punishment that will follow, but because of what it does to your words.'

Lisnhy stands by his chair.

'To be accused like this, when I have done nothing to hurt

anybody . . . it makes me deaf and dumb,' he says. 'I am deaf and dumb.'

I can barely breathe. I tell him about what happened to me at the Bells'. He listens in stunned silence, in awe, his eyes full of tears.

'Your words count to me,' I say, my voice flat.

We stare at the fireplace.

'Will you sit on the floor with me for a while?' he asks. 'I want to complete something.'

'Yes,' I say.

We sit on the floor, legs crossed, opposite one another.

'Close your eyes,' he says. 'This is how it should have happened.'

I close my eyes.

'It is a Sunday morning and you have found a way to escape from the hostel. You decide to go to the big library in Chicago and immediately you see me sitting on the steps. You are happy and so am I. You walk up and hold out your hand. I take you inside the library, to a place where I have been sitting for many, many hours. I show you the books I have read. We sit on the floor. We stare into each other.'

He stops. 'Will you tell me the rest of our story? Could you?'

'Yes,' I say. 'I'll tell you what happens next. We close our eyes and hold each other's hands.'

'Like this,' he says.

'Yes, like this.'

'We kiss the way we wanted to kiss in the hostel, but never could.'

We have only a few minutes. Maybe we have five minutes left. It isn't long.

'The librarian walks by and we hold our breath. She is speaking to somebody near the door. I say that we need to be somewhere more private and you tell me you have an uncle who lives in the city and that he has a mansion. We get into a taxi. Your uncle is away but the maid lets us in. We lie on the bed and drink what we like and smoke cigarettes. We are naked, but we don't touch. We fall asleep and when we wake we are holding each other, as though we have done this for a long time.'

I continue.

'We are in love and we can feel it in the room, as though it were watching over us. We decide we will wait a little longer. We have a long time before your uncle is due back. He will probably let us live with him in his mansion. We have a long time. We decide to come downstairs and we light a fire. The butler will be here in a minute, to tell us it is time to eat. We enjoy the waiting.'

I pause.

'Should we open our eyes?' I ask.

'You can, but I will not ever,' says Lishny.

'Then I won't either. You will be the last thing I ever see.'

Lishny lets go of my hand, and whatever it was holding us together is gone.

'Leave the room,' he says.

I keep my eyes closed, stand up and walk backwards to the door. I find the handle, turn it and walk outside and into the long hallway. The guard is waiting.

'Are you finished?'

'Yes,' I say.

Gertie drives me back to the hostel, her short arms held out stiff and straight at the steering wheel.

'Your mother has sent an urgent fax to head office,' she says.

My heart pounds.

'A fax! My mum has never used a fax machine in her life!'

'She has now. It's quite long and marked confidential. It's waiting for you on your bed.'

'Do you know what it says?'

'No, it's marked confidential. Somebody else might have read it, but I haven't.'

When we get back to the hostel I want a coffee, but the kitchen door is locked. Rennie Parmenter must be in there holding one of his 'How many people are sitting at this table?' sessions. I don't want to read the fax. I go to the barred window. Gertie walks up behind me and I put my hand out for her to hold it. She does. I'm not nervous at all. I want to stand with her at the window, in silence, and that's what we do.

'Look,' I say. 'The Italian waiter is across the road.'

Every day the Italian waiter flicks his restaurant's blue and white check tablecloths to free them of crumbs. He grins at the people passing by, standing firm and proud, with legs apart, under the long plaits of garlic which hang in the window.

I tell Gertie that I like to send the waiter psychic messages because I have become fond of him. He is an old man, thin and small with a round potbelly.

I tell her that if I get out of bed early enough, I like to watch him before breakfast when he comes onto the street with a basket full of bread loaves.

He takes each loaf in its turn and bashes it hard against the restaurant's brick wall. He beats each loaf exactly three times and then returns inside. At first I regarded him as morose and superstitious, but now when I watch him, I count each loaf with exacting care, holding my breath with worry, afraid that one day he might not beat each loaf three times and that this miscalculation might lead to misfortune.

I tell Gertie that sometimes at breakfast, when I take a bite of cold toast, I close my eyes and pretend that I am inside his restaurant and that I am sitting at one of his tables, with blue and white check tablecloths, eating soft white bread and drinking strong coffee. I try to imagine that he and his family are sitting at a nearby table and when I run out of coffee he immediately offers me more.

I tell Gertie that I sometimes close my eyes and see a white and blue check cloth in front of me and I see the Italian waiter move towards me with an egg in an egg-cup.

He says, 'Would you like an egg this morning for a change?' And I say I would. And he gives me the egg and the radio is playing Vivaldi.

Gertie squeezes my hand. 'Thank you,' she says. 'I sometimes forget to look at the world.'

I smile and squeeze her hand, and her warmth feels very good.

'You're going to be just fine.'

'Thank you,' I say.

I go back to my dormitory.

My roommate, Kris, is Norwegian.

'Hi,' she says as I walk towards my bunk.

Her head is heavy on the pillow.

'I'm so sleepy,' she says.

If I was staying, I think we would get along.

'Did I wake you?'

'Yeah, but it doesn't matter. There's a letter on your bed.'

I sit down on my bunk and hope that Kris will go down to the common-room to watch TV. She has the marks from her jacket across her cheek and her eyes are bloodshot. She sits up for a while and then falls down.

'Shit,' she says, like she always says, as though something bad has happened.

'Are you all right?' I ask.

'I just want my mind to be quiet. I'm so tired of the chaotic sound it makes.'

She has said this before. I know exactly what she means. I like her, but she doesn't remember what she has already told you. I have an idea that might help both of us. I pick up the fax.

'How about you read this for me?' I say. 'But don't read it out loud. Just read it to yourself and only tell me if there's any information that a person in my position would absolutely have to know.'

She gets what I mean immediately and grins. She takes the fax and reads it, lying on her back. 'There's something about a baby . . .'

I turn over on my stomach, the pillow under my chest. 'I'm not interested in babies or any of the gossip about what my sisters are doing, or my dad's cricket games or anything like that at all. Only the big stuff. If there isn't any big stuff, then I want you to tear it up and stuff it in the bin.'

She reads for several pages, her face devoid of expression. She has big lips but they don't budge at all. She looks as though she is really thinking, not just reading. She looks intelligent. I try to figure out what it is about her face that makes her look so intelligent. Maybe it's just the size of her eyes; the way they are neither too open nor too closed.

'I think this is sigsnificant,' she says.

'*Sigsnificant*. What a beautiful word,' I say. 'Your English is so good. Why is it so good?'

'Everybody learns it at school. I'm not different.'

Her big lips open on a little smile that makes it look like her teeth are bursting to get out.

'Anyway,' I say. 'You'd better tell me about the important bit.'

'Should I read it out loud or tell you in my own words?'

'Your own words.'

She puts the fax paper on her chest and closes her eyes. She lies still.

'Your mother says she has left your father. She is sick of her life at home and is fed up with your sisters too. She has met a man and this man has won . . .'

She picks the paper up and reads a word, 'Lottery?'

But something tells me she is not really stuck on this word at all.

'Yes,' I say. 'A lottery. A sweepstake. People pick numbers and can win millions of dollars.'

She puts the paper back on her chest and the paper lifts up and down.

'This man, he has won three and a half millions and your mother says you will find it funny that he was already rich before he won.'

I don't find this funny.

'She says she has gone to live with him and that if you want you can stay with them in their house. It has a swimming pool and a spa and a private cinema and a library and horses, and you can stay for as long as you like, and she says she can pay for you to go to university. She says he is not a criminal or anything else you might be thinking.'

I sit up and reach for my cigarettes, but they aren't there. I take in a big breath of air and it tastes quite good, considering. Now I will give up smoking.

I wonder about my dad. I wonder how he is.

'She says she will pick you up at the airport.'

'Is that all true?' I ask.

She sits up and looks at me. 'How would I know if it is true?'

I take the pages and tear them up.

She says, 'There was a last page I did not read, you know.'

I lie down and close my eyes.

Kris stands up and opens the door. 'I could have made it all up,' she says.

I look at her; her big lips staying open in case they'll be needed again.

'It doesn't really matter,' I say. 'I'll have to pack my bags either way, and I'll have to sit in the same seat as myself on the plane.'

We smile at one another, and she leaves.

I lie on my bunk and I think. I think hard about what I have done and what I will do next. The room is darkening slowly with the gloaming. A purple stain drips down the polluted sky; the streetlights not yet on.

I let it get dark and I don't turn on the light. There's a light on outside, in the hall, and it's coming in under the door. A warm, orange band of light. And there's a smell of cooking too.

I lie on my bed through dinner, even though I'm hungry. I expect Gertie to visit, to tell me to come down and eat, and yet I don't feel sorry for myself when she doesn't.

I'm cold, so I get under the blankets. I decide I will lie on my bunk all evening, comforted by the muted din of the TV and laughter and talking downstairs. I hear two boys in their dorm, laughing, and I hear Gertie coming up the stairs to tell them to come back down.

I like this. I like this listening to people moving around downstairs, in other rooms, listening to what they do. If Gertie comes in to ask me how I am, I'll tell her. I'll tell her everything. And we can talk until I fall asleep.

If she doesn't come, I'll look out the window for a while. I'll watch people walking in the street below, and wonder which of them I might like to follow home.